CW00506281

A CORNISH INTRIGUE

THE LOVEDAY MYSTERIES
BOOK TWELVE

RENA GEORGE

Copyright © 2023 by Rena George

All rights reserved.

This book is a work of fiction. The characters, incidents and dialogue are of the author's imagination and should in no way be construed as real. Any resemblance to actual events or persons living or dead is fictionalised or coincidental.

No part of this book may be reproduced in any form or by any electronic or mechanical means, including information storage and retrieval systems, without written permission from the author, except for the use of brief quotations in a book review

Cover design by Craig Duncan

www.craigduncan.com

INTRODUCTION

Loveday, now fully immersed in the joys of motherhood with little Rosie, finds herself entangled in a web of deceit and revenge when an unexpected reunion with old friend Lawrence Kemp takes a dark turn. Drawn into the clutches of an old adversary, Brian Teague, who harbours a grudge over a past tragedy, Loveday must navigate a dangerous game of deception. As the stakes rise and old wounds are reopened, she and her detective partner, Sam, must unravel the twisted truth before it's too late.

CHAPTER 1

*C*lemo's Old Book Emporium could easily be missed, tucked away as it was in Truro's maze of quaint streets between Granny's Attic Antiques and Tilly's Traditional Pasty Shop.

Although not herself an avid collector of second-hand books, Loveday was drawn to the ambience of the old place, with its labyrinth of over-stuffed shelves and smell of leather and aged tomes.

Glimpsing herself in the antique mirror on the far wall, she smiled. Baby Rosie looked so snug in her sling as she gazed about her, the wide, blue eyes eagerly absorbing the secrets of the world. At eight weeks old, Rosie already bore a definite resemblance to her father, Sam, a fact that warmed Loveday's heart.

She continued to wander, delighting at the miscellany of leather-bound volumes, dog-eared paperbacks, crime novels, romances, and history books of old Cornwall. It wasn't this variety that drew Loveday to Clemo's Old Book Emporium. The shop served as the perfect vantage point for people-watching, especially since her maternity leave provided ample opportunity for leisurely strolls with Rosie.

Seeing the familiar figure took her by surprise. Lawrence Kemp had been one of Loveday's closest friends, but over the years, they had grown apart. They hadn't met in ages, so stumbling upon him in the foreign travel section caused her to gasp. He looked different, thinner and more dishevelled than she remembered, but there was no doubt it was him.

'Lawrence?' Loveday approached, a grin spreading across her face. 'Hello, stranger.'

He turned abruptly, surprised. His eyes widened. 'Loveday! What on earth are you doing here?'

She laughed. 'It's a bookshop, Lawrence. I *can* read, you know.' She glanced at the book in his hand, *The Madagascar Trail* by Ruben Lavelle. 'Planning your next adventure?'

'It's a gift for a friend,' he said, his gaze drifting towards Rosie, who blinked her long, blonde lashes at him.

'Lawrence, meet Rosie.' Loveday gently caressed the petal soft cheek. 'My beautiful daughter.'

His eyebrows went up. 'This is your baby?'

His look of astonishment made her smile. 'Don't look so surprised, Lawrence. I'm actually quite a good mother. Ask Rosie.' She playfully nudged her baby's button nose.

Lawrence touched his forehead. 'God, Loveday. You're a mother. I didn't... She looks exactly like you.'

'Does she?' Loveday tilted her head, gazing at the baby. Rosie responded by blowing. a raspberry.

'She's adorable, she has your eyes.' Lawrence turned, his glance tender. 'Motherhood suits you.'

Loveday swallowed the annoying lump in her throat. These waves of unexpected emotions undermined her confidence. It was one of the less appealing aspects of early motherhood. Her gaze shifted to the mezzanine level of the bookshop, where mismatched tables provided a cosy spot for coffee.

'Fancy a drink?' she suggested. 'If you have the time, that is.'

Lawrence nodded. 'Time is something I do have,' he said as

they made for the wooden stairs. He waited until she had settled the baby and they had mugs of steaming latte in front of them before he cleared his throat and looked at her. 'Do you remember Brian Teague?'

'Teague?' Loveday screwed up her face, and then it came back in a flash – Teague! Of course, she remembered him. Lawrence's association with Teague's family had cost him years of freedom, and the life of the wife he'd adored.

The whole tragic story was replaying in her head. Lawrence's late wife, Anchriss, had tried to be a Good Samaritan, rushing her neighbour, Meredith Teague, to the hospital when she went into labour with her twins. Then the cruel hand of fate intervened when the hospital dash ended in an accident that killed the pregnant woman and her babies. Lawrence took the blame and lied to the court that he had been driving because Anchriss had been drinking. Plagued by remorse and guilt, she took her own life while Lawrence was in prison. Grief-stricken Teague, blamed Lawrence for destroying his family and vowed revenge.

Loveday's eyes filled with shock. She was one of the few people Lawrence had trusted with the truth about that accident. 'Teague's not after you, is he? Not after all these years?'

'I had a letter. He wants to meet me,' Lawrence said. 'But I'm not comfortable about it...unless, perhaps...' He raised imploring eyes to Loveday. 'Unless you could come with me.'

She was about to hold up a hand and say she couldn't get involved, but what kind of friend would that make her?

She paused, taking a breath. 'All right,' she said. 'When?'

LATER THAT DAY, back home in Marazion, Loveday and Sam had bathed Rosie together before settling her in her cot. 'Goodnight, my darling,' Loveday whispered, leaning over to gently drop a kiss on the baby's cheek. She felt Sam's arms come around her and snuggled into them as they both gazed down at the sleeping child.

'You do know we're the luckiest people in the world, don't you,' Sam said quietly.

'I do.' Loveday smiled.

A year ago, she'd no thought about having a child – but then it happened. She'd dreaded telling Sam. He had a grown-up family from a previous marriage. Was it fair to rock his world with a new baby? But to her joy, Sam had been delighted. He was also the most supportive partner she could ever have wished for.

They were no longer just a couple; they were a family. And Loveday was happier than she'd ever been. At least she would be once she was back at her editor's desk on *Cornish Folk* magazine.

'Want a drink?' Sam asked, joining her on the sofa with his after-supper glass of malt whisky in his hand.

'No thanks.' She smiled up at him. 'You'll never guess who Rosie and I met today.' She moistened her lips. She'd have to be careful how she worded this. 'Lawrence Kemp. He was in that funny old bookshop in Truro.'

Sam put his glass down on a low table and gave a leisurely stretch. 'How is he?' he asked, yawning.

This was her chance to repeat her earlier conversation with Lawrence. He'd been invited to meet his old enemy, Brian Teague, but he worried about going on his own.

Sam's reaction was predictable. His head jerked up, and he stared at her in disbelief. 'You're doing what?'

'I'm helping an old friend.'

His brow wrinkled in concern. 'You're getting involved in something that's not your business, you need to stay out of this, Loveday.'

'It'll be a chat in a St Ives café. Maybe Teague finally wants to bury the past.'

'I'm still not happy about it.'

.   .   .

A WEEK PASSED before the meeting had finally been arranged. Late spring sunshine had attracted thousands of visitors to St Ives, and Loveday skilfully manoeuvred Rosie's buggy along the busy seafront, avoiding the throngs of holidaymakers. Pausing for a moment to adjust Rosie's white sunhat, Loveday squinted ahead as she spotted the café where she had agreed to meet Lawrence. The place seemed to buzz with activity.

To her relief, Lawrence was already there, having secured a table in the crowded café. He stood up, waving them over. 'Teague suggested meeting at my cottage,' he explained, 'but that would have been too overwhelming for me. Meeting on neutral ground feels more appropriate.'

Loveday could understand that, but glancing about her she wondered if a packed café was a suitable setting for a meeting like this. Perhaps the man wouldn't tun up. None of the faces around them remotely resembled the images she had seen of Brian Teague. And then she saw them entering the café, a man and two children.

'Is that him?' She looked at Lawrence, but he was already on his feet.

The man saw him, pausing briefly before shepherding the children to their table. His voice, low and well-spoken, caught her off guard. 'Lawrence Kemp?' he inquired, raising an eyebrow. 'I'm Brian Teague.'

'I know who you are,' Lawrence said stiffly. 'What I don't know is why you're here.'

There was an uneasy silence as the two faced each other, wary panthers ready to strike. Loveday had to do something. Her hand shot out. 'I'm Loveday, and this is Rosie,' she smiled brightly. Since Teague had brought children along, she hoped there would be no confrontation.

Teague took the proffered hand. 'I brought my family to meet you,' he said. Through mops of dishevelled blonde curls, Loveday saw two pairs of innocent blue eyes staring up at them. 'The older one is Emily.' He placed a hand on the smaller child's head. 'And this is Olivia.'

They smiled at the girls.

'I wanted you to know I've moved on. I've reclaimed my life. I've been given a second chance.' Loveday watched Teague scratch his stubbly beard, aware of his brief glance to Rosie. 'I can see you've moved on too and have a family of your own now.'

Loveday was torn between telling the truth or letting the lie remain.

'I never blamed you for Meredith's death you know, not really.'

She saw Lawrence shift uncomfortably. 'That's remarkably generous of you,' he responded curtly.

Loveday's eyes moved from Teague to Lawrence. She should have anticipated this awkwardness. 'Why don't we all sit down?' she said, gesturing for them to pull up additional chairs.

But Teague shook his head. 'No, I've said what I came to say.' He fixed Lawrence with a stare. 'I don't expect we'll ever be friends, but perhaps we can leave the past behind us.'

Did the smile twitching at the corners of Lawrence's mouth, suggest the merest glimmer of a change? 'I'll go along with that if you really mean it,' he said.

And that was it. They didn't shake hands, and there were no pats on the back. Teague had declined their offer of tea. Loveday couldn't hide her frown as she watched them leave. She hadn't really been expecting confrontation, not in such a busy café, but this bland indifference was something else.

Lawrence had also been watching them go. 'D'you think he knows I wasn't the one driving that car? Maybe he's stopped blaming me for the death of his wife and babies.'

'Perhaps,' Loveday said slowly. She didn't know what to make of this. It hadn't been the friendliest of meetings. In fact, the entire encounter felt too odd to put into words. But she knew Lawrence was pleased as he turned to her, his old smile returning. 'Thanks for coming today, you're a real pal, Loveday. That policeman of yours is a lucky man. The three of us should get together for a drink sometime.'

'Yes, let's do that,' she said. Her eyes were on his back as he went out. She wished she could share her friend's positivity. The meeting had been trouble free, but she sensed there was more to come. And she wasn't at all sure they were going to like it.

CHAPTER 2

'What are you doing at home – and gardening?' Loveday called to Cassie. She had arrived back in Marazion and was unclipping Rosie from her car seat. 'Shouldn't you be out tarting up some rich dude's boat?'

Cassie shook her head, tutting. 'Such disrespect. I'll have you know, madam, that I don't tart up boats, I refurbish luxury yachts.' She put a hand in the small of her back and stretched before struggling up from her knees.

'You're forgetting I have an assistant now, the lovely Harriet Wild, She does the tarting up when I'm treating myself to a day off.'

Loveday laughed. 'I'm not questioning whether you deserve time away from work, Cassie, I'm just surprised to find you pulling weeds in the flower beds. Can I tempt you away from all this to come inside for a cup of tea?'

'That's the best offer I've had all day.' Cassie stretched her back again and stepped out of the garden. 'And after I've had a cuddle with this little lady,' she said, smiling down at Rosie, 'I might even put the kettle on.'

She took Rosie from Loveday's arms, carrying her into the house and making cooing noises as she went.

Renting what had originally been a tiny cottage across the drive from Cassie and her GP husband Adam's, impressive big house had been one of the best moves Loveday ever made.

Soon after she'd met DI Sam Kitto, he'd moved in with her, and last year, after they'd bought the cottage from Cassie and Adam, they made extensive renovations.

Loveday's smile was indulgent as she looked down at her daughter. 'This child is going to be so spoiled.'

Cassie shook her head. 'It's a well-known fact that aunties cannot spoil their nieces.' She gave Rosie a little jiggle. 'Your mummy knows nothing, does she?'

Rosie gave a responding gurgle, her little feet kicking out as she was put into the baby rocker.

Her eyelids were soon drooping as the comfy wobble of the chair did its job.

Loveday gave her an affectionate glance. 'That little chair is worth its weight in gold.'

'I can see that,' Cassie said, dunking a ginger snap into her teacup. 'How was your day?'

'It was busy,' Loveday said. 'We were with Lawrence Kemp.'

'Lawrence?' Cassie looked surprised. 'Is he well?'

Loveday put down her cup, a tinge of worry creeping into her eyes. 'I'm not sure,' she said slowly. 'He was thinner than I remembered, and scruffier too. I don't think he's looking after himself.'

'I thought artists were meant to be scruffy. Isn't it part of the ethos?'

Loveday laughed. 'You're such a snob, Cassie. The artists I know would more probably describe themselves as bohemian.'

Cassie's eyes rose to the ceiling. 'I thought bohemian *was* fashionable.'

'Exactly,' Loveday said, shaking her head. 'Anyway, I was

telling you about Lawrence. He had some good news.' She looked across at her friend. 'Remember Brian Teague?'

Cassie dunked another biscuit. 'The name's familiar. Who is he?'

'The bane of Lawrence's life, that's who. It was Teague's wife who died in that terrible accident.' She paused. 'She was expecting twins.'

'Of course.' Cassie sat back. 'I remember, although I didn't know Lawrence back then. All that happened before he came to Cornwall. Adam and I only got close to him when he painted that picture of our yacht. He told us that he'd been in prison.' She paused. 'He didn't specifically say, but we got the impression that accident wasn't his fault.'

Loveday sighed. 'It wasn't, but Brian Teague didn't know that. He blamed Lawrence for the death of his family. He always said he'd get even.'

'Poor Lawrence. What a terrible thing to carry around with him.'

'That's the strange thing,' Loveday said. 'Teague wrote to Lawrence asking to meet him.'

'I thought you hadn't seen Lawrence for months.'

'I hadn't. We bumped into each other by chance in that funny old bookshop in Truro. He mentioned getting the letter from Teague but said he couldn't face meeting the man on his own.'

Cassie nodded. 'So you went with him. That's where you were this morning. I thought you were taking Rosie for a day out.' Her eyes gleamed with interest. 'So what happened? Did Teague turn up?'

'He did, and he brought his children with him.' Loveday's expression softened. 'Two lovely little girls. Anyway, he said he wanted to move on now he had a family. He told Lawrence it was time to bury the past.'

'That's good, isn't it?'

Loveday screwed up her face. 'I'm not sure. It was all a bit strange. We were meeting in this café, but Teague refused to sit down and have tea with us. And another thing.' She glanced up at Cassie. 'He clearly thought Lawrence and I were together, and that Rosie was his child.'

'And Lawrence didn't put him right?'

Loveday shook her head. 'I don't think he even realized. He was relieved at how well he felt the meeting had gone. He'd been carrying this baggage around for such a long time and suddenly the weight was lifted from his shoulders.' She shrugged. 'I wasn't going to spoil it for him. Anyway, I was probably wrong to be sceptical of Teague's motives. Maybe he really did want bygones to be bygones.'

'I'm sure he did,' Cassie said. 'Teague must have had baggage to offload too. He and Lawrence might never be great friends but if they've reached an understanding surely that's a good thing?'

'I hope so,' Loveday said.

'And what about you, Loveday? I'll bet you're champing at the bit to get back to work.'

Loveday's glance went to Rosie. 'Is that selfish of me?'

'Of course not. Why would you even think that?'

'I can't imagine leaving Rosie with a childminder, but I am missing my job. Does that make me a bad mum?'

'You're my best friend, Loveday, but you do sometimes talk a lot of rot. Besides, you don't have to leave Rosie with a childminder. Take her with you.'

'Take my baby to the office?' Loveday's voice rose as she pulled a face. 'How would that work?'

'Well, that's up to you. I'm not saying it would be easy, and it might take a bit of organizing to set up, but it's certainly possible.'

'Sam might object.'

'Persuade him.'

'Merrick would never agree to it.'

'Merrick might own the magazine, but you're the editor. He

knows how good you are at your job. I think he would bend over backwards to get you back right now.'

'My colleagues wouldn't like a baby in the office.'

Cassie's face cracked into a wide grin. 'Really?'

'It would be distracting.'

'Not if you organize things properly.'

Loveday chewed her lip, glancing back to Rosie. 'What d'you think, kid? Fancy being one of the team?'

Rosie had come to life again and was bouncing enthusiastically in her chair.

'I think that's a yes,' Cassie said.

LOVEDAY AND SAM were clearing up after supper when the call came. She could always tell when it was work by watching his face as he listened to the caller. His expression was one she knew only too well. His brows came down and his eyes narrowed, a deep frown forming. She sighed. 'OK, what's happened this time?'

'It's Lawrence Kemp,' Sam said quietly. 'Somebody's tried to kill him.'

'What?' Loveday stared at him. 'He's not dead, is he?'

'No, but according to Will he's been badly beaten. A neighbour found him unconscious in his cottage and rang 999. He was taken to Treliske Hospital.'

'I should go to him,' Loveday said.

'Absolutely not!' Sam put a restraining hand on Loveday's arm. 'Will says his condition is critical. The medics wouldn't let you anywhere near him.'

Loveday bit her lip, her head shaking. 'That's not right. Lawrence shouldn't be there on his own. What if he comes round and there's not a familiar face to greet him.'

'He's not alone, Loveday. The neighbour who found him is

there. She told Will she'll stay at the hospital for as long as she's needed.'

Loveday's hand trembled as it went to her head. 'It was him. I knew something was wrong about that man.'

'What man? What are you talking about?'

Loveday glanced away, aware she should have told Sam about today's meeting with Brian Teague. She hadn't because after their conversation the other week she knew he wouldn't be pleased that she'd gone, but she'd promised Lawrence, and Loveday didn't let her friends down. Now he was in a hospital bed, critically ill. Was this her fault? Should she have shared her concern about Teague with Lawrence?

She swallowed, preparing for Sam's wrath as she described what happened at the meeting, but his anger didn't come. Loveday had no idea why she was still trembling, because Sam had wrapped his arms around her. 'You should have told me,' he said gently. 'You and I shouldn't have any secrets from each other, not anymore.'

'I'm sorry, I didn't want to upset you. I knew you didn't want me to go.'

'Tell me again what happened today.' He listened intently as she again described the day's events.

When she'd finished, Sam's brows came together in another frown. 'Brian Teague is a name from the past. I know he blamed Lawrence for his wife's death, but that was a long time ago. From what you've said, the man wanted to make amends, so what makes you think he was involved in the attack on Lawrence?'

'Call it intuition. Something about him wasn't right.' She looked up. 'What happens now, Sam? Will you interview Teague?'

He nodded. 'Will's gone to Lawrence's cottage. I'm going to join him there.'

'I'm coming with you. I'll get Cassie to sit with Rosie.'

Sam raised his hands in a defensive gesture. 'Er, no you won't, Loveday. You'll leave this to me. Look, I know you're worried about Lawrence, but you have to let us do our job. Besides, forensics will be all over the cottage and they won't appreciate an extra pair of feet turning up to trample over their evidence.'

She knew he was right, but it didn't make her feel any better. 'I'll want to know everything,' she called after him as he made for the door.

He raised a hand in response. 'I'll keep in touch.'

'Promise?'

He looked back, smiling. 'I promise.'

CHAPTER 3

*S*am had been to Lawrence Kemp's home before, when he'd previously been arrested as a suspect in a murder inquiry.

Lawrence believed his involvement with the law had ended after serving his time and being released from prison, yet there he was, years later, back in the spotlight again this time as a murder suspect. He had Loveday to thank for his release when she'd set out to prove her friend's innocence.

It was the first time Sam had met Loveday. Her interference in his case back then had been like a thorn in his side, and to make matters worse, she was a journalist. Sam fell for her hook, line and sinker.

Detective Sergeant Will Tregellis was leaning against his car, arms folded, and frowning at the activities going on around Lawrence Kemp's fisherman's loft. He looked up as Sam approached, walking to meet him. 'Forensics won't let me near the place,' he said. 'But they say they're nearly finished.'

Sam glanced up at the place and was reminded how much the old building, with its view over the rooftops of St Ives to the busy harbour, must have suited the artist.

Kemp wasn't exactly a recluse, but he did enjoy his privacy. He would hate this current hubbub at his home.

He took the plastic shoe covers from his pocket and bent to pull them on. Will followed suit and they climbed the stairs to the front door.

'Watch where you step, we're not finished yet,' the big forensics officer warned as the detectives appeared. He pointed to the blood on the floor. 'That's where the poor devil was found. If you must come in I'd be obliged if you would stick to stepping on the cards.'

Sam gave the man an irritated scowl. 'We know how to move around a crime scene.'

Will also frowned. 'This is DI Kitto and I'm DS Tregellis.' He paused. 'I don't recognize you.'

The man coloured. 'Scenes of crime officer, Arthur Jacks. I'm new.' He hesitated before adding, 'Sir.'

Sam gave a distracted nod. 'We'll be careful,' he said, looking up as the man's colleague Martin Cleeve came out of the front room and strode towards them.

'It's all yours, Inspector,' he said. 'We're done here.'

They waited for Arthur Jacks to lift his bag and follow his fellow officer out before venturing into the main room.

Will blew out his cheeks, looking at the chaos surrounding them. Lawrence Kemp's home had been ransacked. 'What are we thinking, sir, a burglary that's gone wrong?'

'Maybe,' Sam said quietly. 'But Lawrence Kemp doesn't have many, if any, possessions worth stealing. I don't think this was a burglary, Will. This was done by somebody who's got it in for Kemp.'

'You think we're looking at a serious attempt on his life?'

'I'm not sure. He could have got in the way of the intruder's real reason for being here.'

'What real reason?'

Sam spun round, his eyes scanning the room. 'Our attacker

was looking for something and judging by this mess he didn't find it.'

'You think they could come back?'

'Let's not take any chances. I want a copper posted outside until we know what's going on.' He glanced at his watch. It was after eleven. 'I want to speak to Kemp's neighbour.'

'I think she was planning to stay on at the hospital at least until Lawrence has regained consciousness. He's in a pretty bad way.'

'It's late. We'll catch up with the neighbour in the morning. What ward is our man in?' Sam asked, pulling out his mobile phone.

'Last I heard he was still in intensive care.' Will watched as his boss rang the hospital for a condition check, and raised a questioning eyebrow as the call ended.

'He's still critical,' Sam said, his brow furrowing as he rang Loveday.

'Tell me again what happened at Lawrence's meeting with Brian Teague,' Sam said, next morning as Loveday sat up in bed bottle-feeding Rosie.

She repeated everything she could remember. 'I only went with Lawrence because he was uneasy about meeting Teague on his own.'

'So he was expecting Teague to cause trouble for him?'

'Could be, he didn't say. All I knew was that he would have refused to meet with Teague if I hadn't gone with him.'

'Was Lawrence surprised when the man said he wanted them to be friends?'

'That's not what he said, only that they shouldn't be enemies anymore.'

Sam looked in the mirror, straightening his tie before sliding on his tweed jacket. 'How did Teague contact Lawrence?'

Loveday wiggled the bottle for Rosie to suck out the last dregs of milk and screwed up her face, thinking. 'A letter, I think. Yes, I'm sure Lawrence said the man wrote to him asking if they could meet.'

'So Lawrence has an address for Teague?'

Loveday put the bottle down and moved Rosie onto her shoulder, patting her back until she burped. 'I suppose he must have, because he contacted him to arrange the meeting.'

'Why didn't he invite the man to his home?'

Loveday shrugged. 'Why would he? Lawrence had no idea what to expect. He could hardly be blamed for not trusting the man.' Her eyes narrowed as she met Sam's. 'You're thinking the same as me, that Brian Teague attacked Lawrence.'

'I'm keeping an open mind. You said yourself the man made you feel uncomfortable.'

A tear pricked her eye and she blinked it back. 'This is horrible, Sam. Poor Lawrence. I'm definitely going to see him today, and I don't need your permission.'

IT TOOK Loveday an hour to shower, dress and get Rosie ready for the day. When the baby was snugly buttoned into her hooded cardigan she carried her out to the car, clipping her into her special baby seat, It was another hour before they arrived at the Truro hospital. Not for the first time she reflected on how looking after a baby slowed everything down.

She took Rosie from the car and laid her in her buggy, then pushed her into the hospital and headed for the Intensive Care Unit.

'I'm a friend of Lawrence Kemp,' she told a nurse. 'I don't suppose I could see him for a few minutes?'

The nurse flashed her a harassed look. 'I'll ask,' she said.

It was ten minutes before the nurse reappeared. 'You've got

five minutes.' She threw an uncertain glance to Rosie. 'If the baby cries you'll have to leave.'

'She won't cry,' Loveday insisted, following the nurse as she hurried back into the unit.

'Mr Kemp is in the bed in the corner.' She nodded to the frail shape in the bed, whose face looked as white as the sheets that covered him.

'Lawrence?' Her voice was hardly above a whisper. 'How are you, Lawrence?'

Lawrence Kemp opened his eyes and blinked, a faint smile of recognition flickering across his face.

'Loveday. What are you doing here?'

'I was passing, so I thought I'd call in.' She gave him a teasing nudge. 'I was worried about you, of course. How are you doing?'

'I'm fine,' he croaked. 'Ignore all this fuss they're making.'

'Oh, Lawrence. You're not fine. Somebody attacked you. Was it Brian Teague?'

He touched his head with a shaky hand. 'I was attacked?'

'Yes, Lawrence. I'm so sorry. Did you see who it was?'

'No, it's all a bit hazy. I remember going out for a walk on the cliff path. That meeting with Teague confused me. I needed to think things over, but I still hadn't got it right in my head when I got back to the cottage.' He frowned as though trying to remember.

'What happened when you got home?' Loveday's voice was gentle. 'Was someone there in the cottage?'

Lawrence frowned, again, blinking. 'I couldn't understand why my front door was open. I crept in and listened. Someone was crashing about the cottage. I turned to get my phone from the kitchen and that's the last thing I remember. Everything went black. I don't even know how I got here.'

'A neighbour found you and rang 999.' Loveday bit her lip. 'I can't bear to think what might have happened if she hadn't been there.'

'Neighbour? You mean Cubby? She found me?' A tiny flush coloured his cheeks. 'Is she here?'

'According to Sam she's been here all night.'

A smile stole across Lawrence's face and there was a suspicious twinkle in his eyes that hadn't been there before.

'Lawrence Kemp.' She wagged a finger at him. 'What haven't you been telling me?'

'Nothing,' he said, but he was still smiling.

Her probing was cut short as a nurse appeared at the end of Lawrence's bed. 'I'm sorry, but you have to leave now. The doctor doesn't want our patient to get tired.'

Loveday flashed Lawrence a smile. 'They're throwing me out, but don't think for a minute that I'm letting you off the hook. I want to know everything about this Cubby.'

CHAPTER 4

The woman sitting outside the Intensive Care Unit looked up as Loveday came out. She got to her feet, her expression questioning. 'Are you Loveday?' She didn't wait for a response. An armful of bangles jangled as her hand shot out. 'I'm Cubby Angrove, it was me that found Lawrence.'

Loveday had no idea why she had pictured her friend's Good Samaritan neighbour to be plump, middle-aged and gossipy. She couldn't have been more wrong. Cubby Angrove was tall and friendly. She wore a colourful red Caribbean T-shirt over jeans, and her springy black curls had been brushed back and pinned under a tropical headband.

'You're Cubby?' Loveday smiled, trying to hide her surprise. 'I'm pleased to meet you. I'm afraid I might have used up Lawrence's visiting time.'

'No matter.' The soft brown eyes twinkled. 'I'm going nowhere, and they know that here. They'll let me in.'

Loveday indicated the chairs. 'Shall we sit?'

Cubby followed her lead, stretching down to touch Rosie's cheek. 'She's beautiful, what's her name?'

'Rosie, after my Scottish grandma.'

'You've given your baby a lovely name.'

Loveday smiled. 'Thank you.' Her eyes strayed to the closed ward doors and her brow wrinkled. 'Lawrence doesn't remember what happened.'

'How is he this morning? I've been in the canteen and haven't got into the ward yet.'

'Lucky to be alive I think, and that's all thanks to you.'

'I didn't do anything, I only rang 999.'

'It was fortunate you were there.'

Cubby gave a little shrug. 'I try to keep an eye on him, but Lawrence is his worst enemy.' She looked at Loveday. 'But I'm sure you know that.'

'I'm not sure I do, actually. What d'you mean?'

'Oh, I'm sorry, Lawrence talks about you so much I thought you two were good friends.'

'We are, well, we were.' Loveday shook her head. 'My fault. We kind of lost touch recently.'

Cubby touched her hand. 'Don't blame yourself. It's true that Lawrence has been in a bad place these past months, but that's not your fault.'

'I didn't know.'

'Why would you? Something happened to him, I don't know what it was, but it knocked him for six. He believed somebody was after him.'

Loveday stared at the woman, her eyes wide with surprise. 'After him? What do you mean?'

'I don't know. He wouldn't talk about it.' Her dark eyes slid away. 'The police were here earlier. They wanted to know if I saw anything yesterday that might throw a light on what happened to him.'

'Did you?'

'No, but...' She bit her lip. 'I have something for you. Lawrence gave it to me the day before he was attacked. He said I should pass it on if anything happened to him.'

Cubby dived into a colourful canvas bag and drew out a letter, thrusting it into Loveday's hand. 'It's better if you take this now.'

Loveday stared at the envelope and saw her name had been written there in Lawrence's careless scrawl. She wondered why he hadn't mentioned it.

'It's still sealed,' she said. 'You haven't read this?'

'Of course not, it's addressed to you.'

Rosie began to squirm impatiently in her buggy and Loveday gave it a shoogle. 'I know, little one,' she soothed. 'You've been patient and now you want to leave.'

She sighed, flicking her attention back to Cubby. 'I'll have to hand this over to the police. You know that, don't you?'

Cubby pulled a face. 'I know. The only thing I ask is that you read the letter first. I think you owe it to Lawrence.'

Rosie was becoming fractious by the time Loveday got her back to the hospital car park. Her last feed had been two hours earlier.

'Oh, Rosie, you can't be hungry again.' She gave her daughter a doubtful grin. 'You know there's another bottle in the bag, don't you?'

Rosie pushed her bottom lip out and then started to yell.

'OK, OK,.. I get the message,' Loveday said, reaching into the bag and taking out the bottle before lifting Rosie from the buggy. But with her arms full she struggled to open the car door.

'Looks like you could do with a hand,' a woman's voice said.

She'd been about to get into the parked car next to Loveday's but had stopped. 'Here, let me help,' she said, taking the car key from Loveday and zapped it to unlock the door. She pulled it wide to let mother and child get into the passenger seat before turning to the buggy. 'I presume this goes in here,' she said, expertly folding the thing and stashing it in the boot.

'I can see you're no stranger to babies.' Loveday gave her a grateful smile as Rosie settled into the serious business of feeding.

'I know my way around a buggy,' the woman said. 'I have two little ones of my own. They're at school now, but some things you never forget.' She smiled at the baby. 'Will you two be all right now.'

'We'll be fine. Thanks for your help, Loveday nodded to the woman as she got into her little red mini and gave a final wave before driving off.

Rosie gave a loud burp as she finished the bottle and lay back in Loveday's arms gazing up at her. Loveday blinked. Had that been a smile? Had Rosie given her first real smile? Yes, definitely a smile. It was a special moment. Loveday felt ridiculously proud as she drove back to Marazion.

By the time they reached home, Rosie was asleep again, stirring slightly as Loveday carried her into the kitchen and settled her in the baby seat. She looked down at the small, earnest face, still relishing that special smile. All her little daughter asked was to be fed, changed and tucked comfortably into her cot to sleep. The love that she and Sam lavished on their child was unconditional.

She waited until Rosie had settled before turning her attention to Lawrence's letter. Taking the envelope from her jacket pocket, she turned it over in her hand, not sure she had any right to read the contents. On the other hand it was addressed to her, and Cubby had clearly thought it important that she should read it before handing it over to Sam.

She took the envelope into the study and used the paper knife to slit it open. There was another envelope inside. The Truro postmark was dated five days earlier and was hand printed with Lawrence's name and address. It had been torn open. She slid out the contents and began to read.

Who's Who?
The Innocents? The Guilty? The Killer?
The Choice is Yours

. . .

LAWRENCE KEMP - KILLER of Meredith Teague and her twin babies. This man has no shame!

BRIAN TEAGUE - whose wife Meredith and babies were so cruelly snatched from him by Lawrence Kemp.

RACHEL DAWSON - whose only crime was to be too trusting.

PHILIP DAWSON - medical sales rep for a pharmaceutical company. Philip Dawson tours the country selling mainly to GP practices. This man is having an affair with Mellissa Grantby.

MELLISSA GRANTBY - PRACTICE manager at Hilltop Medical Centre, Truro. This woman is having affair with Philip Dawson!

LOCRYN GRANTBY - MELLISSA'S HUSBAND, an artist working from studio in Marazion.
   This man is having affair with Nessa Cawse.

NESSA CAWSE - RECEPTIONIST for Marazion GP, Dr Adam Trevillick. This woman formerly worked with Mellissa Grantby at Hilltop Medical Centre. This woman is having affair with Locryn Grantby.

. . .

KENAN RETALLICK - NESSA CAWSE'S partner, a fisherman whose boat *Our Bess* fishes out of Newlyn. An innocent man!

LOVEDAY STARED AT THE LETTER, her hand at her throat. What did it mean? She read it again, slowly this time. One name jumped from the page – Dr Adam Trevillick, Cassie's husband! Her brow creased. Why was Adam's name here? None of it made any sense, unless it was some kind of dossier put together by a would-be blackmailer.

But if that was the case, where was the evidence? There were no additional details to back up any of the writer's claims.

She sat down, taking in a deep breath. Poor Lawrence. She was imagining how he must have felt when he read this. Had it been meant as some kind of threat? It might explain why her friend had seemed so out of sorts.

One thing was sure, though. It was definitely something for Sam to consider. She would give it to him when he came home, but not before she made another copy for herself. Sam wasn't the only one who could investigate things. Lawrence may not have asked for Loveday's help, but he was her friend and she had no intention of letting him down, not this time.

CHAPTER 5

*L*oveday was in the nursery preparing Rosie for her bath when Sam walked in.

'Want me to take over?' He smiled, pulling faces to make the baby kick out excitedly.

'No it's fine, I've got this,' Loveday said. 'I think you should read that letter on the kitchen table.'

'What letter? What's happened?'

'Read the letter, Sam. You'll see what I mean.'

He strode off to the kitchen, returning a minute later with the letter in his hand. He held it up. 'You've read this?'

She nodded. Lawrence's neighbour Cubby Angrove gave it to me at the hospital this morning. She insisted I should read it before giving it to you.' Loveday went on, ignoring his irritated scowl. 'Apparently, Lawrence told her to pass it to me if anything happened to him. It could be what his attacker was looking for.'

He followed her into the bathroom, watching as she tested the water in the baby bath before lowering Rosie into it. The baby kicked and gurgled, blowing bubbles as Loveday trickled the warm water over her chubby little body.

'Bless her, she her loves her bath.' Loveday grinned, allowing

27

the baby to splash about for a bit longer before nodding to the fluffy white towel on the rail. Sam took it, holding it out for Rosie to be wrapped in it, the letter momentarily put aside as they returned to the nursery.

'There now, my darling.' She patted Rosie's soft skin dry before putting on her nappy and sleeping suit, and then laying her down in the cot.

'Night, night, sweetheart.' Loveday wiggled her fingers before turning to creep out of the room with Sam. They went back to the kitchen.

'Well?' she asked, sliding a casserole from the oven. 'What do you think? It has to be a blackmail thing.'

Sam spread the envelope and its contents on the table and sat back frowning at it. 'Do you recognize any of these names, Loveday?'

'She put the bubbling casserole on the table and came to stand behind him, her eyes scanning the letter. 'Only Lawrence and Teague, and Adam of course. I've seen his receptionist, this Nessa that's mentioned, come and go, but I've never spoken to her.'

'What about this guy?' He pointed to Locryn Grantby's name. 'It says here he's an artist and has a studio in Marazion.'

She shook her head. 'Never heard of him. But if you're looking for a place to start, it has to be with Adam and Cassie.' She put a dish of vegetables on the table and laid out their warmed plates. 'I think you should show Adam and Cassie this letter.'

Sam gave her a disbelieving stare. 'This is evidence, Loveday. Adam is named here. Of course, I'm not going to show them the letter.'

'You surely don't think Adam has anything to do with this? He and Cassie are our friends.'

'I know,' Sam said, watching as she ladled a generous helping of chicken casserole onto his plate. 'I'm still not going to let them see the letter.'

'What if we show them the names, with no mention of who's bonking who?' She waved a forkful of chicken before putting it into her mouth. 'I can type the names if you like.'

Sam gave a resigned sigh. 'Do I have a choice?'

'Don't be like that.' Her eyes twinkled. 'You know it's a good idea.'

They ate their meal in companionable silence.

When they'd finished, a slow smile spread across Sam's face. 'I suppose I should be grateful you're not suggesting going back to work yet.'

Loveday screwed up her face. 'Actually, I wanted to talk to you about that.'

He'd been scraping the plates clean before putting them into the dishwasher, but now he stopped, turning to look at her. 'Talk about what?'

She began to smile, then decided against it. 'You know how much I love being Rosie's mum, but my maternity leave can't last forever, Sam.' She paused. 'I need to work.'

He swung round to face her. 'You don't *need* to work. My salary can easily support us.'

'It's not about money, you know that. It's about commitment to a career.'

'So what are you suggesting? Working from home?'

'I can't do my job from home, well not all the time.'

Sam took her hands and sat her down at the table, gazing into her eyes. 'I do understand what you're saying, Loveday, but I can't see you going to the office and leaving Rosie with a childminder.'

'Who said anything about leaving Rosie? When I go back to work, I'll be taking her with me.'

H stared at her. 'And Merrick has agreed to this?'

'He will…when I explain my plan.'

'There's a plan?' Sam's eyebrows went up. 'Perhaps you can run it past me.'

'Let's have some coffee,' Loveday said. 'I'll explain everything.'

Sam ignored the offer, pouring himself a good measure of malt whisky. He went back to his chair before taking a sip. 'I'm listening,' he said.

Loveday swallowed. 'You realize this is only my original thinking. But we can create a designated baby area in that corner of the editorial floor no one uses. We'll have everything there that Rosie needs, nappies, wipes, bottles, formula, change of clothes, toys. But best of all, I can keep an eye on her.'

'That sounds fine, but what happens when Rosie gets hungry and cries? Will you be able to drop everything to attend to her?'

'That's where Priddy comes in,' Loveday said. 'She loves Rosie to bits, and Rosie knows her. I haven't sounded her out yet, but you know as well as I do, Sam, that she'd jump at the chance of spending more time with our daughter.'

Sam blew out his cheeks. 'Wow, you really have thought about this.'

THE TAP on the back door was quiet before the door slowly opened and Cassie poked her head into the kitchen. 'I'm not intruding, am I?'

'No, it's fine. Come in, Cassie.' Loveday waved her into a chair. 'Sam's gone into the study nursing a glass of whisky.'

'How did he react to your plan to return to work?' She waved aside Loveday's offer of coffee.

'Tricky.' Loveday pulled a face. 'That's what the whisky is about, but we're getting there. I had this idea to involve Priddy in the plan. What d'you think?'

'Priddy?'

'Well, why not? She's over here practically every day.' She smiled. 'And she adores Rosie.'

Cassie smiled. 'You're very fond of dear old Priddy.'

Loveday nodded. She was remembering the first time they'd met. Priddy had arrived in Cassie's kitchen in a great fluster, looking for Adam. She'd found her old neighbour lying in a pool of blood at the foot of his stairs. 'I think he's dead,' she'd said, her voice shaking as she'd asked for Adam to go back with her.

Loveday had comforted Priddy as she accompanied them back to her cottage at the end of the village. Not only was Jago Tilly dead, but he'd also been murdered.

After that, Loveday had taken to calling on Priddy after her morning jog along the beach, and over time they'd become good friends.

'I think it would work with Priddy coming to the office with us to look after Rosie. My only concern is I don't want to put her on the spot by asking. What if she doesn't want to do this but feels obliged? She might have some cock-eyed idea about letting me down.'

'She'd be more likely to feel insulted if you didn't ask for her help.'

'So you think I should ask her? She'll probably be round in the morning.'

Cassie shrugged. 'Play it by ear. You should be able to sense how things are when you raise the subject of going back to work.' She began to get to her feet.

'Hold on a minute, Cassie. I need to show you something.' Loveday grabbed the hand-written list from the worktop where she'd been scribbling the names. She slid it in front of Cassie.

'Do you recognize any names?'

Cassie scanned the list, frowning. 'What's all this about?'

'I want to know if any of these names, apart from Adam, of course, is familiar to you.'

Cassie looked down again. 'Well, there's Lawrence, and Brian Teague. I obviously recognize those names. And Nessa Cawse. She's Adam's receptionist.' She pointed. 'And this man, Kenan Retallick, he's Nessa's partner. He sometimes calls in to collect her after work. I think he's a fisherman.'

Loveday nodded to the list. 'What about Locryn Grantby? He's an artist with a studio here in Marazion.'

Cassie wrinkled her nose. 'The name's not familiar, although if he's out and about in Marazion then I might recognize him.' She looked up. 'I ask again. What's this all about?'

'Are you around tomorrow?' Loveday asked.

'In the morning I am. I'm not going to the marina until after lunch.'

'That's great. We can catch up then and I'll explain everything, well, as much as I'm able.'

'I can't wait,' Cassie said, getting up and heading for the back door. 'Tell Sam I'm sorry to have missed him.'

CHAPTER 6

'Freshly made this morning,' Priddy Rodda said, coming into the kitchen and putting a foil wrapped parcel of scones on the table. 'Now tell me,' she puffed, slightly out of breath after tramping up the long drive. 'How is our little angel today?'

'Rosie is just fine.' Loveday laughed, nodding to the scones. 'You're spoiling us again.'

'Nonsense,' Priddy's chins wobbled as she shook her head. 'It's only a bit of baking. Besides, I always make too many scones and you know how I hate waste.'

Loveday's eyebrows rose. Priddy's hospitality was legend, as were her baking skills. She couldn't imagine any of those home-made treats going to waste. Her little cottage was like the hub of the village with friends and neighbours popping in for a chat all day long. Could Loveday really expect her to give that up to look after Rosie? She wasn't even sure now she should broach the subject, but she had to give her friend the chance to refuse.

Crossing the room, she filled the kettle, setting out the cups and tea things as the water boiled. 'Sam and I have been discussing my going back to work,' she said lightly.

33

Priddy's expression was guarded. 'So you'll be looking for someone to take care of Rosie,' she said slowly.

Loveday glanced at her. This needed careful handling. She didn't want to put Priddy on the spot by asking her outright to be her childminder. She was happy to babysit now and again, but maybe asking her to take on more duties was expecting too much.

'Well, are you?' Priddy persisted, concern tinging her voice as she took the cup of tea offered and absentmindedly spooned two sugars into it.

'It's more than that.' Loveday sat forward. 'I can't face going into the office every day and leaving Rosie here. So I plan to take her with me.'

Priddy blinked, her blue eyes confused. 'But you can't do that. Rosie will need attention, and if you're busy editing the magazine…' She frowned. 'I'm sorry, Loveday, but I don't see how that would work. It wouldn't be fair on Rosie.'

'It could work,' Loveday began. 'If I had the right person to help me.' She eyed Priddy, but the blue gaze was still worried. 'What I need is for someone Rosie and I both trust to come into the office with us every day. We could create a special baby area, close to my desk, where Rosie could have all the love and care she needs.' She grinned. 'And I could still go across for cuddles.'

Priddy's eyelashes flickered as she considered this. 'When were you planning to start this?'

'No definite date yet, but I'm hoping no more than two weeks from now. I still have to get Merrick on board with idea.' She smiled. 'But I'm sure he will raise no objection.'

'In that case, neither will I.' Priddy beamed at Loveday. 'Let me know when you want me to start.'

Loveday's eyes widened. She hadn't offered the post to her friend, but that was of no importance because she knew she couldn't find anyone better to look after Rosie.

'Are you sure, Priddy? What about all those friends who visit you in Storm Cottage? Won't they miss you?'

Priddy gave an impish grin. 'They might miss the scones and fairy cakes, but they'll get used to it.'

Loveday raised her hand for a high five salutation. 'What a team this is going to be.' She was still in good spirits when she knocked on Cassie's kitchen door an hour later.

'Well?' Cassie said, smiling at baby Rosie. 'I saw Priddy leaving. Did you ask her?'

Loveday's wide smile gave her the answer. 'Come in.' She hustled them inside. 'I knew Priddy wouldn't let you down.'

'I haven't asked Merrick yet. I want to plan it all out and write a schedule of how it will work before presenting the idea to him. But yes, once he knows exactly what I have in mind, and how organized it will be, I think he'll be happy to have Priddy and Rosie in the office.'

She looked up, her eyes shining. 'I'm really excited about this, Cassie. It will be the best of both worlds.' She held her daughter up. 'What do you think, little one?'

Rosie blue eyes twinkled and she chuckled at the raspberry Loveday was blowing at her.

The phone in her pocket rang. 'That'll be Sam. He was going to see Lawrence this morning. He promised to ring and tell me how he is today.'

Cassie held out her arms to take the baby from her.

'Hi, Sam,' Loveday said, and then listened, her face growing serious at what she was hearing. 'Oh no! But that's terrible.'

'What's happened?' Cassie interrupted. 'Is it Lawrence? Is he OK?'

Loveday flapped her hand to quieten her friend. 'Is there anything I can do to help? What about the children?' She paused, biting her lip. 'OK, Sam, thanks for letting me know. Have you told Lawrence?' She paused, listening again as he answered. 'Would you like me to tell him? No? Well, can I at least go to see him?' She sighed. 'I feel so useless. Are you sure there's nothing I can do?' She slid Cassie a look. 'Tell Lawrence I'll visit him later.'

She ended the call and turned to Cassie. 'Brian Teague is dead,' she said flatly. 'It looks like he could have been murdered.'

Cassie's mouth fell open. 'Murdered?' She let Loveday take the child from her arms and sank onto a chair. 'When did this happen?'

'Sometime last night, they think. The postie found him this morning when he tried to deliver a parcel. He was living in a cottage outside Fenwick.'

Loveday's shoulders rose in a confused shrug. 'I didn't take to the man, but I wouldn't have wished this on him.' She bit her lip. 'He lied to us, Cassie. He told Lawrence and I that the children he brought to the meeting were his. Sam's told me Teague didn't have any children, but he did often look after his sister's youngsters.'

Cassie's brow creased. 'Does this have anything to do with the list of names you showed me? Lawrence and Teague's names were there. Lawrence was attacked and now Teague's been murdered.' A look of shock flashed across her face. 'Adam's name was on that list too, Loveday. Could he be in danger?'

'No, of course not.' She reached across to touch Cassie's hand. 'But the list…'

'Those were names I scrawled down from another document.'

'What other document? You're not filling me with confidence.'

Loveday pulled a face. Sam had been angry when she'd suggested showing Lawrence's letter to Cassie. She understood it could be important evidence, especially since Teague had been murdered, but circumstances had changed. Her best friend thought her husband's life could be in danger. She had to show Cassie the copy of that letter.

'There's something I need to fetch from the house. Can you look after Rosie while I run across?'

Cassie was giving her a confused stare. Loveday thrust the

baby into her arms. 'I'll just be a minute. You'll feel differently once you've seen this.'

She was out of the door and hurrying to her cottage before Cassie had time to object. The copy she'd made of the letter was still safely tucked into the pages of the magazine, where she'd hidden it before handing over the original to Sam. She squinted over the names and hesitated. Sam would definitely not appreciate her showing Cassie the letter, but he was coming at this from a different direction. Her friend needed to see it. She ran back across the yard and let herself into the big house. 'Here,' she said breathlessly, putting the note on the table. 'Read this and you'll understand. Adam's name is only here, incidentally. He's not meant to be one of the main players.'

Loveday put out her arms to take Rosie back as Cassie lifted the copy of the letter, her brow wrinkling as she read.

'This is weird,' Cassie said. 'Why would anyone write this? It says here that Adam's receptionist, Nessa, is having an affair with this Locryn character. I've met her partner, Kenan. He's lovely.'

'So you don't think this is true?'

'I hope not. Who's saying this, who wrote it?'

Loveday shrugged. 'It was sent anonymously to Lawrence. He obviously thought it important because he put in an envelope and asked his neighbour to look after it.'

Cassie's frown deepened. 'You don't think...' She shook her head. 'No, it's ridiculous.'

'What?' Loveday encouraged.

'I'm thinking about that intruder who whacked Lawrence. Maybe this is what they were looking for?'

'It's not ridiculous,' Loveday said, her expression concerned. 'How well do you know this Nessa?'

'Not at all really, she's only been with Adam for a few weeks. I probably know her partner better. Kenan sometimes calls to pick her up, so we've chatted.' She paused. 'They live across the bay in Newlyn.'

'He clearly impressed you.'

'Kenan's a nice chap. I really hope this letter is wrong and that Nessa isn't cheating on him.' Cassie glanced at Loveday. 'I know that look. Please tell me you're not planning to do your detective thing.'

'If you mean am I going to help Lawrence, the answer is yes, but I'll need your help, Cassie.'

'I don't like the sound of this. Why don't you leave whatever this is to Sam? You know he won't appreciate you, and certainly not *us*, interfering.'

'Don't you want to know if Nessa is having a fling with this artist person?'

'It's none of our business, Loveday.'

'Lawrence's neighbour made it our business when she gave me that letter.' She sighed. 'Look, Cassie. I'll completely understand if you don't want to get involved, but this is something I have to do. And the obvious place to start is with Nessa. If you introduce me to her I promise I won't ask you to do anything else.'

Cassie eyed her friend. 'I want it clearly understood that I won't be part of anything illegal.'

Loveday grinned. 'Does that mean you're on board?'

'Just listen to this mother of yours.' Cassie pulled a face at Rosie. 'It'll be you she's roping into her adventures a few years from now. Make sure you stand up for yourself, Rosie.'

Loveday tilted her head at the child. 'She's my daughter, Cassie. Of course she'll stand up for herself.' She ruffled Rosie's sparse blonde hair, giving her a fond smile. 'I'll make sure she does.'

CHAPTER 7

'Is Nessa working today?' Loveday asked, her eyes going to Cassie's kitchen clock.

'She's here every time Adam holds a surgery and he's holding one this morning. So yes, Nessa's here.'

'Doesn't he finish about now? He must be with his last patients.'

Cassie gave Loveday a sideways look. 'You're scheming again. What have you got in mind?'

'How does Nessa get home when Kenan doesn't pick her up?'

'I don't know. I suppose she takes the bus.'

'That's what I thought,' Loveday said, smiling down at Rosie as she got to her feet. 'How do you fancy a little run to Newlyn?'

Cassie screwed up her face. 'Newlyn?'

'I know you're due at the marina in Falmouth this afternoon, but I was thinking we could give Nessa a run home first.' She frowned. 'Don't look at me like that. I only want to meet the woman.'

'You want to interrogate her, you mean.'

'I want to know what's going on, Cassie. Lawrence was

attacked and Brian Teague is dead, possibly murdered. Nessa might know something.'

'In that case, shouldn't it be Sam who talks to her?'

'Of course, but Sam's not here.' She sighed. 'Look, Cassie, I have no intention of undermining him. I'll pass everything I discover onto him.'

LOVEDAY HAD CLIPPED Rosie's car seat into Cassie's big four-by-four when Nessa appeared from the side of the house. Loveday gave her friend a meaningful nod as she strapped her daughter into the seat.

Cassie smiled. 'Hi, Nessa. No Kenan today?'

The girl shook her head. 'He's at sea, he won't be home till later today.'

'We're heading out to Mousehole,' Cassie lied. 'Jump in, we'll give you a lift.'

'It's no trouble for me to catch the bus.' Nessa's unsure eyes swept over Loveday in the front and the baby in the back.

'That's Rosie. She won't mind you climbing in beside her. And I'm Loveday.'

Cassie was already starting up the engine, giving Nessa no time to make a choice.

'Cassie mentioned you live in Newlyn,' Loveday said.

'That's right, we have one of those little cottages up the back of the town.' She paused. 'It's not the prettiest place but Kenan, my partner, has a fishing boat, so we're stuck there for now.'

'You don't sound as if you're too fond of Newlyn,' Cassie commented.

'Oh, it's fine. But our cottage is ancient, and with both of us working we don't get time to do any of the repairs it needs.'

'That's annoying,' Cassie agreed.

Nessa frowned. 'No, it's just me. I shouldn't complain. At least we have somewhere to live.'

'It must be a pain having to take the bus to Marazion every day,' Loveday said. 'It's a pity you couldn't you have found work in Newlyn.'

'I like Marazion.'

'But apart from Cassie and Adam, I assume you don't know anyone in Marazion.'

'I...we have friends there.'

'Oh, anyone we might know?' Loveday was aware of Cassie's glance, but unless she asked the questions, they wouldn't get any answers.

'My former boss's husband is an artist. He has a studio in Marazion.'

'I'll probably know him,' Loveday said. 'I know lots of artists. What's his name?'

'Locryn Grantby. He has a studio up on the hill as you leave the village.'

Loveday pulled a face. 'I can't say the name's familiar. My friend Lawrence Kemp will probably know him. He's an artist in St Ives and he knows everybody,' she said, as Cassie stopped at the roundabout, waiting for a gap in the Penzance traffic.

'St Ives is lovely. Your friend's fortunate to be living there. The seafront is beautiful, and I love all those quirky little shops in the back street.'

'I don't know if you would have loved it a couple of days ago when Rosie and I were there. It felt like every visitor in Cornwall had crowded onto the beach.'

'But isn't that the charm of the place?' Nessa said. 'I always feel like I'm on holiday when I'm in St Ives.' She turned to smile at Rosie. 'You're a lucky little girl having a mummy who takes you for days out like that.'

'It wasn't exactly a day out,' Loveday said, glancing to Cassie. 'Lawrence was meeting up with an old acquaintance and he asked us along.'

'I was going to ask how that went,' Cassie broke in, as Loveday stretched into the back of the vehicle to retrieve the rattle Rosie had dropped. 'How is Brian Teague?'

Nessa's flinch was unmistakable.

Loveday looked up at her. 'Are you all right?' She raised an eyebrow. 'You don't know Brian Teague, do you?'

They were driving along the Penzance seafront. A wind had struck up, ruffling the surface of the water. Nessa was frowning at the waves creaming onto the shore. 'I don't know him, not really. It's complicated. He's a friend of a friend, that's all.'

Loveday was aware of Cassie's glance. They were almost in Newlyn. If she was going to discover anything helpful, she had to get Nessa talking about this.

'It really is a small world. Fancy you knowing Brian. I wasn't aware he even lived in Cornwall.'

Nessa narrowed her eyes at the billowing sails of the yacht they could see out in Mounts Bay. 'He's a very distant acquaintance. Kenan and I met him at a party in his sister Rachel's house.'

'I know what you mean. You're in the same social circle.'

'Hardly that. Rachel's husband Philip is a medical rep. I know him through the medical practice in Truro where I used to work.'

Loveday laughed. 'Any excuse for a party, eh?'

Nessa shrugged. 'I suppose it was networking on Philip's part, but he invited my boss Mellissa and her husband, to a party in his house. Kenan and I were included in the invite.' She paused. 'Brian Teague was there in the house. He was drunk. I'm not sure why he bothered to turn up because he didn't mix with any of us.'

Nessa pointed ahead. 'Take the next right, Cassie. You can drop me off at the top of the hill.'

'You sound like you felt sorry for him,' Loveday persisted.

'No, why should I? He wasn't in the least friendly. To be honest, I never gave the man another thought.'

They had reached the top of the hill and Cassie swung the vehicle around. 'Are you sure this is where you want dropping off?'

'This is great, thanks, Cassie.' The girl was already climbing out. 'See you in the morning,' she called, turning to give them a wave as she walked away.

'Did that sound like I was pumping her?' Loveday said. 'I really didn't want to do that. And I certainly don't want to make things awkward for you and Adam.'

'I don't think so. You and I know why we were asking questions, but as far as I could tell, Nessa didn't appear to be suspicious, although she was keen to stress, she didn't really know Teague.'

'Did you believe her?'

'I'm not sure. She did look a bit uneasy when you mentioned him.'

'Maybe,' Loveday said slowly. 'She was certainly surprised, but I could see no evidence that she knew Teague was dead, not in the way she spoke about him.

'Interesting though that all the people mentioned in that note sent to Lawrence know each other.'

Cassie bit her lip thoughtfully. 'I wonder if all of them received a copy?'

BRIAN TEAGUE'S COTTAGE, Windy Ridge, lived up to its name. The dwelling was only half a mile from the village of Fenwick, but situated by itself on the hill. A battered looking old green Ford Fiesta was parked by the side. The place would have been isolated if it hadn't been for the police activity.

'Is the body still here?' Sam asked, pulling in behind the scenes of crime van, and rolling down his window.

'They're waiting for the recovery team to collect him,' Will said.

The portly figure of Dr Robert Bartholomew, the Home Office pathologist, was emerging from the cottage door as the detectives approached. 'I suppose it's too early to expect any helpful information,' Sam called to him.

'There's no obvious physical trauma if that's what you mean.' Bartholomew turned back to the cottage, frowning. 'It could have been a heart attack. If we are to believe the evidence strewn around him the man was a heavy drinker. But I'm not ruling out poison. I'll know more when I get him on the slab.'

As the pathologist left, the undertaker's vehicle arrived, but Sam put up a hand, instructing them to wait until he and Will had viewed the body. They pulled on disposable shoe covers and gloves before going in. The front door led directly into the room where the late Brian Teague's twisted body lay on the floor.

'What are you thinking?' Will said, his eyes on the dead man. 'Are we looking at a murder?'

Sam screwed up his face. 'Well, I don't think he died of a heart attack.' His attention flicked from the near empty vodka bottle to the glass lying beside the body. 'Have we got photographs of all this?' he asked the forensics officer who was still working in the room.

The man nodded. 'I was about to bag these items.'

Sam glanced to the desk beneath the window, watching his step as he crossed the floor. 'Can we also bag these pens and the notebook.' He pointed. 'And those envelopes.'

'Why are we taking these?' Will asked, and then it dawned on him. 'Lawrence Kemp's anonymous letter. You think Teague wrote it?'

'I don't know,' Sam said. Even if he didn't it was another box ticked. He looked around the room. 'Remind me again, who found him?'

A young PC standing by the door stepped forward. 'The postie, sir, he's still waiting outside if you want to speak to him.'

'I'll be with him in a sec,' Sam said, turning to Will. 'Can you check out the bedrooms while I have a word with this chap?'

Eddie Carne was watching the cottage from the front seat of

his post van. He glanced at his watch and released a loud sigh. He'd been here for two hours and nobody had even bothered to speak to him. He wasn't planning to wait for much longer, and if the police didn't like that, then it was too bad.

He looked up, surprised when his window was tapped, the door opened and assessing dark eyes studied him. 'Mr Carne?' The big detective climbed into the passenger seat. 'I'm sorry you've had to wait, we won't keep you much longer.' Sam paused, studying the man. 'Can you tell me what happened?'

Eddie Carne's eyes went the undertakers wheeling out the body. He winced, clearing his throat. 'The man who lives here doesn't get a lot of mail, well apart from the official stuff, but today there was a parcel. There was no reply when I knocked on the door, so I went to tap on the window.' He hesitated. 'That's when I saw him.'

'How well did you know Mr Teague?'

'I didn't. He's only been here for a few months. I may have met him a couple of times. If he saw my van, he'd come to the door and collect his mail. You should speak to Janet.'

'Janet?' Sam queried.

'Janet Harris, his cleaner. She lives in Fenwick. Everybody knows Janet.'

'We'll be speaking to her,' Sam said. 'But to get back to what happened here, tell me what exactly you saw when you looked in the window.'

'Him.' The postman nodded to the body. 'I saw him, poor devil. My initial reaction was that he'd had a fall, then I realized his eyes were wide open and staring. That's when I knew he was dead.'

'Did you attempt to go into the cottage?'

'What? God, no. I rang 999. When the coppers arrived, I was told to wait, which I did. But I'm getting a little worried now. I still have my postal round to finish. When can I go?'

'One more question,' Sam said. 'Where is the parcel?'

'Parcel?'

'The one you came here to deliver to Mr Teague.'

'Oh, that one.' He screwed up his face. 'I'm not sure. I must have dropped it.' He pointed. 'Over there in those shrubs under the window. It'll be there.'

'OK, Mr Carne. Thanks for your help.' Sam made to get out of the van.

'Is that it?' Eddie Carne said. 'Can I go now?'

'Have you left your details in case we need to contact you again?'

The man nodded.

'Then yes, you're free to go,' Sam said. 'Thanks again for your patience.'

CHAPTER 8

*J*anet Harris's cottage was a squat grey building on the edge of the village. The busy-looking woman who was in the garden tending pot plants from a red watering can looked up as Sam and Will approached. Guarded blue eyes swept over them. 'I never buy at the door and I'm quite happy with the church I attend, thank you,' she said.

Sam smiled, producing his ID. 'I'm Detective Inspector Kitto and this is my sergeant, DS Tregellis. We're looking for Janet Harris.'

The woman put down the can, narrowing her eyes at them. 'You've found her, although I don't know what business the police have with me.'

'We understand Brian Teague employed you as a cleaner?'

'Mr Teague?' She looked from one to the other. 'No, the agency employs me. Mr Teague is one of several people I clean for.'

'When did you last see him?' Will asked.

'Yesterday.' Janet's expression was wary now. 'What's this about? Has something happened to him?'

'Why would you ask that?' Will said.

'Well, I don't get many visits from the police. I can see something's going on. Just tell me.'

Sam met her stare. 'Brian Teague was found dead this morning.'

When people were informed that a family member or an acquaintance had died, a range of shocked and then distressed emotions usually followed. But Janet Harris merely nodded. 'I'm sorry to hear that, but I'm not surprised.'

Sam and Will exchanged a look. 'Why is that?'

Janet Harris's kindly face turned away. 'I was fond of the man, even though he made it clear he needed no affection from anyone. I doubt if he spoke more than a handful of words to me all the times I was in his cottage.' She sighed. 'I didn't know much about him, but it was clear he was troubled. The way he sat in that chair drinking vodka, and staring out at the sea was enough to set your teeth on edge.' She looked up. 'How did he do it?'

'Do what?' Sam frowned.

'Kill himself. Isn't that what we're talking about?'

Sam paused before answering. He kept his voice low. 'We're still investigating how Mr Teague died.'

A flicker of uncertainty crossed the woman's eyes. 'You mean he had a heart attack, something like that?'

Sam was aware he could be pre-empting the results of the post mortem, but he was interested to see if any news shocked this woman. 'It's possible he did not die of natural causes,' he said quietly.

Janet Harris frowned as she absorbed this. 'Are you saying Brian Teague was murdered?' The colour was draining from her face. 'No, I can't believe it. Nobody would do that.' Her hand was at her throat. 'I mean why? The man never went anywhere. He was a virtual recluse.'

'So he didn't leave the house much, as far as you know?' Will asked.

'As far as I'm aware, he didn't leave the house at all. There wasn't much cleaning involved because he was fairly tidy, but it was part of his tenancy agreement to have a cleaner. I went in for an hour twice a week.' She bit her lip, thinking. 'I suspect the agency wanted someone to keep an eye on the property. If the tenant was causing any damage, I was expected to report that back.'

She paused, her head shaking. 'Poor man. He may have been strange, but he wasn't any trouble. So long as he had his supply of vodka he was satisfied.'

Sam's mind flicked back to the vodka bottle beside the body. 'If he didn't leave his cottage where did the vodka come from?'

'Mr Teague had his shopping delivered, but he arranged all that himself.' She paused. 'He did have a car, but I don't think he ever drove it. I doubt if it moved from the side of his cottage.'

'Tell us what happened yesterday,' Sam said.

Janet Harris glanced to the door. 'Look, I'm going to have a mug of tea. Would you gents like one?'

Will's hopeful expression answered that question. Sam smiled. 'That would be great, thank you.' They followed her into a bright, immaculate kitchen. The old wooden units had been painted cream, and copper pots gleamed from hooks on the wall. Janet filled the kettle and put mugs onto a tray.

'You were going to take us through what happened yesterday?' Sam was leaning against a unit and crossing his arms.

Janet stopped what she was doing, biting her lip as she thought about this. 'Nothing out of the ordinary that I can remember. I arrived as usual at two o'clock and did the tidying around. There were some dirty dishes in the sink, so I washed them and put them away.'

'Was Teague drinking at that time?'

She thought about this. 'I don't think so because he asked me to pour him a large vodka, which I did. He likes a lot of ice in his first drink, but he must have forgotten to refill the tray because there were only four cubes left. I tipped them into his drink and refilled the ice tray. Everything was normal when I left.'

Janet counted three tea bags into a white, ceramic teapot and poured on boiling water. They waited while she stirred the pot and shook a packet of jammy biscuits onto a plate. After a minute, she poured the tea, indicating they should help themselves to milk and sugar.

'Is the name Lawrence Kemp familiar to you?' Sam asked.

Janet thought about this. 'If you'd asked me this before last month I would have said probably not, but Mr Teague knew him.'

Sam was immediately alert, but kept his expression bland as he eyed his sergeant. 'How do you know that?'

'The letters. He wrote a bundle of letters about two weeks ago and asked me to post them. Lawrence Kemp's name was on the top envelope. I remember looking at the address. It was St Ives and made me think of artists. When I thought more about it, I realized I knew the name. He actually *was* an artist. I'd seen his name in the local newspaper.'

A laptop computer had been found in Teague's desk drawer, but there had been no sign of a printer. Sam's thoughts went back to the hand-written envelope Loveday had presented to him. Not having a printer would explain why the envelope and its contents had been hand written. But a bundle of letters? He hadn't expected that. It was beginning to look like everyone on that list had received a copy of Lawrence's letter.

'I LIKED HER,' Will said later, as they drove back to Truro.

'You like any old ladies who feed you jammy biscuits.' Sam grinned, but he agreed with his sergeant. Janet Harris was a nice, reliable kind of woman.

'Interesting that Teague sent a copy of that letter to the other names on the list.'

'We don't know that for a fact,' Sam countered.

'Not yet,' Will said. 'But it's looking that way, although even if it's right I'm not sure how much it helps us.'

Sam glanced in his mirror before overtaking the slower lorry in front. 'It might indicate another level of bitterness on Teague's part. Whoever wrote that letter was full of it. He wanted to cause trouble. And what better way to do that than giving all those people the chance to hate each other.'

'Maybe none of his accusations were true.'

'It wouldn't matter. Throwing suspicion in the ring would be enough to cause trouble.'

'You think there might be repercussions?'

Sam nodded. 'Don't you? Whatever is going on here, I think we are just at the beginning of it.'

LOVEDAY HAD BEEN WATCHING for Sam's car in the drive that night. She may have promised herself to stay out of this murder investigation, but that didn't mean she couldn't show an interest.

Her head came up when she heard him approach. He sniffed the air appreciatively as he came into the kitchen. 'Someone's been busy,' he said.

'Shop bought, I'm afraid,' Loveday said. 'But it will be burnt black if it stays in the oven any longer. Sit down, Sam.' She took out the steak pie and cut two slices from it, putting one on each of their plates and sliding a dish of vegetables onto the table.

'Smells wonderful,' Sam said, waiting for her to sit before taking up his cutlery.

Despite her undertaking not to immediately leap in with questions as soon as Sam sat down, impatience took over and Loveday couldn't stay silent.

'So, how did your day go? I'm dying to hear what happened at Brian Teague's place.' She was unable to hide the glint of eagerness in her eyes.

'It's a case, Loveday. I thought we'd agreed not to discuss my cases.'

'Are you forgetting it was me who gave you Lawrence's letter?'

'It doesn't look like I'll be allowed to forget.'

'Come on then, tell me what happened today.' Loveday put a forkful of meat and pastry in her mouth and gave a satisfying sigh. 'This isn't at all bad.'

Sam nodded his agreement.

'I'm waiting,' she encouraged.

Sam added broccoli to his forkful of meat and chewed appreciatively before swallowing the food. 'Bartholomew hasn't confirmed it's murder, but Teague didn't appear to have any actual trauma.'

'You mean he wasn't bashed about?'

'Exactly.'

'That doesn't mean he wasn't murdered.'

'It also doesn't mean it wasn't a natural death. He could have had a heart attack.'

'And I'm Good Queen Bess's auntie.'

Sam laughed. 'That wouldn't surprise me at all. Anyway, we're keeping an open mind until we have the results of the post mortem.'

'And that's it?' Loveday couldn't keep the frustration from her voice.

'Not completely,' Sam said. 'Will and I went to see Teague's cleaner. She thought he'd topped himself. She said he was a total recluse who had no relationship with anybody.'

'We know that's not true,' Loveday said, sitting back and fixing him with a frown. 'He came to meet Lawrence and me in that café. And he went to his sister's party.'

'Whoa,' Sam said, putting down his cutlery. 'What's this about a party?'

'That's right. Brian Teague's sister, Rachel.' She flapped a hand. 'She's on that list. Well she lives with her husband and family in Falmouth.'

'You said he went to her party?'

'That's what Nessa said, and she should know because she was there.'

'Nessa?'

'She's another one of the names on that list I gave you. Adam's receptionist, remember? Cassie and I were about to take Rosie on a trip to Mousehole when Nessa came along. She was on her way home to Newlyn after her shift. Naturally Cassie offered her a lift.'

'Naturally,' Sam said, repressing a sigh.

'We had a chat and she told us about the party. Brian Teague was there, and so was everyone else on that list. Well, except for Adam and Lawrence that is.'

'So what happened?'

Loveday screwed up her face. 'Nothing actually happened. It's just interesting that they were all there together. They knew each other. You have to speak to these people, Sam.'

He shook his head, laughing. 'Tell you what. I'll stay home tomorrow and look after Rosie while you go into the station and do my job.'

'That's a great idea, darling.' Loveday blinked at him. 'Are you serious?'

'No.' He smiled, tilting his head at her. 'You know I'm not.'

CHAPTER 9

'Loveday!' Keri Godden called across the editorial floor, her smile beaming as she rushed towards them. She hugged Loveday and reached down to Rosie's buggy to touch her cheek. 'And you've brought this beautiful young lady to see us.'

Other colleagues had left their desks and were crowding round full of questions and baby chat.

'When are you coming back?' somebody asked.

Loveday's gaze moved across the busy office, enjoying the familiar buzz of activity. It reminded her of how much she missed this. 'Looks to me like you're managing fine without me.'

'We're really not,' Keri said, her eyes still on Rosie. 'Merrick is currently doing your job.' She paused. 'Need I say more?'

Loveday understood Merrick Tremayne's position well. He owned *Cornish Folk* magazine and was deeply focused on its success. However, he wasn't a journalist, and while he wanted to support Loveday in creating an exciting and popular monthly magazine, he was hesitant to take risks. She remembered how often she had to persuade him to embrace her trendy new ideas.

With competition all around, they couldn't afford to let the magazine remain stuck in the past.

There was no doubt that the last issue had been rather dull. The interview with Newquay surfers, featured on a double page, didn't bring anything unique to the table. The photos were good, but the content felt repetitive.

'Is he around?' Loveday asked, her eyes going to Merrick's office.

'The boss has got a bee in his bonnet about the behaviour of tourists and he's out doing some vox pops with people in Boscawen Street. He mentioned something about showing the issue like it is.'

'Please tell me he's not planning to criticize our visitors.'

Keri gave a resigned smile. 'What do you think?'

'I think I'm sensing disaster,' Loveday said.

'Speak of the devil,' Keri murmured, nodding to the door.

Merrick was striding into the room. His face broke into a wide smile when he saw Loveday and came towards them, arms outstretched. He held her at arm's length, studying her face. 'You look wonderful, motherhood suits you.'

'It does.' She grinned back. 'I'd been told how boring it could be looking after a baby, but nothing about Rosie is boring.' She glanced down at her daughter, who was intently examining her fingers.

Merrick's expression was suddenly serious. 'This sounds like you're not planning to come back.'

Loveday glanced to his office. 'Actually,' she said. 'Can I have a word?'

She turned to Keri, but before she spoke, her friend was already bending over the baby who was making contented gurgling sounds. 'You and Merrick have your chat. Rosie and I will be fine out here getting to know each other.'

'Thanks, Keri,' Loveday said, turning to follow Merrick to his office.

He sank into his chair with a sigh. 'This isn't going to be good news, is it?'

'That depends on what you think of my suggestion.'

He blinked, a gleam of hope creeping into his eyes. 'Go on,' he said slowly.

Loveday drew in a breath and then exhaled it. She met his gaze. 'My proposal is a bit unconventional. I really do want to come back to work, Merrick, but I don't feel I can leave Rosie.' She paused, eyeing him. 'How would you feel about my bringing Rosie into the office?'

Merrick's mouth dropped open as he frowned.

'I've thought it all out,' she persisted. 'My friend Priddy Rodda has agreed to come into the office with me every day and take care of Rosie while I work. We could kit out that corner of the office nobody uses with a cot and all the other paraphernalia a baby needs.'

Merrick sat back, pouting as he considered this. 'It sounds distracting.'

'We could put screens up.'

'Babies cry,' he came back.

'Priddy will take her for a walk. Honestly, Merrick, you won't know Rosie is here.'

'I doubt that,' he said, getting up and taking a slow walk around the room.

Loveday bit her lip, watching him.

He suddenly swung round to face her. 'Running a creche in a busy office is a touch unconventional.'

'It wouldn't be a creche,' she protested. 'It's just one tiny baby. Won't you at last consider it?'

'I have considered it,' Merrick said, a slow smile starting. 'I think it's a genius idea. When can you start?'

. . .

'WELL?' Keri said, her gaze apprehensive as Loveday approached. 'Please tell me you're coming back.'

Loveday grinned. 'How does next week sound?'

'What? But that's wonderful.'

'It's doubly wonderful, because I'll be bringing Rosie with me.'

'You're bringing Rosie to work? But how…'

'Priddy,' Loveday said. 'It all hinges on the wonderful Priddy. She'll be coming to the office with us and looking after my daughter.'

'And Merrick is happy with this?'

'It's a compromise, but if it means my being able to come back to work then yes, he's happy.'

'That's wonderful,' Keri said, beaming down at the child in the buggy. She gave the rattle she was holding a shake. 'Hear that, Rosie?' Her smile widened. 'You're. joining the team.'

LOVEDAY HAD no intention of dropping in on Brian Teague's sister, Rachel as she drove back to Marazion. It had been an instant decision when she saw the road sign to Falmouth.

After Nessa Cawse had talked about that party the previous day Loveday had made it her business to check up on Rachel and Philip Dawson. She found an address for the couple and jotted it down in the notebook she always carried. And now, finding a safe place to stop, she fished the notebook from her bag and punched the address into the satnav.

The road where the Dawsons lived was on a hill overlooking Falmouth Harbour. Loveday drove past the upmarket properties with their extensive gardens. The house she was looking for turned out to be a large chalet bungalow. Unfortunately, Sam's silver Lexus was parked outside. She hadn't expected that. Surely the woman would have been interviewed yesterday after Teague's body was found?

Her pulse was racing as she drove past. If he saw her, she

would have a job justifying what she was doing here. She didn't know herself, apart from being sure that Teague's sister and her husband were an integral part of the clique of people listed in Lawrence's letter.

Not wanting to drive past the house again, she parked at the end of the road, keeping the property within eyesight as she waited for Sam to leave.

It was another ten minutes before Sam and DS Will Tregellis emerged from the house and got into the car. They sat talking for a few minutes before driving off. Loveday assumed they were discussing whatever impression Rachel Dawson had made on them.

There was no way she could visit the woman now. It had been Loveday's plan to introduce herself as Lawrence's friend, and someone who had recently met her dead brother. But that excuse had grown increasingly flimsy and she was beginning to feel she'd had a narrow escape finding Sam at the house before her.

Rosie was still asleep in her car seat. Loveday smiled as the baby gave a little snuffle. She was about to start the car when she saw a woman appear from the side of the Dawson's house and get into the red Mini parked in the drive.

Was this Rachel Dawson? Surely it must be? A visitor wouldn't park in the drive, not when there was so much parking space in the road. Loveday's hand was on her phone, holding it up to snap a picture before starting the car. There was something familiar about this woman, but she couldn't quite put a finger on. She frowned as she moved off behind the Mini.

Loveday hated tailing another vehicle, probably because she didn't have much experience of the task. She was sure if another car was deliberately following her she would definitely be aware of it. So she kept well back, thankful the startling red colour of the Mini was making it easy to keep it in sight.

She continued to pursue the vehicle through the residential streets. The car didn't turn onto the main road out of Falmouth as she had expected. Her suspicion that the driver was making for the town centre was confirmed when they emerged in The Moor, one of the town's main shopping and parking areas.

Rachel's car dropped to a crawl as she searched for a space. Loveday followed suit, pulling into a spot close to where the woman had parked.

Keeping her distance, she was aware of Rachel collecting a parking ticket. Loveday lifted Rosie into her buggy. She was beginning to wake, which usually meant a grumpy episode was imminent. Taking the bag of baby essentials from the boot, Loveday quickly grabbed a ticket, threw it onto her car dashboard and hurried after Rachel.

Her heart sank when she realized the woman seemed to be heading for the post office. Was this a simple shopping trip with a few chores thrown in? Loveday wasn't sure it was the kind of thing people did when a family member had died so suddenly. On the other hand, maybe Rachel – if this woman really was Rachel – and Brian hadn't been close siblings.

She glanced down at Rosie, who had already pushed out a petted lip. It was the lead in to that first, lusty howl. 'All right, little one, I know it's time for your bottle. Let's find somewhere quiet.' She looked around, her eye flitting over the post office building. No doubt Rachel would be inside by now, but following her was no longer Loveday's priority.

At the side of the building, set back from the road, was what looked like a cosy pub. People were sitting outside having leisurely drinks in the sun. Spotting a free table, Loveday pushed Rosie's buggy to it, and put the bag of baby things on one of the chairs.

A waitress appeared and Loveday gratefully accepted her offer to warm up Rosie's bottle. A few minutes later the baby was contentedly enjoying her milk feed as Loveday looked around. The pub was clearly old and from what she could see, full of character. Flower baskets cascaded with colour and drinkers at the surrounding tables were clearly enjoying the sunshine.

Rosie was now halfway through her bottle when Loveday set it aside to pat her back.

The baby gave a loud belch, searching around for the other half of her lunchtime feed.

As Loveday resettled her daughter on the bottle, a man who'd been sitting in the only shady corner stood up. He held out his arms and a woman rushed into them.

It was Rachel Dawson. Suddenly Loveday knew why she looked so familiar. This was the woman who had helped her cope with Rosie that day in the hospital car park. She sneaked another glance. The pair were sitting, their heads close together - and looking extremely agitated. Whatever conversation they were sharing, it wasn't anything romantic.

Loveday stood up, cradling Rosie and stashing the empty bottle in the buggy as she went in search of the baby changing facilities. Rachel hadn't even noticed her. Snatches of the couple's conversation reached her as she passed them. The man was holding the woman's hand, apparently attempting to be reassuring, but it seemed lost on Rachel.

'It's not right, Phil,' she said, a catch in her voice. 'You have to come home.'

Loveday's head was full of questions as she followed directions to the baby changing facilities. Rachel had mentioned home, and she had also called the man Phil. So, was this her husband? But if he was, then why were they behaving so conspiratorially?

By the time Loveday returned, Rosie's fresh nappy in place, the couple had gone. But the memory of a distressed Rachel Dawson lingered. Something wasn't right. Sam needed to know about this.

CHAPTER 10

*I*t was 8am, two mornings after the discovery of Brian Teague's body, and Sam was in the incident room staring at the murder wall. It could now be treated as murder after pathologist, Dr Robert Bartholomew, confirmed the man had been poisoned.

'A nasty business,' Bartholomew had said over the phone to Sam. 'Strychnine poisoning is not a good death.'

'Strychnine? You mean rat poison? I thought that had been banned years ago.'

'It was.'

'So how did our killer come by it?'

'I think that's more your domain than mine, Inspector, but I suspect bottles of this horrible stuff still lurk in old garden sheds.'

'Could it have been self-administered?'

'I doubt it. Judging by the books I saw in our victim's cottage, he was an intelligent man. Not even an idiot would have chosen this way to die. First there would be the fear, and then painful muscle spasms, an uncontrollable arching of the back, arms and legs would become rigid and the jaw would tighten.' He paused.

'They didn't ban this stuff for no reason, not even a rat should die like that.'

'I get the picture.' Sam cast his mind back to the sight of Brian Teague's twisted body. He could guess the trauma of what the man must have gone through before finally collapsing.

He turned his attention back to the murder wall, focusing on the letter that pointed a finger at each of seven potential suspects. Photos had been added, and he studied each one in turn. Was the face of their killer here? They could eliminate Lawrence Kemp as he'd still been in hospital when Teague died. He put a cross next to Lawrence's photo and turned his attention to the others. Were they really suspects? If their misdemeanours had already been laid bare in this letter, what motive did any of them have to kill Brian Teague? Or was there more? Had the dead man simply been flexing his muscles by demonstrating how easy it had been for him to dig out their secrets? Were the letters a threat, hinting at future blackmail?

His eye went to Rachel Dawson's picture. Her shock and distress when they broke the news of her brother's death had been real enough, but she had refused the offer of a family liaison officer. She'd told them her husband was attending a conference in Aberdeen, but said he would come home as soon as she broke this terrible news.

Across the incident room, Sam was aware of Will on his phone. He saw the sergeant's grim expression as he strode towards him.

'There's been a death at the Hilltop Medical Centre, but it looks like a suicide,' he said.

Sam spun back to the murder wall, his eyes narrowing as he stared at Mellissa Grantby's name. She worked at that medical centre. The woman was also on the list of people he had planned to visit that day.

'Do we have a name?'

Will shook his head. 'Only that it's the body of a woman. She was found in the rest room this morning by one of the GPs.'

Sam tried to keep his mind blank as they sped through the city, but images of Teague's body as they'd found him in his cottage, seeped back into his head. This incident may have nothing to do with Teague's murder, perhaps the dead woman had been a patient at the centre? It was a coincidence though that this had happened at a place specifically mentioned in that letter. Sam didn't trust coincidences, especially when he was investigating a murder.

A SOLITARY POLICE car sat at the entrance to the Hilltop Medical Centre. Sam pulled up behind it. Someone had the sense to stick a hand-written 'Closed Until Further Notice' card on the glass door, but confused patients were still milling about, demanding explanations for what was going on.

Recognizing the two detectives, a uniformed police officer stepped forward, clearing a path through the growing crowd to allow Sam and Will into the building.

'We need more people down here,' Sam instructed. Will was immediately on his phone requesting back-up.

Staff had assembled by the front desk. Some of the younger women were tearful.

A second young PC stepped forward. 'She's in here, sir.'

Sam could see a 'Police Incident' tape had been stretched across a door. The PC shrugged. 'I wasn't sure what to do, I tried to isolate the area.'

'You did well, Constable,' Sam said, ducking under the tape and opening the door to the rest room.

The metallic smell of blood in the enclosed space filled his nostrils. His eyes went to the body of Mellissa Grantby. She was sprawled on the floor by the sink, blood congealing on the two dark gashes to her wrists. A pool of blood covered the floor and was streaked on the wash basin.

Sam stared at the corpse, a wave of revulsion washing over him, 'Call the troops out, Will. We need a pathologist to see this, and forensics too.' His gaze went around the room. 'Who's in charge here?'

'That would be me,' a voice behind him said. Sam wheeled round as a middle-aged woman in a smart, no-nonsense belted navy dress stepped forward. She held out her hand for him to shake. 'I'm Dr Imogene Cornwell, senior partner.'

'Was it you who found the body?'

'No, that was Dr Bentley. He's over there. I suppose you'll want to speak to him. You can use my room.'

Sam and Will hardly had time to look around Dr Cornwell's consulting room when Dr Chris Bentley walked in and introduced himself. He bit his lip. 'It was me who found her.'

'What time was that?' Sam asked, aware that Will had produced a notebook and pen and was taking notes.

Chris Bentley pushed a hand through greying dark hair. 'I'm not sure, exactly. Around eight, I think. I was first here.'

Will looked up. 'If the deceased was in the ladies' rest room, how did you find her?'

'Her phone,' he said. 'I heard a mobile ringing and assumed someone had left their phone there, so I went in to retrieve it.' He paused. 'That's when I found her. I could see straight off that she was dead, but I searched for a pulse anyway.' His grey eyes clouded. 'Poor Mellissa. She must have been going through such a bad time to do this to herself. If only she had confided in one of us.'

'You recognized the deceased?' Will asked.

The GP nodded. 'Of course I did. She's Mellissa Grantby. She's–' He corrected himself. 'She *was* practice manager here.'

'You knew her well then?' Sam raised an eyebrow.

'Only as a colleague. We didn't socialize, well, not outside of practice events. We all went out for dinner at Christmas and there was the occasional presentation when someone retired or moved on. But that was it.'

'How long had she been employed at the medical centre?'

'I don't know. You'd have to ask Dr Cornwell. I've been with the practice for four years, but Mellissa was here before me.'

'From your previous comments I assume you think she was depressed?' Sam said.

Chris Bentley stared at him. 'She must have been to do a thing like this.'

'You're assuming she killed herself?'

'Well, she slit her wrists. What else would you call it?'

Will stared after the man as he left the room. 'He's got a point, sir. This certainly looks like a suicide.'

'We'll see,' Sam said.

IT WAS another hour before Bartholomew had completed his initial examination. 'Well?' Sam asked, watching through the open door as the man packed away his instruments into a black leather medical bag and screwed up his face. 'Please don't expect me to confirm suicide. It may look that way, but I won't know until I have completed my examination.' He waved a hand at Sam. 'It will all be in my report.'

'But we're not ruling out murder?'

The man turned to him, tutting. 'Of course not, Inspector, you should know at this stage we rule nothing out.'

'Bartholomew is such an arrogant sod,' Will said, coming to join his senior officer as the pathologist left. 'Why can't he smile once in a while?'

Sam shook his head. 'I guess smiling isn't in his job description.' He glanced across at the diminishing group of staff members still waiting to be interviewed. 'How are we doing with them?'

'Another hour should see us clear.'

The undertakers had arrived, and Sam nodded his permission for them to remove the body.

He turned to the wall display of staff members and counted six GPs. There was the practice's senior partner, Dr Imogene Cornwell, her deputy, Dr Hamish McEwan, Dr Christopher Bentley, Dr Carolyn Pascoe, Dr Rajesh Kumar and Dr William Thomas. There were six practice nurses and a further five administration staff.

They were still studying the photos as Dr Cornwell approached. 'How much longer is this going to take? We still have patients to see.' She sounded impatient, moving aside for the undertakers to wheel Mellissa Grantby's body past them.

'We all have our jobs to do, Dr Cornwell. And since we are investigating the death of a member of your staff, I'm sure you can bear with us for a little longer.'

She gave an exasperated sigh. 'Is it usual to investigate a suicide quite so exhaustively?'

'It is until a post mortem examination confirms this actually was a suicide.'

The GP looked even more irritated. 'What else could it be? For goodness' sake, you saw the body.'

Sam gave the woman what he hoped was a professional smile. 'We'll know more when we have the PM report. But I see no reason why you can't reopen the medical centre once the forensic officers have completed their work and the rest of the staff have been spoken to. The ladies' rest room will have to be sealed off though.'

'So this afternoon?' Dr Cornwell suggested.

'I would expect so,' Sam said, watching the woman leave before turning back to the display of staff pictures.

'Let's have a copy of all these photos,' he said.

CHAPTER 11

*S*am had arrived home exhausted the previous night. The first days of a murder investigation were like that. Loveday decided not to mention that she'd seen Rachel and Philip Dawson together, she wasn't even sure it was significant. This was another day and she had her own business to attend to as she stood at the door of Storm Cottage facing a delighted Priddy.

'I knew Merrick would agree to having Rosie in the office. He's such a sensible man.'

Loveday pulled a face. 'I didn't leave him much choice. He knew this was the only way I would consider going back to work.'

Priddy was still smiling. 'It was a good decision my lovely, so don't you feel guilty. Your colleagues will hardly know Rosie and I are there.'

'I doubt that,' Loveday laughed. 'My daughter has a knack of drawing the crowds. You and I have lots of work to do. For a start, we'll need an extra set of baby equipment, including another cot.'

Priddy's china blue eyes twinkled. 'We won't need a cot, there's one in my spare room. Rosie can have that.'

'You have a cot?' Loveday's eyebrows went up.

'It belonged to Emily when she was a baby.'

'But your granddaughter is nine years old.'

'Well yes, it's not new, but I have been looking after it and it regularly gets a good clean.'

'But it must be eight years since it was last used.'

Priddy frowned. 'What makes you think that? My little cottage is no stranger to babies you know. I have lots of young friends with babies who regularly visit me. Believe me. Emily's cot still gets plenty use. Come upstairs and see for yourself.'

Loveday held Rosie close as she followed Priddy up to her spare room.

The pretty white cot by the window wasn't at all what she'd been expecting. It was pristine. Even the little clusters of pink roses that decorated the ends were still bright and colourful.

Priddy pulled a face, glancing at her. 'I can see what you're thinking. You're right. It is old. I don't mind at all if you want something smart and new for Rosie.'

Loveday smiled. Despite what Priddy said she knew her friend would be disappointed if she refused the cot. But why would she? It was a kind gesture. 'It's perfect. Thank you, Priddy. I'm sure Rosie will love it.'

'Good.' Priddy nodded, bustling Loveday from the room. She was back in business mode. 'That's one more thing we can tick off the list.'

LOVEDAY WAS in a good place as she pushed Rosie's buggy back home. The sun was shining and she was planning an afternoon in the garden when her mobile rang.

'There's been another death,' Sam said. 'Mellissa Grantby. She's on that list.'

Loveday froze, one hand on the buggy, the other holding her phone.

'Loveday? Did you hear me?'

She shook her head. 'I can't take this in. How did she die?'

'It looks like suicide. She was found in the ladies' toilet at the medical centre where she worked. Her wrists were cut.'

'Who found her?'

'One of the doctors.'

'That's awful, Sam. When will you know?'

'I don't understand what you're asking. Know what?'

'If it really is suicide. Looks like a pretty huge coincidence to me.'

'This exactly why I'm ringing you, Loveday. I don't want you speaking to any of the other people on that list. Or anyone else connected to the case.'

'Why would I do that?'

'I have no idea why you would want to get involved, I'm just asking you not to. You really must leave this to us.'

Loveday's brow wrinkled. She already was involved. Cassie's husband, Adam, was mentioned in that list, and his receptionist, Nessa, worked with him in his and Cassie's house right next door. How could she not be involved?

'Did you hear me, Loveday?' Sam's voice was stern.

'I heard you,' she said quietly.

She was deep in thought as she approached her drive. It would have been comforting to find Cassie's big four-by-four there. She needed advice, but the parking space was empty.

Loveday forced herself not to think any more of the late Mellissa Grantby and Brian Teague until she'd put Rosie down for her afternoon nap.

Satisfied that her daughter was settled, Loveday turned and walked slowly next door to the study. She switched on the computer, intending to make a list of the baby things she would need when she and Priddy set up Rosie's corner in the magazine office. But she found herself Googling Philip Dawson's name. It showed nothing relevant. It was annoying she didn't know the name of his employer. A pharmaceutical company was sure to have an online presence and a picture file of their main employees. She sat back, blinking. Facebook! Of course, she could check that.

Logging in to her social account, she searched for Philip Dawson. He was there, and even better it looked like a family account. There was a picture of the man she'd seen earlier outside the old Falmouth pub. In the picture, the same woman she'd followed from the Dawson house was smiling up at him. And there was a bonus – the two little girls with them were the same children Brian Teague had brought to that meeting with Lawrence. Why had he wanted them to believe they were his daughters?

She sat back, staring at the screen. This really didn't take her much further, but at least she now had a photo of the Dawson family.

Loveday replicated the Facebook search using Teague's name but it produced no results, and the Google search only revealed details of Lawrence's court case and the accident that caused the death of Teague's wife Meredith and their unborn twins.

She had started to type Mellissa Grantby's name into her computer when she heard the familiar sound of Cassie's vehicle pulling up in the drive. She went to the back door.

'I was hoping you might finish early,' Loveday called. 'Can you spare a minute?'

'Sounds intriguing.' Cassie's brow creased when she saw Loveday's serious face. 'What's happened?'

'Nothing, well, nothing that affects the family. Come through,' Loveday said, beckoning Cassie into the kitchen.

Neither of the women sat down. 'Well?' Cassie said. 'Are you going to keep me guessing?'

'It's that list.' Loveday bit her lip. 'Another person has died, Mellissa Grantby.'

Cassie stared at her. 'Died? You mean murdered?'

'Sam says it could be suicide.'

'But you don't believe that?'

'I don't know. Maybe. It's just so creepy.'

'What are you going to do?'

'Nothing. I've promised Sam I won't get involved.'

'Oh, right.' Cassie gave her a sideways look. 'And an angel piddled in my drink.'

Despite herself, Loveday laughed. 'You have such a turn of phrase. But really, I have to stay out of this.' She glanced away. 'Which is why I was wondering if you might have a word with Nessa.'

Cassie's brow wrinkled. 'You want me to speak to Nessa? But why?'

'Mellissa was her boss when she worked at the medical centre in Truro. I'm curious to know why she left.'

'I'm not sure about this. What if Mellissa and Nessa were close? I don't want to be the one to share the news that her friend has died.' She drew in a breath and let it out again. 'I don't exactly think that would get me into your bloke's good books. And then I'd have to explain how I knew about Mellissa. I can see the whole thing escalating.'

Loveday pulled out a kitchen chair and sank onto it, thinking. 'I can't believe these two were best mates when Nessa was pinching her husband.'

'How do you know this?'

'It was in that letter Lawrence was sent. I showed it to you. Remember?'

Cassie sighed. 'Yes, I remember.'

'According to that, Nessa was having an affair with Mellissa's husband, Locryn Grantby.'

'So what are you saying? Are you suggesting they were

enemies?' She swung her eyes to the ceiling. 'This is beginning to sound like you think Nessa killed her.'

Loveday blew out her cheeks. 'I don't know what I think. It's just a feeling that something's not right.'

Cassie pulled a face. 'Tell you what. I won't do anything until you tip me the wink that Sam has spoken to Nessa. I'll have a word with her after that. Who knows, maybe she'll confide in me.'

'Now you're talking.' Loveday grinned.

It was almost eight when Sam walked in that night.

Loveday ran to him and took his hand, plonking him down in one of the comfy chairs. 'You look whacked, my love. Have you eaten?'

'I'm fine. I had a pasty earlier,' he said, rubbing his hands over his face. 'How has Rosie been?'

'Our daughter is absolutely wonderful, of course she hasn't quite managed to read *War and Peace* yet, but I'm working on it.'

Sam laughed. 'How did it go with Merrick today?'

'Really well, actually,' Loveday said. 'He's happy to give up a corner of the editorial floor to Rosie if it means getting me back.'

'Modest, aren't you.' He smiled, taking her hand and pulling her onto his knee. She bent her head to kiss him.

'Want a drink?' she asked.

'After you kiss me again.'

She did, before getting up to pour Sam his evening glass of whisky and then settled to watch him relax. She knew he liked to talk through his day with her, but sometimes he needed a bit of prompting.

'That was bad news about Mellissa Grantby,' she said quietly. 'Are you still treating it as suicide?'

Sam nodded. 'That's the plan, unless we get any evidence to the contrary.'

'You do know that the woman who was once her receptionist now works next door for Adam?'

'Yes, I also know she was having an affair with Mellissa's husband.'

Loveday nodded. 'Of course you do.'

'And before you ask, yes we did speak with her,' he said.

'You mean you interviewed Nessa next door at Adam's surgery?'

Sam raised his eyes to the ceiling. 'Did I say that?'

'Well no, but…'

'We visited her at her home in Newlyn. She'd turned up earlier at the medical centre, saying she wanted to speak to Mellissa. DC Amanda Fox had a word and got her address.'

'Did she tell you anything interesting?'

'Not really. She admitted to the affair, but said she ended it weeks ago.'

'Did you believe her?'

Sam shrugged. 'Why not?'

'What about Brian Teague? Anything new there?'

'Apart from the confirmation that he was poisoned, no.'

Loveday's eyes rounded. 'So it really was murder? Have you spoken to any of his cronies from that party?'

'Will and I visited his sister, Rachel Dawson again yesterday.'

Loveday felt her cheeks colour. 'She must have been devastated to hear Brian was murdered?'

'We didn't have that information when we spoke to her, she only knew he was dead. We'll be going back to see her again in the morning.'

'Were they close as siblings?' Loveday asked.

'The woman was very upset, if that's what you mean. It can't be easy coping with news like that when you're alone.'

Loveday's ears pricked up. 'Alone? But surely she's married?'

'She is, to a travelling salesman who trades in medicines.'

'You make him sound like one of those old peddlers who used

to flog wonder remedies from the back of a wagon. Nessa said he was a respectable rep who works for a pharmacy company.'

'Well, whatever he is, he was away at a conference in Aberdeen when Teague was murdered. His wife was going to contact him.' He stretched. 'He's probably home by now.'

An image of Rachel and Philip Dawson sharing their serious conversation at the Falmouth pub came to mind. She was on the point of blurting out that he couldn't have been away from home because she'd seen him. But if she did that she'd have to explain how she'd recognized him, which meant she'd also have to keep quiet about Rachel helping her with Rosie. How long could she delay telling Sam that she'd seen him and Will leave the Dawson house yesterday?

If that annoyed her detective partner, she could only imagine how concerned he'd be if he heard she had followed Rachel to Falmouth town centre and later researched the couple on Facebook.

She was doing exactly what she'd promised not to do, and now she was involving Cassie.

But this wasn't about her. Rachel Dawson had given her husband an alibi, but it was a lie. Had she done that because she believed her husband had killed her brother? And now Mellissa Grantby – the woman Dawson had been having an affair with – was also dead.

CHAPTER 12

*R*osie's lusty cries woke them next morning. Loveday yawned. 'I think our daughter is trying to tell us something,' she said, stretching.

'I'll go,' Sam said, hopping out of bed and grabbing his dressing gown.

'There's a bottle made up in the fridge,' she called after him. 'Just put it in the bottle warmer.'

She snuggled luxuriously back under the duvet, letting flashes of last night's conversation with herself float through her mind. Philip Dawson had got his wife to say he'd been away on business when Brian Teague was murdered. She understood why Rachel would want to support her husband, but police investigations were sure to expose the lie. She also suspected the couple's behaviour, when she saw them together in Falmouth, could be important, but if she told Sam she would have to explain how she'd recognized them.

Loveday closed her eyes. She had to think of something. And then it came to her. All she had to do was to find an excuse to visit Sam at the police station. If she could get herself in, she might be able to snatch a glance at the incident board. She knew it was police procedure to pin up everything and everyone connected to a case. There was bound to be a photo of Rachel, and hopefully Philip Dawson on that board.

Getting past the desk sergeant and into the incident room would be the tricky part.

She was still thinking about that when Sam came back. 'Rosie needs changing,' he announced, wrinkling his nose. 'I'll let you do that.'

Loveday pulled a face, tossing a pillow at him as he disappeared into the shower.

An hour later she was showered and dressed and Rosie was clean and freshly changed. In the kitchen, Sam handed Loveday a mug of steaming coffee. 'Are you planning to go back to Truro today?'

She nodded, reaching for a piece of buttered toast. 'I'm going to the office. My to-do list is a mile long. Priddy has agreed to look after Rosie while I'm busy sorting out that baby corner.'

'Will you have time to call in at the station?'

'W-h-y?' Loveday stretched out the word, eyeing him.

'I want you to take a look at some photos. You know the kind of people Lawrence associates with. It's a bit of a long shot, but you might see someone you recognize.'

Loveday tried not to choke on her toast. She'd been wracking her brain for a reason to visit Sam and here he was laying it out on a plate for her.

'Sure,' she said, as casually as she could manage. 'I'll look in.'

'Thanks, Loveday,' he said, dropping a kiss on the top of her head as he went out the back door.

Priddy's face was glowing as she held her arms wide to Rosie. 'Come here, my lovely. You and I are going to have such a good time today.' She jiggled the baby up and down and Rosie blinked up at her.

'This is really kind of you, Priddy.' Loveday pushed the buggy into the tiny kitchen and put the baby bag on the table. 'Everything you'll need is there. Call me if you have the slightest problem.'

'Don't worry. Rosie and I will be fine.'

Loveday bent to kiss her daughter's cheek and waggled a finger at her, grinning. 'And you behave yourself, my girl. I don't want to hear you've been bossing Priddy about.'

'You wouldn't do that, my lovely, would you?' Priddy beamed. It was obvious to Loveday that her friend and her daughter were going to enjoy their day together.

She took her time, enjoying the stroll along the seafront as she headed back to the cottage to collect her car. On mornings like this, when the sun sparkled on the water, and St Michael's Mount looked inviting, it was hard to imagine anywhere more beautiful than Marazion. Or was that being disrespectful to her childhood home in the Scottish Highlands?

Her mum, Heather, would be in the kitchen of the Dolphin Inn right now, cleaning up after serving a hearty Scottish breakfast to her B&B guests. Her dad, Duncan, would be stocking up the bar and preparing for another busy day.

Loveday's older brothers, Hugh and Brodie still helped out when needed, but these days their focus was on the little craft brewery they had set up. It wouldn't make their fortune, but then they'd never intended it should. The fact that their beer was so popular was enough success for now.

Loveday smiled, remembering the welcome they had given Sam and her when they travelled north to introduce Rosie to her family.

Hugh and Brodie had not married either, but they had partners and their own little families. Loveday saw how much her parents doted on the collective grandchildren, Ross (five), Daisy (two) and Brodie's three-year-old twins, Robbie and Lucy.

Now they had another granddaughter and their delight couldn't have been more obvious.

Her thoughts returned to the day ahead as she approached the end of her drive and zapped her car to unlock it. The crunch of feet on the gravel behind her had her swinging round.

'Good morning,' the young woman said.

'Good morning, Nessa.' Loveday had not missed the dejected look in the girl's huge brown eyes. She sucked in her bottom lip, unsure if she should mention Mellissa Grantby's death. But Nessa resolved the issue herself.

'You'll have heard about Mellissa,' she said.

Loveday nodded. 'I'm so sorry. Were you close friends?'

'Not really, but we were colleagues.' The brown eyes filled. Loveday took a tissue from her bag and handed it to the girl.

'I'm sorry, but it's been such a shock.'

'I can imagine,' Loveday said.

Both women turned as Cassie emerged from her house. When she saw Nessa's distress, she immediately went to give the girl a hug. 'I heard about your friend,' she said gently. 'Come into the kitchen. The surgery hasn't started yet. Adam won't miss you for a few minutes.' She looked up. 'You come too, Loveday. We'll have a cup of tea.'

Loveday filled the kettle and busied herself with the tea things while Cassie put an arm around Nessa's shoulder. 'If you need to go home I'm sure Adam will manage.'

'No, it's fine.' The girl raised a hand and pushed her blonde hair from her face. 'I can't believe Mellissa would kill herself. I spoke to her a few days ago. There was no hint of any of this. She was buoyant, full of herself even.' She shrugged. 'That was the Mellissa I knew.'

Loveday put a mug of hot, sweet tea in front of Nessa. The

girl was shaking. 'There must be something we can do to help,' Cassie said.

'You said you didn't believe Mellissa killed herself. What did you mean?'

Nessa pushed her hands through her hair. 'Oh, I don't know. I'm all over the place. One minute I'm thinking Mellissa couldn't possible have killed herself and then I'm thinking this was all my fault.'

'Of course it isn't. How could it be your fault?'

'Because I had an affair with her husband.' Her glance moved from Loveday to Cassie, expecting to be met with disapproving looks, but she found none. 'It was over ages ago, but Mellissa still blamed me. I went along to the medical centre yesterday to have it out with her but they wouldn't let me in. The police were everywhere. I had no idea what was going on. I said they had to let me in, these people were my friends.'

She swallowed. 'That's when this female detective appeared asking how I knew everybody there. I told her I had once been the receptionist. That's when she told me it was Mellissa who had died.'

'I left my address and the police came to see me at home later, but I couldn't tell them anything.' She paused. 'I feel sick. This was all my fault.'

'That's ridiculous,' Cassie said. 'Anyway, you said you didn't believe she killed herself.'

'But if she didn't…' Loveday left the sentence hanging.

'If she didn't,' Cassie said. 'Then someone else was responsible for her death.'

Nessa stared at her. 'You think Mellissa was murdered?'

'Do you have a better explanation?' Loveday said.

.   .   .

LOVEDAY WAS STILL CONSIDERING this possibility as she drove to the police station in Truro. Sam wasn't there when she arrived, but he'd asked Amanda Fox to meet her.

'I understand DI Kitto wants you to look at some mugshots,' she said, not waiting for a response. The smile was stiff as she walked Loveday past the incident room and into an anteroom. 'You can wait here while I fetch the books.'

New tiny frown lines were etched into the woman's face making her look years older than the last time they'd met. The corkscrew auburn curls having been scraped back into a severe knot on top of her head did nothing to improve her appearance.

Loveday was thoughtful as she watched her leave the room. The whole station knew about Amanda's crush on Sam. But that had been years ago and Loveday had no idea if the woman still held a torch for him.

The detective returned minutes later with two large photo albums and dumped them on the table. They were clearly heavy.

Loveday stared at the books, her eyebrows going up. 'What exactly am I looking for?'

Amanda shrugged. 'I assume the inspector wants you to flag up anybody you recognize.'

'If you mean anyone connected with your current case, wouldn't it be better if I looked at those faces on your murder wall?'

Loveday didn't miss the fleeting hesitation. 'I've only been instructed to show you these mugshots,' she said curtly. 'Take your time and have a good look at them.' She was already heading for the door.

Left on her own, Loveday began flicking through the pages. Some faces looked familiar, but not in connection with Brian Teague's murder. And any of them could have been responsible for that attack on Lawrence. She closed the books with a sigh. She'd been no help at all.

Loveday got up and opened the door, glancing into the

corridor for someone to tell she'd finished. No one was about so she ventured out. She'd spotted the incident room on the way here. If she found her way there surely no one would question she'd taken a wrong turning. Her pulse picked up as she quickened her step. A man emerged from a door at the far end of the corridor and gave her a nod as he passed. Loveday went through the door and found herself in the large open-plan incident room. The board she was looking for was on the wall to her right. At one of the far desks she could see Amanda, her head bent and a phone to her ear. No one was paying her the slightest attention so she walked on, stopping when she reached the murder wall.

Her eye travelled over the faces. Lawrence was at the top of the board and below him the face of Brian Teague. His sister Rachel Dawson was also there with her husband right next to her. Loveday's hand was on the phone in her pocket. She glanced over her shoulder. She couldn't believe none of these detectives was questioning her presence in their incident room. Slowly she withdrew the phone and snapped a photo, sliding it back into her pocket.

At the same moment, Amanda turned, and seeing Loveday, jumped up from her desk. 'You shouldn't be here,' she snapped, directing her from the room.

'I looked at all those photographs but I can't say I actually recognized any of them.' She shrugged. 'Sorry.'

Amanda sighed, pushing open the door. 'I'll tell DI Kitto you weren't able to help.'

'Where is Sam?' Loveday asked, as they headed for the way out.

'He's busy with enquiries, but thank you for your time.' She held out her hand for Loveday to return her ID pass. She'd been dismissed, but she'd achieved her purpose. She could now speak with confidence when she told Sam the alibi Philip Dawson had given was flawed.

CHAPTER 13

Sam answered Loveday's call immediately. 'I've seen your murder wall,' she said.

'You what? You were in the incident room.' He didn't sound pleased.

She sighed. 'Well it was your idea for me to go into the station and look at those photos.'

'Those mugshots aren't in the incident room.'

'Er, no. I got lost. The point is, I saw Philip Dawson's photo, and I recognized him. I saw him and his wife in a Falmouth pub garden yesterday. So if they told you he was in Scotland when Brian Teague died they were lying.'

'What are you talking about, Loveday?'

'I told you,' she cut him off. 'Rosie and I were in Falmouth and we called in at this place so I could feed and change her and these two people were there. I noticed them because they were arguing. The woman appeared upset and the man was trying to calm her down.'

'What time was this?'

Loveday's brow crinkled as she worked this out. 'Well, I was giving Rosie her lunchtime bottle. You work it out.'

'How is Rosie?'

Loveday smiled. 'According to Priddy, our little girl is loving all the spoiling she's been getting at her place.'

'I can imagine,' Sam said, and she knew he was smiling too as the call ended.

Loveday had already called Priddy for a quick check up on Rosie before she went into the police station. If she rang again this soon, it would look like she didn't trust her old friend. Priddy would contact her if there was a problem. She stuffed the phone into her pocket and drove out of the police car park.

THE HOSPITAL WAS as busy as she'd expected. She knew from her phone contact with the Intensive Care Unit that Lawrence had been moved into a regular ward, but she was chastising herself for not visiting him sooner. She made her way through the maze of corridors until she found the door to the ward where they'd put him. Her face broke into a wide smile as she recognized the woman sitting there.

'Hello, Cubby, it's good to see you again.'

'Loveday!' The woman's face lit up. 'Lawrence will be so glad to see you. We can't go into the ward at the moment because the doctors are doing their rounds, and only family members can be there.'

'How is the patient today?' Loveday was on tiptoe to see through the glass door panel and into the closed ward.

'You mean apart from being cantankerous?' Cubby gave an exasperated sigh.

'That doesn't sound like Lawrence.'

'I'm afraid your friend doesn't take kindly to being kept in hospital. He's all ready to go home, but he has to wait for the final sign-off from the consultant, Mr James.' She smiled. 'He just wants to get out of here.'

Before she had finished speaking, the ward doors flew open

and an important-looking man in a crisp candy-striped shirt and rose pink tie strutted out. A posse of young medics chased after him.

'That's him, that's the consultant,' Cubby whispered. 'He's the one who has the final say on whether Lawrence gets discharged or not, so keep your fingers crossed. He desperately wants to get out of here.'

They waited until the doctors had moved out of sight before entering the ward. Lawrence saw them immediately and gave a delighted call. 'Loveday! It's great to see you.'

'Well?' Cubby said. 'Are we to celebrate your discharge?'

'We definitely are.' He beamed. 'I have to wait until my prescription from the hospital pharmacy is ready, and then I'll be free to leave.'

'That's such good news, Lawrence,' Loveday said. 'I meant to call in sooner, but everything has been pretty full on over the past few days.'

Lawrence reached out for Cubby's hand. 'I know. This lovely lady has been keeping me updated.' He paused. 'Does Sam think Teague's murder is connected to that list I got?'

'Why would you ask that?'

'Because Teague sent it.' His hand went to his head wound. 'I also think he was the one who whacked me.'

'There's no evidence of that,' Cubby cut in. 'I know the man's dead, but he will have family out there, and blackening his name does not help.'

'It wasn't you who got attacked,' Lawrence hit back.

Cubby looked away, blinking. 'I'm sorry. I didn't mean...'

'I know you didn't.' Lawrence reached for her hand and squeezed it. 'And you're right I shouldn't be accusing anyone when I have no evidence.'

'What made you think Brian Teague was involved in your attack?' Loveday asked.

'I would have thought that was obvious. He hated me.'

'But he wanted that meeting with you to make amends.'

'Did he?' Lawrence met her eyes. 'I believe he was setting me up for some other thing he was planning.'

'Like what?'

'Take that list. It only makes sense if it was the opening hit for a bigger plan. Teague was a devious devil, but I don't believe he was all that clever. Like I said, if I'm right there will be a documented plan somewhere. He wouldn't have committed something like that only to his mind.'

Loveday frowned. Could any of this be right? She went back to the wording of that list.

Who's Who?

The Innocents? The Guilty? The Killer?

The Choice is Yours.

Had there been more to come – more revelations, fresh accusations? According to the list, all the main players had secrets. And if Lawrence was right, Brian Teague had held all the clues. Now he was dead…murdered.

She let the implications sink in. Was this something Sam had considered? Maybe he was even investigating the theory. After all, he didn't tell her everything.

'If you're right, Lawrence, why do you think Teague involved you? Why didn't he simply send his list to the police?'

Lawrence raised a surprised eyebrow. 'You know why. The man loved his drama. He wanted the publicity and he was sure this kind of thing would achieve that.'

'But you wouldn't have gone to the newspapers.'

'Maybe not, but Teague was devious. It's clear from his letter that he spied on people. How else would he know about their private lives? '

'So you think he knew you and I were friends before we met in that café?'

'Almost certainly. I'm sure he knew I would give you the letter, and that you would pass it onto Sam.'

'But that just takes it back to the police again.'

'More than that, I think. I know you well, Loveday. You wouldn't have let it go. Even if Sam didn't investigate further, you would have.'

Loveday's smile was slow. He was right. It was exactly what she would have done. But Teague wouldn't have known that – or would he?

'Assuming Teague did write that list. Could there be a reason why he sent it to you?'

Lawrence frowned. 'I'm not sure what you mean.'

'Have you thought any more about the actual names on the list? I mean, is it possible you might know any of them? What about Locryn Grantby, for instance? He's described as an artist who works from a studio in Marazion.'

Lawrence shook his head. 'Never heard of him.'

'Try this,' Loveday said, getting into her stride. 'Teague's sister and her husband had a party, which the other people on the list attended.' She paused. 'Those little girls Teague tried to pass off as his daughters, by the way, were actually his nieces. They were Rachel and Philip's children.'

'Why would he do that?'

'Who knows? Maybe he felt pushed into a lie when he assumed Rosie and I were your family.'

Lawrence's head flopped back onto the pillow and he gave a weary sigh.

'I think we should change the subject,' Cubby said quickly, giving him an anxious look. 'You may be going home today, Lawrence, but you still need to rest.'

Loveday put out a hand. 'Of course you do. I don't know what I was thinking, asking you all those questions.'

'Might have something to do with you being a journalist.' He grinned.

'I'm also your friend, and I should have known better.' She turned to Cubby. 'Sorry.' She was gathering up her bag. 'Call me when you get back to St Ives, and if there's anything you need let me know.'

Lawrence raised Cubby's hand and kissed it, giving it a pat. 'I'm being well looked after.'

'I hope you still think that when I start to lay down a few rules.'

'I'll ignore them.'

'I know you will,' Cubby said, a wry smile curving at her mouth. 'But I'll be doing it, anyway.'

They all looked up when the lunch trolley clattered into the ward. 'I think this is where I get thrown out,' Loveday said. She pointed at Lawrence. 'And you, young man... You do as Cubby says.'

'I will think about those names on the list,' he called after her. 'Maybe we could continue the conversation in another day or two.'

Loveday nodded. 'In the meantime, you concentrate on resting up,' she called back, noticing he was still holding Cubby's hand as she left.

LOVEDAY SIGHED as she sat in the hospital car park. Lawrence had given her much to process. She needed to speak with Sam, but first there was another call to make.

'Priddy? It's me. Has Rosie been behaving herself?' She knew the response would be reassuring, but she still needed to hear it.

'The little love. She's fast asleep now, but she did have a very active playtime on that mat with the mobiles over it,' Priddy said.

Loveday sighed. 'Rosie loves that. So there've been no problems?'

'Not a single one.'

'D'you think she's missed me?'

'Well, she did give me a few strange looks, probably wondering where you were, so yes, my lovely, I'd say Rosie has definitely missed her mum.' The smile in Priddy's voice was obvious. 'You relax and enjoy all the other things you have to do today, and look forward to how excited Rosie will be to see you again when you get back here.'

The call ended but Loveday sill sat back, holding the phone. It was the first time since her daughter was born that she'd left her in a friend's care for the best part of a day. She suspected it was probably affecting her more than Rosie.

CHAPTER 14

$\mathcal{L}$oveday had been about to drive out of the hospital car park when her phone sprang into life again. She smiled when she saw the name of her assistant at the magazine flash onto the screen. 'Keri. How are you doing?'

'That's exactly what I was going to ask you. It's ages since we had a proper catch up.'

'Well, I'm in Truro now. If you can slip out for half an hour we could grab a coffee.'

'I have a better idea,' Keri said. 'Let's make it lunch.'

'Ah, lunch,' Loveday repeated with a sigh. 'A luxury I don't get much time to indulge in anymore.'

'Well, we can sort that right now. What about Benji's Bistro in Lemon Street?'

'The name's not familiar, but I'm sure I'll find it.'

'You will. It used to be the plain old wine bar until its new owner took over.'

'I'm guessing his name is Benji.'

'How did you know that?'

'It's a gift,' Loveday said airily.

. . .

HALF AN HOUR later she and Keri were in the bistro, tall glasses of chilled spritzer in front of them as they waited the arrival of their food orders.

'So when are you coming back to us, Loveday? It better be soon, or else Merrick will run us all into the ground.'

'Poor Merrick. I'm sure he's doing his best,' Loveday said.

'So am I, and that's the problem. Charming though he is, our magazine's esteemed owner isn't the journalist he aspires to be.'

'It's fortunate you're there to keep him in line, then.'

Keri sighed. 'It would be if he ever listened to me, but you know, Merrick. He only ever paid attention to you.'

'I doubt if that's true.' Loveday smiled, knowing how much her boss relied on his wife, Connie's advice. The couple wed following years of friendship when Connie had been the family's housekeeper at Morvah, the old farmhouse they shared with Merrick's father, Edward Tremayne.

'Anyway, I'll be back with my little entourage of Rosie and Priddy on Monday, so we'll see how that goes.'

'We've all been busy scrubbing out and tidying that corner of the office. So if Rosie fancies eating her food off the floor she'll be perfectly safe.'

'I don't think Priddy, or I, will be encouraging that.' Loveday giggled. 'But please thank everyone for their efforts.'

'We want you back, Loveday. The old place isn't the same without you.'

'I hope you're still in that frame of mind by the end of next week.' She knew that converting an area of the editorial office to a nursery was a complete experiment. It had felt like a great idea when Cassie suggested it, but what if it didn't work? What if Rosie was so unsettled at her changed surrounding that she cried all day? On the other hand, she could be her usual endearing self, which could be a different kind of distraction for her colleagues.

'Don't be so negative. I'm sure none of us are expecting this to be easy, but we're all on your side.'

'What if it doesn't work, Keri? I won't leave Rosie at home, not even with the best childminder in the world.' Loveday bit her lip. 'I would have to resign.'

Keri reached out and squeezed Loveday's hand. 'Of course it will work. We're all here for you. Come back to the office with me and check out Rosie's space for yourself.'

KERI WAS RIGHT. Loveday mulled over everything her PA had said as she drove home to Marazion later. It was up to Loveday to make this plan work. She smiled, remembering how her colleagues had transformed what everybody seemed to be calling Rosie's Corner. A couple of old folding screens had been dug out of the office attic, they had been scrubbed clean, and someone had stapled a sheet of colourful comic images and graphics onto them. There was no doubt Rosie would get a welcome.

Loveday's anticipated pleasure at being reunited with her daughter was rewarded by Rosie's instant smile as she reached up from Priddy's cot her to her mother.

'Has she been good, Priddy?' Loveday asked again, hugging her baby.

'What do you think? Rosie and I have been enjoying ourselves today. We went down to the beach and watched the other children playing.' She leaned over Loveday's shoulder to smile at Rosie. 'You liked that, my lovely, didn't you?'

Loveday carried her daughter downstairs and settled her in her buggy as Priddy collected all the baby equipment and put it into her bag. 'You've no idea how good it feels to be able to leave Rosie with someone I trust.'

'You and I are like family, my lovely, and now Rosie is a part of that.'

'Thanks, Priddy.' Loveday bent to kiss her cheek. 'That means a lot.'

Loveday was in a happy frame of mind as she pushed Rosie

back home. She wasn't expecting to find visitors in her drive. Nessa Cawse was waiting by her back door with a man Loveday didn't recognize.

'Sorry if this feels like an ambush, Loveday, but there's someone you need to meet.' She turned to the man. 'This is Locryn Grantby. Mellissa's husband.'

The man nodded, his sad eyes didn't look confident he should be here.

Loveday touched his arm. 'I'm so sorry for your loss, Mr Grantby.'

'I know it's an imposition, but do you think we could go inside for a few minutes?' Nessa said.

'Of course.' Loveday unlocked the back door and manoeuvred Rosie's buggy into the kitchen. 'Please sit down. I'll put the kettle on.'

The man raised his hand. 'Not for us, thanks. We won't be stopping.'

'Locryn has something to tell you,' Nessa said, giving him an encouraging look. 'Go on. Tell her.'

The man swallowed. 'Mellissa and I have not been together as a couple for almost a year. She knew all about Nessa and me. She also knew our affair was over.'

'I'm sorry. I don't understand why you're telling me this.'

'He's telling you because Mellissa didn't kill herself because of us. We don't believe she committed suicide at all.' Nessa hesitated. 'Mellissa had a relationship that no one was supposed to know about.'

Loveday's stare went from one to the other. 'Is this true, Mr Grantby?'

He nodded.

'What evidence do you have?'

'I heard them on the phone, at least I heard Mellissa's side of the conversation.' He looked down, shuffling his feet. 'It was… intimate.'

'You should go to the police with this information.'

'We were hoping you would do that,' Nessa said.

'I don't understand.'

'Cassie told me DI Kitto is your partner. He came to see me.' She shrugged. 'He was considerate enough, but I'm not sure he would understand about this.'

'Are you telling me you withheld possibly important information from the police? If that's the case, you could be in a lot of trouble.'

'The police are treating Mellissa's death as suicide. I told Inspector Kitto I believed she was murdered, but I had no proof and I don't think he believed me. At that time, I was unaware Locryn had heard Mellissa and this mystery lover talking on the phone. He only told me about this later when I rang to offer my condolences. We've come to you because we couldn't risk the police dismissing Locryn's information as irrelevant.'

'I don't know what you think I can do,' Loveday said.

'Speak to Inspector Kitto. Tell him we believe Mellissa was murdered. He'll listen to you. As things stand, for as long as her death is logged as a suicide, Locryn and I will be blamed for her state of mind. Believe me, nothing could be further from the truth.'

Loveday blinked, not sure she should ask the question on her mind, but she launched in anyway. 'Did either of you receive an anonymous letter recently?'

The look that passed between the couple answered the question.

'How did you know?' Nessa asked.

'It was a shot in the dark. Someone who was named in that letter passed his copy onto me.'

'So DI Kitto has also seen it?'

Loveday nodded. 'I'm presuming everyone else named on that list has received a letter.'

'Mellissa certainly did,' Locryn said. 'I don't know about the

Dawsons, but I'd be surprised if they hadn't been sent a copy. Teague was a trouble maker.'

'You believe he sent those letters?'

'Oh, he sent them all right,' Locryn said.

WHEN THEY LEFT, Loveday stood at the kitchen door watching them walk up the drive and turn onto the seafront. It was an unsettling end to her day. She had been looking forward to devoting the rest of the afternoon to Rosie and now these two had given her something else to think about.

She glanced at the wall clock as Rosie wrestled herself out of her light cover. It was time for another feed. Loveday crossed to the fridge where the rest of the day's bottles were stacked. She wasn't waiting for that demanding yell.

Minutes later, with Rosie was feeding contentedly, Loveday allowed her thoughts to drift back to Mellissa Grantby. Could her visitors have been right about murder? They were totally wrong about Sam. If Mellissa had a secret lover he would definitely want to investigate that, but it still didn't point to murder. If she'd had more time, she would have questioned Nessa further, but Rosie was her priority.

Her thoughts filtered back to her earlier conversation with Lawrence. He'd been convinced Teague sent those letters, and the dead man's cleaner said she'd posted a bundle of letters.

But that could be a huge coincidence. What they needed were facts, sadly those were thin on the ground.

She smiled at Rosie's expression of total bliss as she demolished the rest of her feed. 'You and I have had a busy day, my pet, and I sense it's not over yet.'

CHAPTER 15

'Sorry, Sam,' Loveday called when she heard him close the back door. 'You've missed Rosie's bath time, but she's waiting for her goodnight cuddle.'

He looked happy as he came into the nursery, holding his arms out to take the baby. Loveday stood back, watching them. She couldn't believe she had ever doubted Sam's pride at being a father again. His older children were young adults now. Jack and Maddie's delight at having a new half-sister was obvious by how often they seemed to be in Marazion these days.

Sam bent to put Rosie into her cot, tucking her into the light covers. He stroked his daughter's cheek and she chuckled back at him. 'She looks content,' he said.

'She is. She's had a lovely day with Priddy.'

He turned, sliding an arm around her. 'That worked out, did it?'

Loveday nodded. 'Really well, actually. I'm taking all the baby stuff into the office tomorrow to set up Rosie's Corner.'

'So you're really going to do this?'

'I am.' She frowned up at him. 'It's too late for any doubts, Sam. I plan to start work on Monday.'

He pulled her closer. 'No doubts,' he said, kissing the top of her head. 'Not any more. If this is what you want, and you're confident Rosie is being properly looked after, then you have my support.'

'She'll be fine.' She laughed. 'You should see how excited my colleagues are about my taking Rosie into the office.'

'What about Merrick?'

'He's just happy I'm coming back to work,' she said, glancing over her shoulder for a last reassuring look at her daughter.

They moved into the kitchen, working together to prepare their supper.

'I had a couple of visitors earlier,' Loveday said, tipping frozen chips into the air fryer and turning to increase the heat under the heavy black pan ready to sear the steaks.

Sam raised a questioning eyebrow. He'd laid out the cutlery and was splashing an oil and lemon dressing over their salad.

'Adam's receptionist, Nessa Cawse, called in. She had that artist chap, Locryn Grantby, with her.'

Sam stopped what he was doing to stare at her. 'Grantby? The dead woman's husband? What on earth did they want?'

'They don't think Mellissa's death was a suicide.'

'Or maybe they're trying to shift the guilt. Everyone we spoke to today agreed Mellissa was in a bad place before she died, which isn't surprising when her husband and her friend, Nessa, were cheating on her.'

'But that's the point.' Loveday removed the cooked steaks to a warm plate and looked up at him. 'They weren't...having an affair I mean. According to them, that relationship was over some time ago.'

'And you believed them?'

'Well, yes, I did, but things have moved on since then. According to them Mellissa had a secret lover. Locryn heard her speaking to him on the phone.'

Sam's brow wrinkled. 'We know about that. If we're to believe the list, she was having a thing with Philip Dawson.'

'No, this was different. Apparently, they all knew about Mellissa and Dawson, but Locryn was shocked when he heard her talking with this other man.'

'I don't suppose he told you who this secret lover is?'

Loveday sighed, her eyes on the ceiling. 'I think the clue is in the word, secret. Of course he didn't tell me. He doesn't know. I guess they were hoping you would investigate that.'

Sam sat at the table as Loveday dished up the food. 'Why did they tell you this? Why didn't they come to the station and make a statement?'

'Probably for the very reason you've demonstrated. They knew you wouldn't believe them.' She paused. 'Look, Sam, I can understand why you might be sceptical, but don't they at least deserve a hearing?'

'Will and I have already interviewed Nessa Cawse. She didn't mention anything about this phone call.'

'She didn't know about it when she spoke to you. Locryn only mentioned it to her this afternoon.' She tipped her head at him, knife and fork poised. 'Well Sam? Will you check it out?'

He waved his fork at her. 'Your supper is getting cold.'

Loveday sliced through her steak, put a piece into her mouth and chewed thoughtfully. She'd done what she promised. It was up to Sam now. But if Mellissa Grantby really did have another lover, would it change anything? They could have had a falling out, leaving the woman so distraught that she took her own life.

On the other hand. This was the second person from that list who was now dead. She knew Sam didn't care for coincidences like this any more than she did.

Loveday waited until they were relaxing after their meal and Sam had his glass of whisky in his hand, before mentioning that she'd visited Lawrence in hospital.

'He has a theory, you know. For instance, take that list. He believes Teague sent it to him.'

'We already know he did. The cleaner, Janet Harris told us.'

'She told you she posted a bundle of letters for Teague. You have no proof they were this list.'

'They were. I know they were, but of course we'll be working to confirm it.'

He took a sip of whisky and rested his head back on the comfortable chair. 'Is that it?'

'No, Lawrence is also curious about why this list was sent to him. He believes Teague's attempt at reconciliation with that bizarre meeting was the first part in setting him up. The man hated Lawrence. He believed he was responsible for the death of his pregnant wife and unborn twins. His whole existence was about getting revenge.'

'But all that was years ago.'

'Except that in Teague's mind it could have been yesterday.' She screwed up her face, thinking. 'Lawrence says this man was planning his revenge, not only on him, but on everyone on that list. He doesn't have any evidence, but it is possible, isn't it?'

Sam shrugged. 'If it is, then we'll never know. No one could know what was going on in Teague's mind.'

'What if he'd written it down?' Loveday asked. 'That was another of Lawrence's theories. If there was such a plan, he believes Teague would have put it together on paper. Or there could be a file in his computer, or even on a memory stick.' She shrugged. 'For all we know, he could have stored it in the cloud.'

'OK.' Sam sighed. 'We'll have another search of Teague's cottage. Our techie guys are already looking at his computer.'

'Can I come with you to the cottage?'

'No.'

'But I know what to look for. I can help you.'

Sam gave his most patient smile. 'We both know that won't be happening.'

. . .

LATER, in bed that night, Loveday stared into the dark. Something wasn't right and she couldn't put her finger on it.

She agreed with Sam that Brian Teague had written and sent those intriguing lists, but what if Lawrence was right and they were the start of a much bigger campaign of fear. She blinked, trying to set everything out logically in her mind.

All the names were there – Rachel, her husband, Philip, Mellissa and Locryn, Nessa and her partner, Kenan. Four of those six people were being unfaithful to their partners. Nessa and Locryn insisted their affair was history. That left Philip and Mellissa. Philip had lied to give himself an alibi for the time of Brian Teague's murder – and now Mellissa was dead.

She turned, eyeing Sam with a stab of irritation and punched at her pillow. How could he sleep so soundly when her mind was in turmoil over *his* case?

It was no good. She would have to get up. Loveday slid quietly from the bed, and ignoring her dressing gown she went through to the nursery. The night light was casting a soft, assuring glow over the little room. A smile flickered on her mouth as she peeked into the cot. Rosie had kicked off her covers and was lying, arms thrown out, her button nose twitching as she dreamed her baby dreams. She didn't wake up as Loveday gently repositioned her and drew up the covers again.

She crept from the nursery and went into the study, closing the door quietly behind her so as not to disturb Sam. He'd be concerned if he found her on the computer in the middle of the night.

Logging into her Facebook account, she began searching. Mellissa Grantby's page. It was full of condolences. Loveday scrolled through the messages. Many of them seemed to be from her colleagues at the medical centre. One of these people had found her body. Sam had said he was one of the doctors, but which one? Her eye travelled down the names, singling out the doctors. Dr Imogene Cornwell, Dr Hamish McEwan, Dr Christopher Bentley, Dr Carolyn Pascoe, Dr Rajesh Kumar, Dr William Thomas. There was no way she could know, and certainly nothing in the messages suggested more than a professional relationship.

She pulled a notebook from the desk, lifting one of the pens, and began to jot down the list of GPs. On another page, she wrote down the names from the list. Loveday sat back, staring at her notes.

Brian Teague had been murdered, Lawrence had been attacked and Mellissa Grantby was dead. Teague had known Lawrence and he would have met Mellissa at Rachel's party. Her mind went back to what Nessa told her and Cassie about that party. She and Kenan had been invited together with Mellissa and Locryn. Philip Dawson had issued the invitations. Nessa had suggested it was a networking thing, as the man was a pharmacy rep and supplied the medical centre with prescription drugs. She chewed the end of her pen. Surely he would have extended the party invitations to the GPs?

She would need another word with Nessa.

CHAPTER 16

*N*ext morning, minutes after Sam's Lexus had turned out of the drive, there was a knock on Loveday's kitchen door. 'Come in, Cassie,' she called, balancing Rosie with one arm and taking the bottle from the warmer with the other. The knock came again. She sighed. 'What's wrong with you, Cassie? I said come in.'

The door opened slowly, and Nessa Cawse poked her head in. 'It's not Cassie, it's me.' Her expression was hesitant. 'Is this a bad time?'

'Not if you don't mind chatting while Rosie's has her breakfast.' Loveday nodded to the coffee pot. 'Help yourself to a drink.'

Nessa did and then sat watching them.

'I told Sam what you and Locryn said yesterday.'

Nessa gave her an anxious stare. 'Does he believe us that Mellissa was murdered?'

'I wouldn't go that far,' Loveday said, taking the bottle from Rosie's mouth and holding it up to squint at the remaining contents.

'But he is going to investigate?'

'That's up to Sam. You need to trust him, Nessa. He knows

what he's doing. If there's any suggestion Mellissa could have been murdered, he won't ignore it.'

Loveday looked up. 'That party Philip Dawson organized.' She paused. 'Was anyone else from the medical centre there?'

Nessa put down her coffee mug. She was looking hopeful again. 'Why? Is it important? Have you thought of something?'

'No, but Sam said it was one of the doctors from the surgery who found Mellissa. Do you know which one it was?'

'It was Dr Bentley, he found her in the rest room with her wrists slashed.' Nessa shook her head. 'Obviously, he tried to resuscitate her, but it was too late. Mellissa was dead.'

'I have to say,' Loveday started gently. 'It does sound like suicide.'

'But it doesn't make any sense,' Nessa said. 'Why would she be in the rest room at the medical centre at all? Even if she had been planning to kill herself – which I don't believe for a minute – she would surely have done it at home.' She leaned forward. 'And why slash her wrists? Mellissa couldn't bear the sight of blood.'

Loveday blinked. 'You never said that before.'

'Well, no, I've only just made the connection. The pair of us got rat-arsed one night and she let it slip. It was connected to something that happened in her childhood.' Nessa bit her lip. 'She tried to gloss over it of course, saying it had been a joke, but I'd seen that look in her eye. It was real all right.

'After that, I began to watch her at work and I noticed how she avoided any incidents that might involve blood. For instance, she would never deliver a message to any of the nurses if she knew injections were being given or blood samples taken. How bizarre is that?'

'Could it have affected her job if it was known?'

'D'you mean would she have been sacked? Probably not, but it wouldn't have gone down well with the doctors if they'd known the manager of their medical centre had a fear of blood.' She glanced at the clock. 'I'd better go, or the patients will be arriving before the receptionist turns up.' She got up, looking back as she reached the door. 'Will you tell Sam know about this blood thing?'

'Of course, I will,' Loveday said.

WHEN ROSIE WAS BATHED, changed and ready for another day in Priddy's care, Loveday set out along the front. She tried to banish thoughts of Mellissa's death as she pushed the buggy, but they kept sneaking in. Would someone with this woman's serious aversion to the sight of blood really slash her wrists? Even if it was a cry for help that went wrong, surely she would have chosen a different way to reveal her pain?

Anyone who contemplated killing themselves would have to be in a really bad place mentally, but nothing she'd heard about Mellissa suggested she'd been depressed. She was unlikely to have been a secret drug user because Sam told her the post mortem hadn't shown this. It had also ruled out serious illness. According to Locryn, their marriage was over and Mellissa had been in a relationship with Philip Dawson. Was there really a secret lover? They only had Locryn's word that such a person existed, and now she had to tell Sam that the woman had an aversion to the sight of blood.

She frowned, annoyed for allowing herself to become so distracted when there were other, more important things to think about. Today's priority was to prepare Rosie's corner of the editorial floor, and she intended to give that her full attention.

As she approached Storm Cottage she could see Priddy waiting for them by the open front door. She looked excited.

'Are you sure this is all right? I don't want to impose on you.'

'What nonsense.' Priddy brushed away her concerns with a flap of her hand.

'This young lady and I are going to have another wonderful

day together.' She smiled down at the child. 'Aren't we, my lovely?'

Loveday's heart gave a sudden lurch at the sight of Rosie's huge blue eyes staring so trustingly up at her. An unexpected flash of guilt shot through her that it would be Priddy enjoying the fun of her daughter's company today and not her. But the hours ahead were all about preparing for them to be together, so leaving Rosie with a trusted friend should be no hardship.

She kissed her daughter before turning to hurry back along the seafront to collect her car. 'I'll ring when I get to the office,' she called back, giving them a final wave.

Loveday frowned as she approached her little car, wondering if she had overdone the amount of baby equipment she'd packed in. She stared at the bulky items crammed into the back seat, trying to estimate how many trips up and downstairs it would take to unload this lot when she reached the office.

But as she arrived in Truro's city centre her excitement mounted. As soon as she entered the editorial floor her eye was drawn to the colourful corner. The folding screens, previously retrieved from the office attic, looked amazing with their eye catching pictures, Someone had painted 'Rosie's Corner' in bright pink.

Loveday gulped back the lump in her throat, turning as she saw Keri approach. 'We've left the screens free standing until all the equipment has been placed,' she explained. 'But the lads will be securing them and making sure they're safe before Rosie arrives.' She slid an arm around Loveday's shoulders and gave her a squeeze. 'This is going to work.'

Loveday fought back the surge of emotion. 'I hope we'll still be thinking that while we're humping baby equipment up all those stairs.'

'Ah, we have a fiendishly clever plan for that.' Keri nodded across the office as two male colleagues came towards them. 'Ray and Allie have volunteered their services. All you have to do is hand over your car keys.'

Loveday gave them an unsure look as they strode towards her. 'There's quite a lot,' she said. 'It could mean several trips.'

Ray flexed his muscles, giving her a grin. Allie told her it would be a doddle.

'I'm not so sure about that,' Loveday muttered, staring after them as they made for the back stairs. She turned to Keri. 'I feel guilty taking them away from their work.'

'They'll be fine,' Keri said. 'Anyway, it's Friday. We can afford to be a little laid back.' She caught sight of Merrick beckoning to them from his room. 'I think you're being summoned.'

CHAPTER 17

'I hope you're not having second thoughts about this.' Loveday gave Merrick a concerned look as she glanced out at the activity still surrounding Rosie's Corner. 'I know it looks like my daughter is taking over out there, but things will settle down.' She bit her lip, hardly daring to look at him.

'I'll hold you to that,' Merrick said, a wry smile creeping over his face. 'But it's not why I called you in.'

'Sounds ominous,' Loveday said, sinking into the chair across from his desk.

He slid open a drawer and took out a large package, placing the tissue-wrapped item on the desk between them, and gave an embarrassed cough. 'It's for Rosie,' he said. 'A little thing Connie made.'

'Really?' Loveday grinned up at him.

'Well, go on. Open it.'

Loveday unwrapped the parcel, taking care not to tear the tissue. And then she gasped, holding up the pink and white crocheted cot blanket. 'It's absolutely beautiful,' she breathed. 'I had no idea Connie was so gifted.'

Merrick allowed his smile to deepen. 'I've learned never to under estimate my wife.' His eyes went to the blanket, and Loveday didn't miss his look of pride.

Romance and marriage may have come later in life for Connie and Merrick, but what they had together really worked.

Connie had established herself as an intrinsic part of the Tremayne family household long before Loveday entered the picture. Her genuine warmth and geniality had not gone unnoticed by Merrick, his younger, wayward sibling, Cadan, and their father, Edward Tremayne.

Connie still had a soft spot for Cadan, even though his questionable lifestyle barely kept him on the right side of the law. To Connie he was a troubled young man who needed guidance, and not the criminal in the making that everyone else saw.

Loveday hadn't been surprised when Merrick and Connie announced their engagement. She and Sam were frequent guests at Morvah, and she hadn't missed those fleeting shy looks that passed between the couple.

They were made for each other. It was a joy to see how successful their marriage was.

Loveday touched the soft wool of the blanket and blinked back the annoying sting of tears. 'Please thank Connie for me. Tell her I love her beautiful gift, and so will Rosie.' She gathered up the blanket, determined not embarrass Merrick by getting emotional in front of him. 'I'll call her later.'

Merrick let her reach the door before calling after her. 'Just for the record, Loveday. It will be good to have you back with us… You *and* Rosie.' He cleared his throat. 'Before I completely run the magazine into the ground, that is.'

TEARS WERE ANNOYINGLY STILL THREATENING when Loveday got back to her desk.

'Everything all right?' Keri nodded to the tissue-wrapped blanket.

'Connie made it for Rosie.' She displayed the blanket. 'Isn't it beautiful?'

'Wow,' Keri said, fingering the soft wool. 'Wish I had a talent like that.'

'Me too.' Loveday glanced across the office to where the flurry of activity was tailing off.

'They've done as much as they can, but you'll need to organize things as you want them. Let's have a look.' Keri started across the office and beckoned Loveday to follow.

They crossed the editorial floor and Loveday stood back as Keri moved the room divider aside to allow access to Rosie's Corner.

Loveday's eyes lit up. 'This is absolutely perfect,' she said. Priddy's cot had been assembled, with the bedding and new mobile play mat neatly stacked inside it. The little changing table was there and the bins of essential items. The window on the back wall made the space bright and cheerful, but it would need a blind for Rosie's sleep time.

'Well, what do you think? Will this do?' Keri asked.

'It will more than do,' Loveday said slowly, her gaze travelling around the space. 'Priddy will need a comfy chair of course, but we'll bring that on Monday.'

'What about Rosie's bottles?'

'I'll make those up daily here at the office and store them in the fridge in the kitchen.'

'And soiled nappies?' Keri pinched her nose.

'I'll deal with them.' Loveday laughed.

Her mobile phone rang and she fished it out of her pocket. 'Sam! You won't believe how good Rosie's Corner looks. I'll take some photos and send them to you. We can look at them over a quick pub lunch if you're free.'

She waited, crossing her fingers. She didn't believe for a

minute that Sam's workload would allow that. But to her surprise, he agreed.

'I can't spare more than half an hour. What about the Crab and Creel?'

It was the pub where they used to share working lunches in the days before Rosie's arrival. She felt like her old self was returning, and her spirits rose. 'That would be great, Sam,' she said.

Loveday wondered how he would react when she retold her conversation with Nessa. She still hadn't processed her news about Mellissa's aversion to blood. She had done some quick research in the car before leaving Marazion. The condition had a name. Haemophobia. It was something that could be overcome, but from what Nessa had said, in Mellissa's case that hadn't happened. It was still playing through Loveday's mind as she walked along the city streets to meet Sam.

IT FELT strange to be back in the Crab and Creel. Loveday looked around her and saw their preferred table was free. She slid into the familiar bench seat, keeping an eye on the door, but she couldn't stop her attention straying to the cathedral. It wasn't as old as the great Gothic edifice might suggest. She had always felt a bit cheated about that and often wondered about the original St Mary's Parish Church that had once stood on the site. It wouldn't have been as grand as this cathedral, and it wouldn't have had the three soaring spires, and it definitely wouldn't have looked down on so many holidaymakers buzzing around in its shadow.

She smiled at the young couples wandering hand in hand, the office workers, enjoying their hour of lunchtime freedom, and the mums pushing prams and buggies.

An idea was beginning to form in her mind, a plan that was exciting her more with every passing minute.

'You were miles away, Loveday,' Sam said. She hadn't noticed he'd come into the pub and was now standing in front of her, an amused look on his face. 'What were you thinking about?'

She looked up at him. 'I was people-watching.'

'Nothing new there then.' He grinned, raising an eyebrow. 'Glass of white wine?' He was already heading for the bar. 'Make it a spritzer…and a toasted cheese sandwich,' she called after him.

Sam returned within minutes and put their drinks on the table, taking the seat opposite. 'The food's on its way,' he said, tilting his head at her. 'I'm guessing it all went well today?'

'It was amazing. Have you seen the photos?'

Sam got out his phone and began scrolling through the images again. 'Your mates have really pushed the boat out. This is very impressive.'

'They've all been fantastic, including Merrick,' she said, her eyes shining.

'So everything is good to go?'

'Definitely. I can't wait for Monday.'

Sam reached across the table and squeezed her hand. 'You look happy, my darling.'

'I am. It's exciting to be going back to work, especially when Rosie will be right there with me.'

'How do you fancy an extra pair of hands to get you both settled in?'

'If you're offering to come with us on Monday that would be fantastic.'

'Consider it done.' Sam grinned.

She watched him as she sipped her drink. Tiny worry lines creased his forehead and a there was a restless edge to him. Loveday recognized the stressed look. It was a sign that not all was going well with his investigation. They had a murder, an attack on Lawrence Kemp, and a death that might well prove to be another murder. No wonder Sam was tense. Loveday knew he couldn't really afford the time to meet her for this drink, but he had anyway, and she loved him for it.

She leaned forward, lowering her voice. 'Did you know Mellissa Grantby had a fear of blood? Nessa told me.'

He put down his beer, the frown lines deepening as the significance of what he was hearing sank in. 'She didn't mention this when I spoke to her.'

'Probably because she'd never thought about it,' Loveday said, looking up to thank the barman as he handed over their sandwiches. She waited until he was out of earshot. 'It's quite significant, isn't it? I mean if she hated the sight of blood why would she cut her wrists?'

'The point hadn't eluded me,' Sam said.

'It gives you another line to pursue, doesn't it?'

Loveday could tell by his body language, by how the earlier defeated slope to his shoulders had disappeared, that this news could be something significant.

It was a good feeling, and she smiled. But this wasn't the only reason for the light in her eye. The idea tugging at her mind was in its infancy and she had more thinking to do, but it was a definite possibility.

CHAPTER 18

*J*anet Harris's brow creased at the unexpected knock on her cottage door. She didn't encourage callers as late as this. She went to the window and eased back the curtain, but the lane was so dark she could barely make out the shape of the person on her doorstep.

'Mrs Harris? Janet?' The voice didn't sound threatening, and they knew her name.

'I'm so sorry to call this late, but I was worried about you.'

Worried? What were they talking about?

Janet opened the door a crack and peered out at the caller.

'Don't you remember me, Janet?'

Janet stared at her visitor. There was something familiar about them. 'I'm not sure,' she said. 'Have we met?'

'Only briefly, but I was visiting a friend in the village and thought I should call by to make sure you're OK. What happened to Brian must have been a terrible shock.'

'Mr Teague? You knew Mr Teague?'

'We were friends. I still can't take it in. I know you looked after him. You're bound to be upset.'

'Well, yes. I...' She opened the door wider and peered again at the caller, and then her face broke into a wide smile. 'Oh, it's you. I didn't recognize you at first.'

'Look, I know it's late, but I wondered if we could talk? There isn't anyone else I can share this with.'

Janet hesitated for a second. 'Come in,' she said. 'I'll put the kettle on.'

'That's very kind of you.' The caller glanced down the lane, making sure no one was out there in the dark watching them, before stepping into the cottage.

'I'm sure you didn't make many cups of tea for Brian.' The caller had followed Janet into her kitchen.

She shook her head. 'You know Mr Teague. He didn't drink tea, not if he had a supply of vodka to hand, even though he knew it did him no good, but he wouldn't be told. I...'

She broke off mid-sentence. 'I remember now. You were there that day! I passed you on the track to Mr Teague's cottage.' She looked up, blinking. 'It was you, wasn't it?'

The visitor moved closer, the genial expression was slipping, features became distorted. Suddenly, hostile eyes mocked her. Janet backed away, unsure what was happening. She drew her dressing gown closer around her, but there was no comfort in the movement. She didn't know why she was shaking, except that this person had unnerved her. 'It's late and I'm feeling quite tired,' she said. 'I think maybe you should go now.'

'But we were going to have tea.' The words were sneering.

'Please leave now!' Janet tried to sound assertive, but her heart had started to pound alarmingly. Why had she allowed this character into her home? She edged away, but the figure moved closer.

'I wasn't sure you recognized me coming from Teague's cottage, so I gave you the chance. If you didn't remember me, you would have turned me away at the door, but you didn't. You invited me in. Big mistake, Janet...huge.'

She could feel the rasp of hot breath on her face. Her eyes

moved frantically around the room, desperately searching for a way out of this situation. But she found none. Her oppressor was now only inches away.

'I really didn't want to do this, Janet, but you must see you have left me no choice.' The voice was chilling.

Janet's eyes widened in terror as she saw the hammer. She reached behind her, desperately scrabbling for the knife rack, but it was too far away.

'You know I can't allow you to go to the police.'

She gripped the sink, screaming for help, but no one heard. She cowered back as the blows rained down on her head. Searing pain shot through her as she slid to the floor and the blackness enveloped her.

UNAWARE OF THE callous murder of Janet Harris, Loveday and Sam were preparing for a family day out.

Rosie kicked out her legs, hands flapping as she jiggled excitedly in her baby seat.

'She knows we're off for a picnic.' Loveday laughed.

'I'll take your word for that,' Sam said, raising an amused eyebrow as he finished packing the car boot.

Loveday slid down the window and gave Cassie a wave as her friend emerged from the big house. She raised a hand, shielding her eyes from the early morning sun. 'Going somewhere nice?' she called.

'St Ives. We're having a day on the beach.'

'Ah, hence the untimely hour.'

'Untimely? Well, maybe for you, Cassie.' Loveday pulled a teasing frown. 'Nine o'clock is halfway through the day for some folk. Besides, you know what St Ives is like. You have to get there early to nab a space on the beach.'

Adam appeared from the side of the house, a garden rake in his hand. The voices of their children, Sophie and Leo, drifted to them from the back garden. 'They're setting up the barbecue,' Adam explained.

'Sounds like a plan.' Loveday grinned. 'Have a great day.'

'You too,' Cassie called after them as they set off up the drive.

SAM PARKED on the St Ives seafront to unload the boot as Loveday lifted Rosie from her car seat and settled her into her buggy. Loveday found a spot on the beach near the harbour, spread a blanket on the sand and secured a yellow parasol to protect Rosie from the sun while Sam drove up the hill to Barnoon Car Park.

He returned fifteen minutes later as Loveday was giving Rosie a drink of milk.

'You'll find sun block over there.' She pointed. 'We've been lathering it over ourselves.'

Sam spread the sun protection on his arms and white legs and stretched out on the blanket beside them. 'What's so funny?' he said, screwing up his face at Loveday's giggle.

'Your legs in those shorts. Very tasty.'

'I'm going to ignore your mummy, Rosie, she doesn't appreciate me.' He lay back again, closing his eyes.

Rosie finished her drink and Loveday put the bottle into a plastic bag and looked around her. The beach was really busy now. She held up her face to the blue sky and felt a light breeze touch her cheek. She closed her eyes, soaking up the sounds of children playing, the soft crunch of sand under bare feet, the distant swish of the waves. A jingle from an ice cream van drifted over the seafront and somewhere overhead a gull cried. Loveday sighed. It was a perfect day, or it had been until someone blocked the sun. She sat up, lifting an arm to shield her face from the shadow that had fallen across them. Her mouth dropped open as she peered up at the man. 'Lawrence! What are you doing here?'

'I live here. Remember?'

'I meant on the beach. I didn't think a day on the sand was your thing, well not without your easel.'

He gave them a sheepish grin. 'Sorry. I didn't mean to interrupt your family time.'

'Nonsense,' Loveday said. 'Sit down.'

But Lawrence remained standing, his gaze straying to the expanse of blue sea. 'Cubby's gone to meet one of her old pals in Penzance. It felt like too good a day to stay indoors.'

Sam propped himself on his elbow and squinted up at the man. 'Loveday's right. Why aren't you out painting?'

'I'm not sure.' Lawrence sighed. 'Maybe I'm just not capable anymore.' His defeated tone had Loveday staring at him.

'You'll get back to it. Don't be so hard on yourself, Lawrence. You're still recovering from that attack.'

'That's what Cubby says.'

'Well, Cubby talks sense. You should listen to her.'

He shrugged. 'I suppose.'

Loveday patted the blanket. 'We're about to have our picnic. You should join us.'

Lawrence looked away, embarrassed. 'No, it's fine. You're having a family day.'

'Sit down, Lawrence,' Sam ordered. He wasn't taking no for an answer. 'There's plenty of food.'

'Definitely,' Loveday chipped in, glancing at Sam. She hadn't expected him to be so insistent. She was impressed.

Lawrence brushed sand from the blanket and did as he was told, eyeing the spread of cheese flan, sausage rolls, and salad sandwiches being set out in front of him. 'This is a banquet,' he said. But Loveday suspected his participation in the meal was more out of politeness than hunger. He hardly ate a thing.

Sam, on the other hand, had tucked in with gusto and was now patting his stomach in satisfaction.

Lawrence nodded to Rosie, who was sleeping contentedly in the shade of her parasol. 'She looks so peaceful.'

Loveday smiled. 'She's due a bottle any time now. You can give it to her if you like.'

'What? Me? No!' He stuttered, overcome by shock. 'I might drop her.'

Right on cue, Rosie stirred, and stretched before the first wails of hunger came.

Sam took a bottle from the cool box as Loveday gently placed Rosie into Lawrence's arms.

'I'm not sure what to do,' he said, clear panic in his voice as she presented him with the bottle.

'Don't worry,' Loveday said, sliding a grin to Sam. 'Rosie knows the score. Just follow her lead.'

'Wait till she asks you to change her.' Sam winked.

Lawrence's eyes flashed alarm. 'I can't do that.'

'Don't listen to Sam.' Loveday laughed. 'He's teasing you.'

It was ten minutes before Rosie finished her bottle with a satisfied burp. Lawrence watched as Sam took her from him and gently laid her back in the buggy while Loveday reached for the changing bag. She'd noted the sign for baby changing facilities along the front and gave the men a backward wave as she set off for them.

Sam reached back into the cool box and produced two cans of beer. He handed one to Lawrence. 'I think you deserve this.'

'You might be right,' he said. 'I've never fed a baby before.'

'Well, it looks like you both survived the experience. We might call on your services again.'

'I don't know about that.' Lawrence grinned, brushing sand from his jeans.

They drank their beer in silence for a few minutes.

Lawrence narrowed his eyes, staring out to sea. 'I was in your part of the world yesterday. I went to see Locryn Grantby. He has a studio in Marazion, you know.'

Sam sat up. 'Go on.'

'You're probably wondering why I did that.'

Sam didn't answer. He waited, giving the man time to continue.

'I was curious about why that list was sent to me. I didn't know any of the people mentioned, apart from Dr Adam, and Teague himself of course. But there had to be a connection otherwise it didn't make sense.

'I figured I could see Grantby without raising his suspicions. We're both artists, after all. So I went to Marazion yesterday and found his studio. He was there and we got talking.'

He looked at Sam. 'I was right. We did have a connection. It's pretty obscure in my case, but it's there.'

He set his empty beer can down in the sand, propping himself up on his elbows. 'We got talking about our work and exhibitions we'd had. That's when I remembered who Grantby was. His work was exhibited in a Plymouth gallery. I was there at the opening. When I mentioned this, Grantby looked upset, and then the whole story came out.

'His wife, Mellissa had hired a minibus and roped in a few friends from the medical centre where she worked that included her assistant, Nessa Cawse, and her partner. She also invited a friend of the centre, Philip Dawson and his wife. He worked for a pharmaceutical company and supplied the centre with prescription drugs.'

He shot Sam another look. 'It was them! Don't you see?' His eye glistened with excitement. 'They were all on that list – and Grantby had just mentioned them.'

'OK,' Sam began carefully. 'So the six of them were at Locryn's exhibition. I don't see–'

'It's what happened after the opening, when they were leaving the gallery,' Lawrence interrupted. 'Grantby had been driving the minibus. Apart from him, they were all a bit tipsy after the cheese and wine party. More partaking of wine than the cheese I believe.' He waved a hand. 'Anyway, there was an accident outside the gallery and a woman was killed. According to the evidence Grantby gave at the subsequent inquest, she stepped out in front of the minibus. He said she didn't stand a chance.

'He was breathalysed of course, but the results were negative because he'd only had one glass of wine all day. The coroner later found it was an accident.'

Sam nodded.

'What d'you think, Sam? Is any of this helpful?'

'It might be. Thanks, Lawrence. Leave it with me,' he said, raising a hand to wave at Loveday as she and Rosie came back to join them.

THEY HAD FINISHED their picnic and were putting things away when Sam's mobile phone rang. He pulled it from the pocket of his shorts, frowning at the list of missed calls. Loveday's heart sank as she watched his expression change when he answered Will's call. She knew what was coming. 'Oh no, Sam. Please don't say you have to work.'

'I'm sorry, Loveday.'

'But it's Saturday!' she protested.

'Janet Harris is dead,' he said.

Loveday screwed up her face. 'Who?'

'Janet Harris. She was Brian Teague's cleaner. She was found by a neighbour this morning.'

Loveday stared at him. 'Oh no, but that's awful.' She frowned. 'You don't think this is another murder, do you?'

'That's exactly what I'm thinking,' Sam said.

CHAPTER 19

'I'll take Loveday and Rosie home when they're ready to go.' Lawrence offered. 'My car's up at the loft.'

Sam hesitated, glancing at Loveday. She gave a shrug that suggested a reluctant agreement.

'Well, if you're sure, Lawrence, and Loveday doesn't mind, it would certainly save me time.'

'Oh, all right then.' Loveday relented. 'But you'll have to drop off Rosie's car seat.'

She watched the two men leave. They were friends now, but it hadn't always been the case. She recalled how the first time she met Sam he'd arrested Lawrence as a suspect in a murder investigation. He was completely innocent, of course, and Loveday had played her part in proving it.

Back then Sam had thought she and Lawrence were more than friends, even though it wasn't true. And despite their own growing relationship, that suspicion lingered.

Loveday wasn't sure what had eventually convinced Sam that her friendship with Lawrence was purely platonic, she was simply thankful that he no longer questioned it.

She sat on the beach, gazing thoughtfully out over at the

rolling waves for another five minutes before stretching to collect their belongings. Being on the beach without Sam was no longer fun. She gave a resigned smile as his Lexus arrived with the car seat. He dropped a gentle kiss on Rosie's cheek and wrapped his arms around Loveday.

'Sorry about this. You know I have to go, don't you?'

'Of course I do.' Loveday's eyes dropped to his shorts. 'Your fashion choice might be tricky, though.'

'Lawrence said he'd loan me something more suitable.'

'Really?' She smiled, thinking of her friend's relaxed dress style.

Lawrence arrived minutes later in his battered old jeep and thrust a pair of new looking jeans at Sam. 'Cubby bought them,' he explained. 'She's trying to tidy up my appearance.' He pulled a face. 'I'm not even sure I'll wear them.'

'If there's no trendy ripped knees they'll suit Sam just fine,' Loveday said, aware that he was off to investigate another possible grim murder.

'Thanks,' Sam said, turning to install the baby seat in the back of the old jeep. 'You didn't have to do this, Lawrence. We really are grateful.'

'Not a problem,' he said, as Loveday strapped Rosie in, and Sam put the other bags on the seat beside her. He sighed as he watched them take off up the hill out of St Ives. It wasn't how he'd planned for their family day to end.

TRAVELLING in Lawrence's jeep was as uncomfortable as Loveday had imagined. She tried not to grip the edge of her seat when they bumped up the hill and turned onto the country road to Penzance.

'Sam will probably tell you about this, but you should know that I went to see Locryn Grantby yesterday.'

'Really?' She swung round to stare at his profile. 'I'm intrigued. Are you going to tell me why?'

Lawrence retold his story, looking proud of himself for discovering that link about the six people on the list being together at Locryn's exhibition. His expression turned serious as he recounted details of the subsequent fatal accident.

'That's awful.' Loveday was genuinely shocked. She wondered why neither Nessa nor Locryn had mentioned it. 'How long ago did all this happen?'

'About six months. I pulled up the details of the inquest online.'

Loveday was getting used to the jolting movement of the jeep, but when they passed the village of Nancledra, she felt relieved they didn't have much further to go.

It was mid-afternoon when they drove into Marazion. Her glance went the crowds on the beach, the colourful wind breaks and flapping sun brollies. It looked almost as busy as St Ives.

'I know,' Lawrence said, following her gaze. 'It's the start of the summer and already Cornwall is being deluged by tourists.'

Loveday slid him a chastising look. 'Or maybe what you see is ordinary folks like us enjoying a day on the beach.'

'Maybe.' Lawrence turned into her drive. He didn't sound convinced.

'Come in for a drink,' she offered, as they unpacked the jeep.

'No, I'll get back, Cubby will be there now and she'll be wondering where I've got to, but thanks anyway.'

'It's us who should be thanking you.' Loveday smiled, stepping back as Lawrence manoeuvred a U-turn at the top of the drive. She returned his wave as he took off.

LOVEDAY TOOK A SLEEPING ROSIE, still in her car seat, into the study and switched on the computer.

She got comfortable at the desk, a mug of coffee to hand and tapped in 'Locryn Grantby Artist'.

A list of options appeared and she scrolled through them.

The Plymouth exhibition was there, and a newspaper story from the inquest into that poor woman's death.

She clicked the link for the official inquest report and sat back to read it. From the evidence presented, it looked like Locryn was right. The woman had stepped in front of the minibus. He really hadn't stood a chance of being able to stop in time. The inquest had absolved him of any blame, but it was a difficult thing to live with.

The dead woman was named as Tamsin Lamphier. Loveday bit her lip. She was only 23 years old. The name was unusual. She typed it into the search bar and began to scroll through the results. From what she could see, Tamsin had been a primary school teacher in Cambridge. So what was she doing in Plymouth?

Loveday scrolled back to the inquest details. They told her that Tamsin had been visiting family in the area. So who was the family? Try as she might, she could find no other reference to identify any family.

Surely if they had attended the inquest they would have got at least a mention in the media? On the other hand, not everyone wanted their name splashed across a newspaper, neither would they appreciate being interviewed for the TV news.

Perhaps they had considered their privacy so important that they stayed away from the inquest. They hadn't been called as witnesses, but if they hadn't been with Tamsin at the time of the crash they wouldn't be witnesses.

Her eye went to the clock in the top corner of the computer screen. She had been sitting there for more than an hour. No wonder she was stiff. She was about to shut down the computer but decided to have one more try.

She entered Tamsin Lamphier in her Facebook account and punched the air when the young woman's photo came up.

Loveday studied the pretty face. She looked so happy. There was a flurry of condolences from Facebook friends after the accident and a response from her brother-in-law, Jason.

Scrolling beyond these posts, she was pleased to see Tamsin had been very active on Facebook and popular from the responses she could see. But this was a job for another time. There was a meal to prepare and a baby to organize.

JANET HARRIS's body lay in a pool of blood on her kitchen floor. The Home Office pathologist, Dr Robert Bartholomew, had been and gone. The undertakers were standing discreetly outside the cottage, waiting for Sam's permission to remove it.

DS Will Tregellis tutted as he glanced down at the body. 'Why would anybody want to kill a nice old lady like her?'

'Well, somebody did,' Sam said, his expression grim as his gaze travelled around the room. He sighed. 'Whoever did this was known to her. Why else would she have admitted them to her home so late? She's in her dressing gown, so she was clearly getting ready for bed.' He glanced at the two mugs set out on the worktop. 'Looks like she was about to make a drink for her caller, which explains why she was attacked here in the kitchen.'

Will blew out his cheeks. 'This has to be connected with Brian Teague's murder.'

Sam agreed, but he wasn't sure how it helped them. 'We have to concentrate on the more than strong possibility that Janet knew her attacker, so possibly Teague knew them as well, which means it could be anybody that visited Teague's house.'

'But Janet said nobody visited him.'

'He got groceries delivered,' Sam reminded him. 'Janet could definitely have met whoever made those deliveries.'

They moved out of the cottage and Sam gave the undertakers

the nod to remove the body. He beckoned one of the white-suited forensic officers over. 'Can we have a photograph of the kitchen worktop, in particular those two mugs. And I want them checked for prints.'

The officer nodded.

'I can see why we need to look at whether these two murders - and this is definitely murder - are connected. But they are completely different.'

Sam agreed. 'This one definitely doesn't have the finesse of the Teague murder. It looks more like our killer panicked, which suggests Janet was targeted because of something she knew, or saw.'

Will gave a wry smile. 'And all we have to do is figure out what that is.'

Sam put a hand on Will's shoulder. 'It's not like you to be so defeatist, Will. Who knows, maybe the forensic boys will find the killer has left us a big fat clue.'

'Yeah?'

Sam pulled a face. 'You never know.'

But Will suspected his senior officer wouldn't be holding his breath.

LOVEDAY SLID a chicken casserole into the oven and wiped her hands on her apron. There wouldn't be so many hot suppers once she'd started back at the magazine. She wondered how Sam would appreciate her relinquishing the domestic goddess role she'd taken upon herself. Loveday adored caring for her little daughter, and she didn't mind the cooking, but she definitely couldn't exclusively commit to being chief homemaker. She was the editor of a magazine and she loved that job, too. Everything might not run smoothly at first, but with Sam's support she knew she could make it work.

The lure of the research she'd started was still tugging at her when she looked in on Rosie. She was sleeping soundly. Sam had called, saying he was on the way home. She checked her watch, estimating he would arrive in ten minutes. There was time for another quick check on Tamsin Lamphier's Facebook page.

Loveday scrolled through the posts. The only mention of a family member was Tamsin's brother-in-law, Jason Rowe.

She glanced to the list of Facebook Friends, her eyebrow arching when she saw there was more than a hundred of them. Tasmin had clearly been a popular young woman online. The faces of all the people she had connected with scrolled past. Loveday was fascinated by the images, even if she wasn't sure any of them would be familiar. And then she stopped, scrolled back and stared at the screen. She blinked. What was he doing there? She checked the name…Jason Rowe. If this was the brother-in-law mentioned in an earlier post, he must be using a false name, because there was no doubting the identity of the man she was looking at.

The back door opened as Sam came in. Loveday called to him. 'I'm in the study, Sam. I think you should have a look at this.'

He came to stand beside her, his eyebrow lifting at the computer screen. 'OK, what's going on? What am I supposed to be seeing?'

Loveday pointed to the name. 'It seems this person was calling himself Jason Rowe. But that's not the name we know him by.' She turned, looking up at him. 'This is Brian Teague.'

CHAPTER 20

'What does it mean, Sam? Why was Teague calling himself Jason Rowe?'

'I'm not sure,' Sam said slowly. 'Unless it was a spur-of-the-moment thing.'

'Rowe is only mentioned by name in the inquest, but what if Teague witnessed the accident. Think about it. In his mind, his wife was killed by a careless driver. We know it wasn't Lawrence, but he still believed it was, and he hated him. Now his dead wife's sister has suffered the same fate.'

Loveday paused, thinking over what she'd said. 'All this happened after Locryn Grantby's art exhibition where the wine would have been flowing.'

'But according to the newspaper report of inquest, Locryn was driving the minibus and he was stone cold sober,' Sam said.

'It doesn't mean the others were. In fact, we know from what Lawrence said that they were all quite tipsy after the event. What if Teague saw them at that accident? He wouldn't exactly have been happy at the sight of a bunch of drunks piling out of the minibus that had just mowed down his sister-in-law.'

Sam's brow creased. 'That's a lot of assumptions, Loveday.'

'Maybe, but it might be the reason Teague was targeting these people.'

'It doesn't explain why Teague was murdered, though.'

'Maybe not, but there's a connection in there somewhere and we need to find it.'

Sam tilted his head, blinking at her. 'We?'

'OK, you,' Loveday conceded, but he was still watching her. She put up her hands. 'I know that look. You're telling me to back off, but it's difficult to ignore this stuff. What if Teague was calling himself Jason Rowe to protect Tamsin from any intrusive publicity should a newspaper decide to revisit her sister's tragic story?' She was ignoring the frown playing on Sam's face. Loveday had no intention of plunging headlong into this, but she couldn't ignore what was going on.

'I'm not saying your insight isn't helpful, Loveday. I just don't want you playing Miss Marple again.'

'I wasn't planning to,' she said stiffly. Doing a spot of freelance sleuthing may not have been her intention, but there was nothing to say she couldn't do a bit of online investigating.

Persecuting the six friends by sending those letters would also have been totally in character for Brian Teague. She wouldn't have put it past him to hire a private detective to spy on them. Maybe that was how he discovered those secret affairs?

And now three people were dead!

Later that night, after checking that Sam was sleeping soundly, Loveday slipped out of bed and went into the study. She took a sheet of printing paper and wrote six names in landscape across the top. She drew a line between each of them and began to list what she knew about the people.

Philip Dawson / Rep for pharmaceutical company and frequent visitor to GP surgeries and health centres / Lied to police about where he was when Brian Teague was murdered / Spotted having an apparently clandestine meeting with wife in

Falmouth pub when he was supposed to be out of area / He was having affair with Mellissa. **Suspicious!**

Rachel Dawson / Philip's wife and sister of Brian Teague who organized a party attended by all six of the group / Gave Philip an alibi for Teague murder. **Worth watching!**

Nessa Cawse / Former receptionist at Hilltop Medical Centre, Truro, who left when her boss, Mellissa Grantby discovered her affair with her husband, Locryn / Now Dr Adam Trevillick's receptionist / Told self and Cassie about Dawson's party / Visited self with Locryn to say affair was over and insisted Mellissa was murdered / Said Mellissa couldn't stand sight of blood. **Worth watching!**

Kenan Retallick – Nessa Cawse's partner / Fisherman who owns his own boat *Our Bess* in Newlyn / Nice quiet man who sometimes meets Nessa from work in Marazion. **Not Suspicious!**

Locryn Grantby – Husband of Mellissa / Artist with studio in Marazion / Previously had affair with Nessa Cawse / Had his own art exhibition in Plymouth / Driving the minibus that killed Brian Teague's sister-in-law, Tamsin Lamphier and later cleared of any blame at inquest. **Worth Watching!**

Mellissa Grantby – Late wife of Locryn / Philip Dawson's mistress / Does she also have secret lover? / Practice manager at Hilltop Medical Centre, Truro / Former friend of Nessa until she discovered affair with her husband / Found dead with wrists cut in ladies' loo in medical centre by one of the GPs, Dr Christopher Bentley. **More investigation needed!**

Loveday ran her eyes over the names. Philip Dawson seemed the most suspicious of the six. Her mind went back to seeing him and Rachel at that pub. The woman had dashed to meet him immediately after Sam and Will had left her house. That in itself was surely odd. If Dawson was having an affair with Mellissa, had Rachel known about it? If she did, then why was she still supporting him?

And then there was Nessa. Loveday wasn't sure she trusted the woman. Teague had spilled the beans about her affair with Locryn, but what if he'd revealed his knowledge to Mellissa before he sent those letters? If this was why Nessa was forced to leave her job, she'd have a reason to hate the man. But was that a reason to kill him?

The brutal murder of Janet Harris was another thing. And if Sam was right that both murders were down to the same killer it would surely rule Nessa out.

The least suspicious of all was Nessa's partner, Kenan. Loveday could think of no reason this man would want to kill Brian Teague, but no one was that innocent. Maybe they should take a look at him.

Her eyes again slid over the names she'd written down. Mellissa Grantby! Could she have killed Teague and then committed suicide in a fit of guilt? Or, as Nessa and Locryn suggested, was she another murder victim? By all accounts, the woman hadn't been popular. If Rachel Dawson knew about that affair with her husband, she certainly wouldn't have been happy. And if she'd been sent Teague's list she must have known. Could Rachel have killed Mellissa?

Loveday sat back yawning, rubbing the back of her neck.

It would be helpful to have a chat with Rachel Dawson, also with the GP who discovered Mellissa's body. All she knew about him was his name, Dr Christopher Bentley, but unless she actually became one of his patients – which wasn't going to happen – she couldn't justify arranging a chat with him.

She checked her watch. It was 4am – too early for Rosie to be awake and demanding a feed. Loveday tiptoed to the nursery and silently peeked in. All was quiet. She went back to bed, slipping in without disturbing Sam.

It was two hours later when Rosie gave her first whimper. Loveday squinted at the clock, reluctant to leave the comfort of bed again. Beside her, Sam let out a groan. 'It's fine,' she said, crawling from under the duvet. 'I've got this.'

'Are you sure?' he murmured sleepily, pulling the bedding over his head.

Loveday looked back with a frown. She knew he would be going into the station today, even if it was Sunday. Murders didn't solve themselves.

By the time Sam came striding into the kitchen ready to face his day, Loveday had a plate of grilled bacon and tomato keeping warm in the oven. She topped up the dish with a good helping of lightly scrambled eggs and put a couple of slices of bread in the toaster.

'Hope you're hungry.' She looked up at him, presenting her cheek for a kiss.

'I don't deserve you,' he said, pulling out a chair and sitting down.

She put the plate of food in front of him, buttering a slice of toast for herself. 'Don't get too comfortable,' she warned. 'All this stops when I go back to work.'

'Now she tells me,' he said, forking up the bacon and scrambled eggs.

She watched him eat as she nibbled her toast, pleased to see he was clearing his plate.

He stood up, patting his stomach. 'That was exactly what I needed this morning.' He paused, looking at her. 'I'm really sorry, Loveday. I know I offered to help move the rest of the baby equipment into the office today, but that was before Janet Harris got herself murdered.'

'You make it sound like it was something she arranged.'

Sam pulled a face. 'You're right, that came out more callous than I meant it to be. Maybe I've been a copper too long.'

Loveday slipped her arms around him. 'We both know that's not true.' She lifted her head, meeting his eyes. 'You liked her, didn't you.'

'She was a nice woman.'

'Go and find her killer, then. And don't worry about what's happening back here. I'm on top of it.'

Sam wrapped his arms around her, snuggling his face into her hair. 'I'm the luckiest bloke in the world.'

'No argument from me on that score.' Loveday laughed, but a twinge of guilt crept over her as she watched him leave. She'd agreed to no Miss Marple tactics, but Sam had admitted her insight was valuable. So she would try to help him, but maybe not today. She'd be far too busy putting the finishing touches to Rosie's Corner.

Loveday felt pleasantly weary by the end of the day. Priddy had once again looked after Rosie while Loveday packed her car and drove to the magazine office with the extra bits and pieces a baby might need.

Sam rang to say he'd pick up fish and chips. Loveday set out plates and took a bottle of Chardonnay from the fridge. They ate, and sipped their wine, both content not to discuss the murders that evening.

'Sorry I couldn't help you with Rosie's stuff today,' Sam said, as they finished their food and lingered over their wine.

Loveday smiled at him. 'Don't be, there wasn't that much to do. It was more about my getting my head around the fact that I'll be back at work tomorrow.'

'Are you OK with that?'

'Yes,' Loveday said thoughtfully. 'I am.'

'What about Rosie? D'you think she'll settle into a busy office?'

Loveday blinked, cocking her head at him. 'You're not worried about this, are you Sam? You did agree to it.'

He reached for her hand, smiling. 'I'm not worried, not really. I'm sure Rosie will love it.'

Loveday's gaze was earnest as she met his eyes. 'She will, Sam,' she said softly. 'We'll make sure she does.'

CHAPTER 21

*L*oveday could feel her excitement mounting as she drove to Truro with Priddy and Rosie. They had set off early, but when they reached the magazine Loveday was pleased to see Keri had already arrived in the editorial office. Her PA's eyes immediately went to Rosie.

'This is going to be such fun.' She grinned. 'Can I help with anything?'

Loveday glanced to Rosie's Corner. Sam had said he would call by. She was surprised to see Sam was still there, and looking clearly impressed with everything he saw.

'I think we're pretty well organized,' Loveday said, Rosie in her arms as they followed Priddy to the corner.

'It's great,' Sam said, turning at Loveday's approach. 'Well what d'you think, Rosie? You've got your own personal nursery corner.' Wide blue eyes gazed up at him as he touched her cheek.

'I have to go, but keep in touch,' he said, giving Loveday a peck on the cheek. 'Leave messages if I'm not available, I'll want to know everything that happens today.'

'I will,' Loveday called after him distractedly, as she glanced around her to make sure everything was in place.

It took some time for Loveday and her colleagues to settle down to their morning routine. Her eyes kept straying to Rosie's Corner.

At ten o'clock, Merrick signalled the heads of departments to his office for the Monday conference.

Loveday followed her colleagues in as everyone took their seats.

Merrick looked around the assembled faces. Keri already had her pen poised to take notes.

He smiled. 'I'll start with the good news that Loveday is back with us.'

Everyone smiled a welcome and Loveday tried not to blush as he continued. 'Our readers may be too polite to tell us the quality of our editorial content may have slipped somewhat these past few months, even with the sterling efforts of Keri and our free-lance contributors.' He gave a little cough. 'And I have done my best to step up to the mark, but we have definitely missed Loveday's steadying hand on the tiller.'

Loveday saw heads nodding in agreement. Merrick was a great boss, and although he'd be first to admit he was no journal-ist, he had definitely kept the team motivated.

'All these comments are very flattering, and it's great to be back, Merrick,' she said. 'But *Cornish Folk* hasn't exactly collapsed in my absence. I can see everyone here has done a fabulous job. I'm looking forward to hearing the details of how that all happened.'

Merrick smiled his thanks for her comments as he spread the contents of his file across his desk. 'Let's start with our advertis-ing,' he said. 'I'm delighted to say the last edition actually made money. Most of our advertisers have taken more space and we have a full page from Benzies advertising their TVs. So well done Gil and your team.

Gil Morrish inclined her head. 'We're also speaking with some new businesses with a view to them being part of our current "New to Cornwall" advertising feature,' she said. Loveday didn't miss the twinkle in her eye. 'It's going very well. I don't think anyone we've approached has declined to take space.'

'Excellent,' Merrick said, turning his attention to the magazine's line-up of freelance contributors. 'I like the graphics of that salmon leaping up the falls for the "Out-of-Doors" column.' He gave a thumbs up to graphic designer Mylor Ennis, who was also responsible for most of the magazine's photography.

'Now then,' Merrick said, his chair creaking as he leaned back. 'We need ideas for a new series. Keri and I have been out and about doing vox pops in the centre of Truro, asking our readers what they want to find when they open their copies of *Cornish Folk*. The word most people mentioned was *family*. They want a family themed series they can all relate to.' He looked up. 'So, ladies and gentlemen, ideas please.'

Loveday raised her hand. 'They must have been reading my mind. This is exactly what I've been thinking,' she said, glancing to Rosie's Corner. 'What if I document my experience of working while my baby is close by in the office? You said yourself, Merrick, that this arrangement isn't exactly traditional. It's an experiment which relies on the support of all my colleagues. I think our readers would enjoy sharing the experience with us.'

For a second nobody spoke, and then a broad smile crossed Keri's face. 'What a brilliant idea,' she said.

Loveday's eyes went around the room. Everyone was nodding.

'It might work,' Merrick said slowly.

'Does that mean we're going for it?' Loveday asked.

'Why not? Let's give it a try,' Merrick said.

Out of the corner of Loveday's eye, a familiar figure was striding across the office and heading for them.

Merrick looked up, frowning as the new arrival burst in. 'I think you all know my brother, Cadan.' He paused, throwing Loveday a resigned look. 'He'll be joining us.'

A surprised look went around the team.

'Well, I didn't expect a round of applause, but I'm not that bad,' Cadan said.

Loveday tried not to show her feelings. It was her job to present a united front. She gave an embarrassed cough, managing a quick smile. 'It's good to have you on board, Cadan.'

Merrick held Cadan's eye. 'My brother is sitting in on today's conference. He won't be taking part in any planning.' The warning, as he eyed his brother was unmistakable.

Loveday could already sense trouble in the wind. Cadan had never permanently lived in the family home. The occasions when he did move in always meant trouble, and judging by the current arrogant gleam in his eye, he was going to be up to more mischief.

She held back as the meeting broke up and people returned to their desks.

'So, Cadan. You'll be joining us.' Loveday raised an eyebrow. She knew him of old and still didn't trust the man.

Cadan Tremayne smiled. 'That's right, but despite what my brother says, I intend to play my part. This magazine needs some new guidance and I'm here to pull it into shape.'

Loveday frowned. 'I wasn't aware we needed to be pulled into shape, nor did I know Merrick had given you the authority to make changes.'

'I haven't,' Merrick said coldly.

'Maybe not yet, but I have ideas and once he hears them he'll agree my suggestions make sense.' There was challenge in Cadan's voice. 'For instance, we could launch a new opinion page. It would be good to stir things up.'

Loveday could see Merrick was holding his temper in check. 'We're not that kind of magazine,' he hissed.

'Well, maybe it's time we were.' His eyes had gone to Rosie's Corner. 'I see we've now turned the office into a creche.'

Loveday could feel herself bristling. 'It's hardly that,' she said stiffly.

'Whatever it is, it's not professional,' Cadan snapped. His words were barely out when Rosie's lusty wail resonated across the office. 'I rest my case,' he said, the corner of his mouth lifting in a sneer.

Priddy's round face poked out from the screen. 'Sorry, folks. Rosie's telling us she wants her bottle. We'll be sorted in a jiffy.'

Cadan turned and was striding out of the office, Rosie's demanding yells in his ears.

'Ignore him,' Merrick said. 'He has absolutely no say around here, even if he thinks otherwise.'

Loveday remained in her seat after the meeting dispersed. 'What's Cadan doing here?' she asked, noting Rosie's cries had stopped. She was remembering his last visit when he'd been locked up for a week following a pub brawl.

'We don't know for sure. According to Connie, the latest girl-friend has turned him out.'

'Isn't he a bit old for that kind of thing? Why doesn't he have his own place?'

'Good question.' Merrick sighed. 'I guess my brother has never quite grown up. He says he needs someone to look after him.'

Loveday pulled a face. 'Does he.'

'Never mind him. I met Sam on the way out earlier. He was telling me he's right in the middle of another murder investigation.' He stopped, looking up at her. 'I hope you won't be getting involved, Loveday.'

'It's Sam's business, not mine,' she said curtly.

'That hasn't stopped you before. I'm thinking of the scrapes you've got yourself into when you get mixed up in Sam's cases.' He paused, shaking his head. 'You put yourself in danger. And now your old artist buddy, Lawrence Kemp, has been attacked. Is that connected to what's happening?'

'Probably.' She screwed up her face. 'And before you say any more, I know I have to consider Rosie now.'

Merrick squinted at her. 'So you won't be doing any amateur sleuthing?'

'Not the way you mean, but Sam told me he welcomes my insight.'

'Your insight? What does that mean?'

'It means Sam knows I'm good at working things out.'

'I thought you said you wouldn't be getting involved.'

Loveday heaved a sigh. 'I won't, well, not in a physical way.'

Merrick gave her a sideways look.

'Of course, if Sam asks for my advice I won't refuse.'

CHAPTER 22

*L*oveday spotted Cassie skulking behind her big four-by-four as soon as she pulled into the drive. She'd dropped Priddy off at her cottage and was looking forward to reflecting on her first day back at work. It seemed this was not going to happen.

'Thank heavens you've arrived,' Cassie said excitedly. 'I was worried you might miss him.' She nodded to the light grey BMW Loveday had parked behind. 'It's him.' Her voice was low and conspiratorial.

'Who?' Loveday swept her gaze over the vehicle. She was used to her friend's often whacky behaviour but this was confusing.

'*Him*,' Cassie repeated. 'That rep chap, Philip Dawson. He's calling on Adam.' She gave a frustrated sigh, planting her hands on her hips and tilting her head at Loveday. 'Don't you want to catch him as he comes out? I thought he was one of Sam's suspects. You could speak to him, make it look natural…get him chatting.'

Loveday knew exactly who Philip Dawson was, she just didn't expect to find him here on her doorstep. But why wouldn't he be here? He was a rep for a pharmaceutical company. It was his job to sell drugs to GPs like Adam.

Her mind flashed back to her earlier promise to Merrick not to get involved in Sam's case, but surely it was different when something fell into your lap like this? It wasn't as if she'd gone out of her way to find the man.

'Here, let me take Rosie.' Loveday had unclipped the baby from her car seat and Cassie was already lifting her from her mother's arms. 'I'll get Rosie settled inside.' Her eyes slid to the man emerging from the side of her house. 'That's him,' she hissed.

Loveday swallowed. She could hardly accost the man, demanding to know his connection with the dead Mellissa Grantby. Her car was blocking him in and she saw him scowl at it.

'I'm so sorry,' she said, following his irritated gaze and spread her arms in an apologetic gesture. 'There's not a lot of space in the drive.'

'If you could reverse your car back…' he began.

Loveday jangled her keys, indicating that she would do as he asked. It was the moment Rosie chose to let out a bad tempered yell.

Instantly evaluating the situation, and seeing Loveday's chance to delay moving her car by appearing to be the harassed mum, Cassie thrust Rosie back into her mother's arms. 'Look, I'm sorry, but I have to go. I'm already late.' She wrinkled her nose. 'I think Rosie may also need changing.' She flashed Dawson a smile. 'I'm sure this gentleman won't mind waiting.'

Dawson gave an irritated sigh, his hand shooting out for Loveday's car keys. 'Give me your keys. I'll move the thing myself.'

'No!' Loveday looked shocked. 'I'm not covered for another driver.' She turned towards her kitchen door. 'Let me settle my daughter and I'll sort it. You'd better come in.'

She could feel Dawson's exasperation, but he followed her

into the kitchen. 'I'll have to change her,' she said. 'It would speed things up if you could stick the kettle on, would you. You'll find a bottle in the fridge. If you could wash your hands and warm it for her, we'll be with you in a minute.'

Loveday hurried the still crying Rosie away to the nursery, imagining Philip Dawson staring open-mouthed after them.

The nappy change did nothing to improve her daughter's mood. She was still howling for food when she carried her back to the kitchen.

To Loveday's surprise the man had actually filled a plastic jug he'd found with hot water and Rosie's bottle was warming in it.

'I can see you've done this before,' she said, seating herself comfortably with the baby in her arms as Dawson handed her the bottle.

'How many children do you have?'

The man frowned, and for a moment Loveday wondered if she'd be told to mind her own business. But he merely nodded.

'We have two little girls, Emily's seven and Olivia's six.' The mention of his children appeared to have a settling effect on his urgency to drive away.

'I take it you're not one of Adam's patients,' Loveday said, her eyes on the man's black leather case.

'I'm an advisor to health centres and GP surgeries. It's my job to inform doctors of the latest prescription drugs available.'

Loveday hid her amusement that he'd elevated himself from the ranks of a lowly rep. 'You visit health centres?' She paused. 'Like the one in Truro where that poor woman killed herself?'

She waited, watching Dawson swallow. She took a punt. 'You knew her, didn't you?' she said softly. 'I can see how it's saddened you.'

Philip Dawson bowed his head. 'Yes, I knew Mellissa. We were friends.' He spoke as though only to himself, his words so quiet that Loveday had to strain to hear them.

'I'm sorry. I can see you were close.' She was studying him, not sure if his reaction to the woman's death was more guilt than grief. The woman's husband Locryn, and his former lover, Nessa Cawse, were convinced Mellissa had been murdered. Had she rejected Dawson and had he staged her death to look like a suicide? It couldn't be ruled out.

Loveday thought Locryn probably had more motive to murder his wife. She was, after all, being unfaithful to him. But then, his own morals were hardly whiter than white.

Rosie finished her bottle as they spoke and was looking contentedly satisfied as Loveday patted her back.

Philip Dawson was staring at the floor. The memories, prompted by Loveday's probing, had apparently swept him back to the past.

'Did your wife know about you and Mellissa?' she asked gently. It wasn't a question she would normally have been bold enough to put, but she suspected he was a man who was done with secrets.

His nod was sad. 'Rachel knew all right, her brother made sure she did.'

'Her brother?' She could feel her pulse picking up, he was talking about Brian Teague. 'What did he have to do with it?'

'He was blackmailing Mellissa and me.' He shrugged. 'Although I don't know why he bothered when he'd planned to tell Rachel all along.'

'Your brother-in-law doesn't sound like a very nice man.'

Dawson's nostrils flared as he drew in a deep breath. 'I hated him, but that hardly matters now he's dead.'

His eyes went to Rosie. 'Look, can you put the baby down now and move your car? I think I've been patient long enough. I need to be on my way.'

'Of course.' Loveday got to her feet. 'Let me settle her in the cot and I'll be right with you.'

Dawson was fidgeting by the kitchen door when she

returned, briefcase in his hand. 'I shouldn't have said all that stuff. It was private.'

'It's fine.' Loveday smiled at him. 'Sometimes it helps to unburden yourself to a stranger.'

But Dawson was shaking his head. She could see him frowning as she reversed her vehicle, freeing space for him to get out.

'Just a thought before you go,' she said, as he went to his car. 'Do you believe Mellissa killed herself?'

The man's frown deepened. He met her stare with steely hard eyes. 'She cut her wrists.'

'That's not what I asked.'

'You want me to say if I believe she was murdered?' He paused, sighing deeply. 'Then yes, the answer is yes. I believe Mellissa was murdered.'

Loveday stared after the big BMW as it crunched up the drive and turned off at the top. Well, that was definite enough, she thought, wondering if anyone still believed Mellissa Grantby had died by her own hand.

She felt guilty at how she'd led Dawson into sharing those confidences, but nothing he said had ruled him out of being the killer. He and Rachel had already lied to Sam and given him a false alibi for Brian Teague's murder.

Now Dawson had admitted he hated the man, but was it a strong enough reason to kill him?

She reached for her phone and tapped out a text message to Cassie, warning her not to come over as Sam was about to arrive and she hadn't yet decided what to tell him about her encounter with Philip Dawson.

Cassie texted her agreement, suggesting they could meet in Truro at lunchtime the next day.

Loveday was trusting she could keep that appointment. Now that work days were, by necessity, more structured to encompass

Rosie's needs and the commitment to collect Priddy in the morning and drop her home each afternoon, Loveday had to be super organized.

Time would tell if she could actually do that.

CHAPTER 23

*C*assie had suggested they meet in Aldo's, a popular Italian restaurant in Boscawen Street. She was already there when Loveday arrived.

'It'll have to be a quick coffee, I have a mountain of work at the marina,' Cassie said as Loveday sat down.

'This meeting *was* your idea, Cassie,' she reminded.

'I know, but I got a call from the Dalrymples this morning. They want us to start on *Lively Lady* today. That's two whole days ahead of schedule.'

'Maybe you should have reminded them of that.'

Cassie's look was scathing. 'It's a full interior refurb, Loveday. You don't say no to people with their kind of cash. Anyway, they need their yacht. They're planning to sail her to Cannes for the film festival this month, and I've promised the *Lady* will look spanking new by then.'

Loveday shook her head. 'You do sail close to the wind.' She grinned. 'If you'll pardon the pun.'

It was almost noon, and Aldo's hadn't yet filled with the lunchtime crowd, but Cassie still lowered her voice. 'So what happened yesterday?' she whispered, making it clear they were sharing a confidence. 'I thought the way you conspired to get Dawson into your kitchen was brilliant.'

'I wouldn't exactly describe it that way.'

'We won't quibble over how you describe what you did. Tell me what he said. Is he our killer?'

Loveday sat back, laughing. 'If he is, he was hardly likely to admit it to me.'

'Well, what *did* he tell you?'

'Not a lot, really.' Loveday looked up as their coffees arrived. She smiled her thanks to the girl and waited until she was out of earshot before continuing. 'He said his brother-in-law Brian Teague was blackmailing him over his affair with Mellissa.'

Cassie's eyebrow went up. 'Blackmailing? You mean he wanted money?'

'No, blackmailing probably isn't the right word, but it's the one Dawson used. He probably meant Teague was threatening him.'

'Threatening?'

'He said he'd tell Rachel if Dawson didn't break off his affair with Mellissa.'

'I thought Rachel already knew about her husband's bit on the side.'

'She did,' Loveday said. 'That's what made Teague's threat so pointless.'

Cassie spooned sugar into her cup. 'If Dawson broke up with Mellissa, for whatever reason, it might explain her suicide.'

'I doubt if it was suicide,' Loveday said. 'Remember, Nessa told me the dead woman had a hang-up about blood. And I'm guessing her last moments involved quite a lot of that. But that's not all.' She looked up at Cassie. 'Philip Dawson also believes his lover was murdered.'

'Did he offer any evidence?'

'No, but he was quite adamant about it, and I believed him.'

Cassie's eyes had strayed to the far side of the restaurant

where Aldo was engaged in serious conversation with an attractive young woman. 'That's his daughter, Gabriella, she said, her eyes narrowing. 'I wonder what's going on there?'

'Probably family business and nothing to do with us,' Loveday said, but her gaze lingered on the pair. She saw Aldo shake his head and walk away, waving his hands in a gesture of frustration. His daughter called out after him, but the man didn't turn back, and Gabriella sank down at a corner table.

Cassie checked her watch. 'I must go.' She reached for her bag.

Loveday had turned, gesturing for the bill, so she hadn't noticed the man who strode past their table.

'Well, look at that,' Cassie said, nodding in Gabriella's direction. 'Isn't that your boss's brother?'

Loveday's head swivelled round. Cadan Tremayne was holding Gabriella's hand. Even at this distance, she could see the woman was crying.

Cassie gave an affected tut. 'And her a married woman.'

Loveday was more interested in what Cadan was up to. Was he having an affair with this Gabriella? Was this what had brought him back to Cornwall? He'd told Merrick he'd been kicked out by a girlfriend and had nowhere else to live. But was this true? She wouldn't be surprised if he was on the run from some criminal misdemeanour or other. That was usually the reason when he turned up unannounced at the family home. But now she was considering something completely different.

'I don't suppose you know who Gabriella is married to?'

Cassie shook her head. 'Only that he's a GP. Adam and I saw them together at a function, but we weren't in their company.'

'But you know Gabriella?'

'I don't *know* her, only that she's Aldo's daughter. He introduced us one day when I was here for a business lunch.'

Loveday looked back at the couple as she and Cassie were leaving. They appeared cosy now. Cadan was stroking the woman's cheek. His head came up quickly, like he sensed he was being watched. Loveday had glanced quickly away, but she knew he'd seen her.

'I must get on,' Cassie said when they'd stepped out of the restaurant and into the busy town centre. 'How's Rosie, by the way?' She pulled an apologetic smile. 'Sorry, I should have asked sooner. Have all your colleagues been smitten by her charms?'

'A bit,' Loveday grinned. 'But so far, so good.' She lifted a hand to show her fingers were crossed.

SAM WAS THUMBING through the witness statements on his desk for the third time when Will walked in. His shoulders rose and fell in a sigh. 'There's nothing here, at least nothing that helps us.'

'It might not be a suspicious death,' Will said.

'Oh, it's suspicious all right.' Sam frowned, getting up and moving to the window before turning on his heel to stare at his sergeant. 'We both know this woman didn't kill herself. We have to stop pussyfooting around these people at the medical centre. Somebody must know something.'

Will shrugged. 'Maybe there's nothing more to know. We can't pick out bits of evidence that suit us.'

'What evidence?' Sam shot back. 'Everybody at that centre has clammed up. As far as that lot are concerned, Mellissa Grantby slit her wrists because her marriage wasn't working.'

'Well, it wasn't, her old man was having an affair with Nessa Cawse. Isn't that why Mellissa sacked her?'

'That was weeks ago, and she was having her own little fling with Brian Teague's brother-in-law, Philip Dawson.'

'I doubt if that was ongoing,' Will said. 'Don't forget, they were all outed in that letter Teague sent.'

Sam indicated a chair. 'Sit down, Will. We need to talk this through again. Two people connected to that letter are dead and a third man, Lawrence Kemp was attacked.'

'Don't forget poor old Janet Harris. She was definitely murdered.'

'OK, let's start with her,' Sam said, dropping into his chair. 'Her only connection to all this is that she cleaned for Teague.'

'What if she knew more than she told us? The killer could have been someone she knew and she was protecting him.'

'If she was prepared to protect the killer why would he murder her?' Sam sat back, steepling his fingers as he processed this. 'Maybe she wasn't protecting him. Janet could have seen something but didn't realize its importance.'

'What kind of something?'

'I don't know, but if the killer believed it identified him, well…it could have got poor old Janet Harris murdered.'

Will's brows knitted together. 'OK,' he said. 'If we accept the same killer murdered both Teague and Mrs Harris, it still doesn't explain why he killed Teague in the first place? Nothing was stolen from his cottage, well, not that we're aware of. So it wasn't a burglary that went wrong. His killer knew him.'

'Exactly!' Sam said. 'Let's rule out the possibilities. Teague was a loner, so it's unlikely he was in a relationship. We have no evidence of a disgruntled lover out there.'

'He did make it his business to know stuff about people though, which takes us back to that letter.' He paused. 'Mellissa could have killed him and then cut her wrists in a fit of remorse.'

'Anything's possible,' Sam agreed. 'But why would she? She wasn't the only one accused of being unfaithful in that letter. And since the accusations were all out in the open, there was no need to silence Teague.' He lifted the pen on his desk, his brow wrinkling as he subconsciously twirled the pen in his fingers. 'What if Mellissa had to be silenced for something she knew,' he said slowly. 'Something that wasn't in that letter but something that Brian Teague also knew about?'

Will shrugged. 'I suppose anything's possible.'

Sam sprang out of his chair. 'We need to speak to Nessa Cawse again.'

LOVEDAY WAS aware of Cadan's approach as she typed. She ignored him, hoping he was on his way to see Merrick, but he stopped at her desk, a hand on the back of her chair as he leaned over her. 'It wouldn't be in your interest to repeat what you saw this morning. I still have some clout around here. Think on that if you want to keep your job.'

Loveday spun round, her eyes furious. 'Don't you dare threaten me, Cadan Tremayne.' Keri was staring at her now, and Loveday saw no reason to keep her voice down. 'And if you believe I intend to keep quiet about your little liaison with Aldo Ricci's daughter, then you have another think coming.'

Cadan's face contorted in fury. 'You'll be sorry for this, lady. You can depend on it!' He shot a glare to Rosie's Corner. 'And make sure you collect your *menagerie* on the way out.'

He spun on his heel, watched by the entire editorial team as he stalked out of the room.

Loveday, her heart still pounding, was aware that Merrick was on his feet and calling her into his office.

Keri leaned across her desk. 'Cadan's full of hot air,' she said. 'Ignore him.'

'He threatened me, Keri. Nobody gets to do that.'

She could see Merrick was still standing, staring anxiously out at her. She took a deep breath, calming herself. Getting upset was helping no one.

CHAPTER 24

*N*essa Cawse was sitting in her garden staring over the rooftops and out to sea when Sam and Will arrived. Sam saw her start, her body language uneasy as they approached.

'Unless you're here to tell me you've arrested Mellissa's killer, I don't think I want to speak to you.'

'Good view,' Sam said, ignoring her comment as he followed her gaze out over St Michael's Mount to Marazion. If he narrowed his eyes and concentrated on the far shore, he could almost pick out the cottage where he, Loveday and Rosie lived. The thought made him smile. He turned away, mustering a more professional stance.

'We'd like you to tell us about Mellissa. I believe you were friends.'

Nessa squinted up at him. 'Mellissa sacked me.'

'We know all about that, but you were still friends, weren't you?'

'I don't know if Mellissa would have agreed with that. I had an affair with her husband.'

'I wouldn't have thought that would have bothered her too

much,' Will cut in. 'Wasn't she also having a fling with Philip Dawson?'

'It wasn't anything serious. She was using him to get her own back on Locryn. It's what Mellissa did. She got her own back on people who annoyed her.'

'Are you and Locryn Grantby still in a relationship?' Sam asked.

'God no.' She flashed him a shocked look. 'And in case you're interested, I'm sorry I got involved.'

'Why did you?' Will asked.

'I don't know. It was stupid. Kenan and I were going through a bad patch and Locryn…well, he was there.'

'Did Kenan know about you two?'

'He does now. I told him yesterday. He…he didn't take it well.' She bit her lip, her voice trembling. 'If fact, he didn't come home last night. I think our relationship is over.'

Sam could see tears glistening.

'I'm sorry. We didn't mean to upset you.'

'You didn't. I managed that all by myself.' She pulled a tissue from her pocket and blew her nose. 'You wanted to ask about Mellissa. Does this mean you now accept she was murdered?'

'It means we are still investigating what happened to her,' Sam said.

'Well, she *was* murdered. Like I said before, she wasn't a popular woman. She made enemies because she didn't suffer fools gladly. But she didn't let differences she had with people simmer away. She acted and dealt immediately with what she saw as problems. That usually meant dismissals.'

'Having an affair with someone who didn't work at the centre was surely not a sacking issue,' Will said.

'Maybe not, but if Mellissa had it in for you, she could make life intolerable. Believe me, I know.' She sighed. 'What I'm saying is if you're looking for a killer you will be spoilt for choice.'

Sam looked for a glint of revenge in the woman's eyes but saw only pain. 'I know you're serious about what you say, but you don't know Mellissa's state of mind when she died.'

'I don't,' Nessa agreed. 'But I do know that people who have the kind of obsessive fear of blood that Mellissa did do not slit their wrists to die in a blood bath.' She raised a hand to stop Sam's further questions. 'She was absolutely paranoid about blood. Oh, she was good at hiding it, but people knew. Ask her colleagues.'

She flashed Sam a frustrated look. 'You must already know all this. Locryn and I asked Loveday to pass it on to you.'

He did know. Loveday had clearly believed Nessa's story.

They'd gone back to re-question staff from the medical centre. The team of detectives carrying out the interviews had been specifically instructed to ask if Mellissa had any hang-ups about blood. Not one person had confirmed knowing this.

The question had also been raised at Locryn Grantby's interview. And although he'd told them he agreed with Nessa Cawse insistence that it was true, he could offer no actual personal evidence.

'You know, of course, that Mellissa had another man on the go?' Nessa said.

Sam nodded. It was another nugget of information Loveday had passed on. They'd checked it out and could find no evidence that it was true, but they were still keeping an open mind.

'I haven't helped you at all, have I?' Nessa said. 'You're still putting Mellissa's death down as a suicide.'

'You're wrong, actually. We don't know it's suicide, nobody does.'

'But you'll find out?'

'That's why we're here,' Sam said.

But Nessa's attention was fixed on the tanned face of the young man in the fishing smock who was striding towards them.

She hadn't noticed them walking away as she rushed into Kenan Retallick's open arms.

Sam glanced back as they reached the car and smiled. 'At least somebody's day just got better,' he said.

'I SUPPOSE you heard all that stuff earlier,' Loveday said to Priddy as they drove home later with Rosie.

'I imagine they heard it in Newquay.' Priddy grinned. 'But you certainly sent that young rascal away with his tail between his legs.'

'D'you think so?' Loveday pulled a face. 'The thing is I wouldn't have told anyone I'd seen Cadan with Aldo's daughter. It was his business. I shouldn't have exploded like that, but he did threaten to get me dismissed in front of the whole office. He shouldn't have done that.'

'I doubt if he'll be crossing you again, my lovely. He's learned his lesson. I'm sure Gabriella won't be happy when she hears about his little outburst.'

Loveday slid her a surprised look. 'You know her?'

'I know *of* her. Merrick knows her too, I thought he would have told you. He and Connie are friends of Gabriella and her husband.'

'He didn't mention that,' Loveday said slowly, wondering why he'd kept that information to himself.

The traffic on the A39 was heavy and the slow crawl of vehicles frustrating. She tried to wipe thoughts of the upsetting clash with Cadan from her mind but it was impossible. She was remembering that earlier conversation with Merrick.

'I'm sorry about that,' he'd said as she'd entered his room. 'My brother has a lot to learn about manners.'

Loveday's heated reply had been clipped. 'He threatened me!'

'I heard. We all did.' He'd glanced out across the office. The eyes that had followed her into Merrick's room were being quickly averted.

'What I don't understand is what prompted such an outburst.'

Loveday had given a baffled shrug. 'Nothing really. It was a confrontation that came out of nowhere. I wasn't planning to tell anybody about Cadan's latest little affair, but he pressed all the wrong buttons.' She'd bitten her lip. 'He suggested my job would be at risk if I told anyone what I'd seen in Aldo's.'

Merrick had raised an eyebrow. 'What exactly did you see?'

She'd repeated the sequence of events, including how she'd seen Cadan put his arms around a distressed-looking Gabriella.

'And that's it?' The eyebrows were still raised.

'I thought it was another of Cadan's little dalliances, but now I'm wondering if there's more to it.'

Merrick's brow had knitted, and she could tell how angry he'd been. 'Cadan will apologize for his behaviour,' he'd said. 'I'll make sure he does. In the meantime, I would chalk this up to experience. Whatever is going on here is my brother's problem, not yours.'

He was right, but Cadan having trouble with women was not exactly new. He wasn't the most moral of men.

Priddy's voice snapped Loveday back to the present. 'I hope Gabriella isn't having an affair with that Cadan. He's a bad lot.' She tutted her disapproval. 'Her husband is such a lovely man.'

'You know Gabriella's husband?'

'I met him when Hannah worked at that medical centre in Truro.' She shook her head. 'That poor woman. Hannah was really shocked. She said Mellissa was the last person she'd believed would take her own life.'

'Hang on! I didn't know your daughter worked there. I thought she was a librarian.'

'She is. The medical reception work she did was between jobs.'

'And she knew Mellissa Grantby?'

Priddy nodded. 'I didn't mention it because it was last year. According to Hannah, Mellissa was not popular. She ruled the roost, ordering everybody about, which was probably why they couldn't keep admin staff.'

'You said Hannah introduced you to Gabriella's husband at the medical centre.'

'That's right, Dr Bentley works there. He's one of the GPs.'

Is he now, Loveday thought, wondering if this information would interest Sam.

'Hannah also worked for Gabriella. She has boutiques, you know.'

'I didn't know,' Loveday said. 'I'm still processing how much your Hannah gets around.'

'Oh, she's settled now,' Priddy said. 'She loves that library job. The reason Hannah left the medical centre was because Gabriella offered her more money to work in her Truro boutique.'

'You said she had boutiques, plural.'

'That's right. She started off with a shop in Newquay, which is close to the cottage she and her husband have in Crantock. According to Hannah, Gabriella has another shop in Falmouth.' Priddy's brow creased. 'I'm trying to think what she calls them.'

Her eyes narrowed. 'I've got it. Bonita, yes, that's it.'

'Gabriella Bentley owns Bonita?'

'You know the boutiques?'

'I know *of* them, but they're too pricey for me. I can barely afford M & S.' Loveday was picturing the exclusive shops, the tall potted palms that stood by the doors and the minimalist whiteness of the interiors. Her brow creased into a frown. Why would a woman like that have any interest in Cadan Tremayne?

Rosie was splashing excitedly in her bath when Sam walked in later. He kissed the cheek Loveday held up to him and bent to plant another on their daughter's wet head.

'Well timed.' Loveday stood up, handing Sam a plastic duck as she went to attend to their supper. 'Don't let Rosie boss you,' she called back.

An hour later, with Rosie settled after her bath, and their supper plates stacked in the dishwasher, Sam followed Loveday out to the garden.

Her smile was relaxed as she took the coffee he brought. 'Smell that lavender,' she said. 'Isn't it wonderful?'

'Wonderful,' he agreed, stretching out on the lounger next to her. 'Have you recovered from your little spat with Cadan?'

She sat up, staring at him. 'Who told you about that?'

'Merrick rang. He wanted to make sure you were all right. He said Cadan was very rude.'

'That's putting it mildly.'

'So I gather. I think Merrick and Connie are planning to excommunicate him from the family.'

Loveday frowned at him. 'Really?'

'No.' Sam grinned across to her. 'I made that up. But he's definitely not flavour of the month.'

'He disgraced himself today, and all because Cassie and I saw him with Aldo Ricci's daughter Gabriella, in the restaurant.' She wriggled round to face him. 'Did you know she was married to one of those doctors at Hilltop Medical Centre?'

'Which one?' Sam's smile had gone.

'According to Priddy, it's Dr Bentley. You and Will must have spoken to him when you were there.'

'We did,' Sam said thoughtfully.

CHAPTER 25

'Brace yourself,' Keri warned, her eyes on the door of the editorial suite. 'Prince Charming has just come in, and he's heading this way.'

Loveday didn't need to turn her head. She knew exactly who her PA was referring to. It was Cadan Tremayne.

Talking over yesterday's events with Sam the previous night had helped to put things into perspective. The man's behaviour had been outrageous, but it was his problem.

However, if he'd come back for a second round of confrontation, then bring it on. She was ready for him.

She waited, determined to keep her attention on the computer screen. He approached her desk and gave a nervous cough.

'Could I have a word, Loveday?' He sounded hesitant.

'Depends on what the word is,' she said stiffly, aware that every pair of eyes in the room was watching them.

'How about sorry?'

'I'm listening,' she said, not turning to look at him. She had no intention of making this easy.

'Not here,' he said. 'In private.'

Her fingers were still tapping at the keyboard. 'Privacy wasn't very high on your agenda when you stormed in here with your threats yesterday.'

'I know, and I'm sorry for that. Please allow me to explain,' he said, his eyes sweeping the room. 'Without this lot lugging in.'

Loveday sighed. 'You've got five minutes,' she said, saving her work before getting up and striding past him out of the office.

Neither of them said any more until they had walked across to the café in Lemon Quay and found a table.

'Well?' Loveday folded her arms, looking up at him. 'I'm listening.'

Cadan forced a smile. 'You're not going to make this easy for me, are you? I thought we were friends.'

'Friends? Is that what you thought?' Her stare was incredulous. 'There was nothing friendly about your behaviour yesterday, Cadan. You threatened me.'

'I panicked,' he said, hanging his head. 'I was shocked when you and your friend appeared in Aldo's and saw me there with Gabriella.'

'Cassie and I didn't just *appear* in Aldo's. We were there when you walked in.'

'Well, whatever,' he came back, flapping a hand that suggested the details were not important. 'The point is, my meeting Gabriella wasn't what it looked like. She'd asked for my help. It was a sensitive business.'

'Then maybe you should have chosen a less public rendezvous for such a *sensitive* meeting.'

'The venue was Gabriella's choice. Aldo's is her family's business. It was a place where she felt safe. So you can imagine how horrified she was at the thought of rumours about us being spread around Truro.'

'And who did she think would spread those rumours?' Loveday said coldly. 'Apart from me, that is…me being such a notorious rumour-monger.'

Cadan spread his arms in a contrite gesture. 'Look, I've said I'm sorry. I was all over the place yesterday.'

'For heaven's sake, Cadan. I couldn't care less who you're having a fling with, I–'

'But we're not having a fling!' he interrupted, his voice rising. 'I told you. We're just friends.'

Loveday didn't believe a word of that. She was remembering the couple's tender embrace in the dark corner of the restaurant. But more curiously, she wondered why he was making such a fuss about insisting their liaison was innocent.

Priddy said Gabriella was married to Dr Bentley from the Hilltop Medical Centre – the man, as she now knew, who'd discovered Mellissa Grantby's body. Was this another coincidence, or was it all linked?

Loveday was thinking about this when she left Cadan in the café, still wondering if his behaviour the previous day had been forgiven.

Priddy was negotiating the buggy through the glass doors of *Cornish Folk* when Loveday spotted her and hurried to help. Rosie gazed up, her little fists thrashing about excitedly as she recognized her mother.

'You don't mind if I take Rosie for a walk?' Priddy asked. 'She loved our little outing yesterday.'

An unexpected flush of guilt swept over Loveday. She should be the one taking her daughter for a walk. It wasn't the first time she'd encountered this feeling of remorse. Her gaze constantly strayed from her desk to Rosie's Corner as she worked. And she was trotting across the office to check up on her far more than was necessary.

Priddy's understanding blue eyes had been watching her. She put a hand on Loveday's arm. 'You're fretting about your baby, my lovely,' she said. 'Rosie knows you're here. Look at her. I've never seen such a contented child.'

Loveday glanced away, blinking back a sudden tear. She knew

Priddy was right. No one could be with their child every minute of every day. She had found a wonderful solution to being a working mum while still having Rosie close by, and it was working. 'I know,' she said.

'Well, blow your nose and get into that office.' Priddy gave her a little push. 'There's a visitor waiting for you in reception. I told her you probably wouldn't be long. She said she'd wait.'

Loveday peeked over Priddy's shoulder to the young woman who had spotted her and was now on her feet.

'Thanks, Priddy, I'll deal with this.' She gave Rosie a wave. 'You two enjoy yourselves.' She watched them go, swallowing a lump in her throat before turning to walk into the magazine building.

'Nessa. This is a nice surprise,' she said, forcing a professional smile. She wondered what reason the young woman could have for seeking her out at work.

'Can we talk?' Nessa asked. 'I have a favour to ask.'

Loveday indicated the reception's corner seating area. 'It's more private over here.' She nodded to the drinks machine. 'Can I get you a coffee?'

'No thanks. This won't take long.' She bit her lip. 'I hope you won't take this the wrong way, because it's not meant as a criticism of Inspector Kitto. But I had a visit yesterday from him and Sergeant Tregellis about Mellissa's death. I'm worried they're still treating it as suicide.'

Sam had mentioned his interview with Nessa Cawse. As far as she was aware, he still had an open mind.

'You probably think I'm being a pest. I know I've already told you about the problem Mellissa had with blood, and Locryn overheard her talking to some man on the phone that definitely wasn't Philip Dawson.' She gave Loveday a desperate look. 'Mellissa didn't kill herself. I know she didn't.'

Loveday sighed. She couldn't get any more involved in this.

'Detective Inspector Kitto will be conducting a thorough investigation. There's really nothing I can do.'

'You can come with me to the medical centre,' Nessa said, touching Loveday's arm. 'I'm going there now to catch up with some people I used to work with. You wouldn't have to do anything, just come with me.'

Loveday glanced away, her brow creasing. 'It sounded innocent enough. Why shouldn't she go? She had to admit she was curious to know more about Gabriella's husband, Dr Bentley. According to Cadan, the woman was paranoid about any suggestion that she was cheating on him. It made Loveday wonder if it was true.

'It's close to here. We could walk,' Nessa said hopefully.

'OK, I'll come, but only on the strict understanding that I'm not there to interview anyone.'

'That's fine by me,' Nessa said.

'Wait here. I'll have to tell my PA I'll be out of the office for an hour.'

HILLTOP MEDICAL CENTRE was a modern single-story building. There didn't seem to be a patients' car park, which probably accounted for the number of vehicles cruising the area as their drivers looked for a parking spot.

'Looks busy,' Loveday said, noting how many people were coming and going through the glass doors.

The face of the young woman on the reception desk broke into a wide smile when she recognized Nessa as she walk in.

'I'm just calling in to say hello,' Nessa said. 'And I've brought my friend, Loveday.'

The young woman nodded to Loveday. 'I'm Merryn, she said, turning to the two women working on computers behind her. 'Look who's here,' she called.

Nessa gave them a wave. 'Hi, Helen... Hi, Sally.' Both women waved back, clearly pleased to see her. 'How is everybody?' she asked.

Helen, the older of the two women whom Loveday estimated to be in her early fifties, pulled a face. 'Not so good. It's pretty awful here at the moment. It's like we have this great cloud hovering over us, and most of us didn't even like Mellissa.'

Loveday lowered her voice, glancing back to make sure none of the patients waiting for their appointments overheard. 'It must be worse for the person who found her,' she said.

Merryn's nod was sympathetic. 'Poor Dr Bentley. He's been going around like a zombie since it happened.'

Loveday followed her eyes to the man in jeans and blue striped shirt who had ducked his head into the waiting area and asked for his next patient by name.

'God, is he still doing that?' Nessa tutted. 'He's the only doctor who calls for patients in that way. There's a perfectly efficient electronic system that flashes up the patient's name on a board.'

Apparently sensing he was being watched the GP turned, his eyes lingering for an uncomfortable split second on Loveday.

Merryn smiled at him. 'Dr Bentley has his own way of doing things,' she said defensively. 'The personal touch gives patients that extra bit of confidence.'

'Is that what he told you?' Nessa said, making it clear she didn't share her friend's high opinion of the handsome doctor.

Loveday allowed her eyes to stray around the reception area, pausing when she saw the photos on the staff board. She moved away for a closer look. Dr Christopher Bentley was there, smiling confidently into the camera. There was a definite glint in his eyes and she wondered, not for the first time, if the good doctor might fancy himself as a bit of a gigolo. If she was right, and he had an eye for the ladies, his ego wouldn't take kindly to any suggestion that his wife was unfaithful. She glanced away, silently chastising herself for making such an assumption. But she hadn't been wrong about that adoring look in Merryn's eye when the doctor had briefly appeared in the waiting room. Dr Christopher Bentley had an admirer. She wondered if he knew, but more importantly, had he taken advantage of the situation?

Loveday caught Nessa's eye, and tapped her watch, indicating she had to get back to the magazine. She gave the women a wave, pleased to see Nessa had done the same and was heading towards her at the door.

'Well, what did you think?' Nessa said as they left the building.

'About what?' Loveday asked, her expression bemused.

'Him, of course. Dr Bentley.'

Loveday turned to answer and immediately spotted the familiar shape of the big silver grey car rounding the corner. She grabbed Nessa's arm. 'Duck!' she ordered, pulling the woman behind a parked car. 'It's Sam, and he won't be pleased to see me here.'

The two crouched lower as Sam and Will Tregellis cruised past. Loveday watched them pull into a parking space. 'Sorry about this,' she said, still keeping low until the two detectives had left their car and disappeared into the centre. 'I told you Sam was investigating.'

'That's great,' Nessa said. 'But I still want to know what you think about Christopher Bentley.'

Loveday's eyes were cautious. 'What am I supposed to think? I didn't even speak to the man.'

'But you saw him,' Nessa said. 'You must have noticed Merryn is besotted with him.' She sighed. 'Look, Bentley's a flirt. He loves that women fancy him. What if he was Mellissa's secret lover?' She shot Loveday a knowing look. 'I wouldn't put it past him.'

NESSA'S WORDS had stuck with Loveday for the rest of the afternoon, and the possibilities were still darting around her mind as she drove Priddy and Rosie home to Marazion later. Any suggestion of an affair between Mellissa Grantby and this GP was grasping at straws. Nessa had no evidence to back up such a claim. It was all a figment of her imagination and Loveday had allowed herself to be swept along with it.

Her thoughts turned to Gabriella, and Cadan's insistence they were not a couple. She was a beautiful woman, and Cadan wasn't known for turning his back on a situation that could benefit him. Added to that, Gabriella's apparent vulnerability would be irresistible to him.

By the time they had reached Marazion, Loveday had decided. She would find a way of speaking with Gabriella.

CHAPTER 26

'Y ou two look happy,' Cassie said, pulling up a chair and joining Loveday and Rosie in the sunny front garden.

The wild rabbits, which had initially scampered to the safety of the hedge when Cassie arrived, were venturing back and beginning to nibble the grass again.

'How's it going at work? Is this young lady running the magazine yet?'

'Just about.' Loveday laughed. 'She's certainly making her mark with my colleagues.'

'I knew that decision to take her to the office with you would be a success.'

'I couldn't do it without Priddy. She's been amazing.'

'Ah, bless.' Cassie smiled indulgently at Rosie, whose eyes were fixed in fascination on the rabbits. 'What about the other stuff, has Sam arrested anyone yet?'

Loveday remembered Sam's expression when she'd told him Cadan's friend Gabriella was married to a GP at the Hilltop Medical Centre. He'd looked interested but he hadn't confirmed it was even helpful.

'Not yet, and it's really getting to him,' Loveday said. 'Nessa is still trying to convince everybody that Mellissa was murdered, and Locryn insists she had another lover, apart from Philip Dawson that is.'

'It could be a smoke screen,' Cassie offered. 'They could have murdered Brian Teague together and be up to their necks in the other deaths.'

Loveday gave her a questioning look. 'That would mean Adam is employing a murderess and letting her loose on his patients.'

'I know.' She screwed up her face. 'Terrifying, isn't it.'

Loveday looked up. 'Remember Cadan Tremayne turning up as we left Aldo's?'

'When he was with Aldo's daughter, yes, of course I do. Why?'

'Because he had a right go at me in the office later, warning me not to spread any rumours about him and Gabriella. He was furious that we'd seen them together.'

Cassie's eyebrows went up. 'Was he now.'

'Oh, he'd calmed down by this morning and apologized for his behaviour, insisting there was nothing untoward between them, but I don't believe that for a minute. Turns out the lady is married to a doctor at the medical centre where Mellissa Grantby died.'

'Really? I didn't know that.'

'It gets better,' Loveday said. 'He was the one who found her. Nessa and I went to the centre today so I could meet the staff she used to work with.'

Cassie's wide-eyed expression urged her on. 'So did you meet this doctor, the one Gabriella's married to?'

'I didn't actually meet him, but I saw him. And I saw the effect he has on women. Nessa said he's a flirt. In fact, she suggested he and Mellissa could have had a thing going.'

'Charming.' Cassie tutted. 'Is nobody connected to this business faithful to their partners?'

'It doesn't seem so, but this Dr Christopher Bentley is interesting. I was thinking of having a word with his wife tomorrow. Cadan said she was worried we'd seen them together and was paranoid I might spread gossip about them.'

She smiled down at Rosie, who was gazing back at her with huge, adoring blue eyes.

'Being a mother agrees with you,' Cassie said.

Loveday nodded, her eyes still on her child. 'I wouldn't argue with that.'

SAM'S TEENAGE DAUGHTER, Maddie, rang as Loveday was preparing potatoes for the evening meal. 'How's my gorgeous little sister? Is she missing me?'

'Absolutely.' Loveday grinned at the phone. 'When are you coming to visit us?'

'I was hoping to come down tomorrow,' Maddie said. 'I could babysit and give you and Sam a night off.'

'You don't have to bribe us, you know,' Loveday scolded. 'Just come. We'd love to see you.'

'So you won't want me to babysit,' Maddie said, a tease in her voice.

'I never said that.'

They both laughed. Loveday liked the easy relationship she had with Sam's older daughter.

When Maddie first announced her ambition to follow Loveday into journalism, her mother, Sam's first wife, Victoria, hadn't hidden her disappointment. She'd wanted their daughter to take over the family hairdressing business in Plymouth. But Maddie's brother, Jack, who at twenty-one was studying to be a vet, had given his full approval.

'Is that editor still slave-driving you?' Loveday asked.

'Ed is not a slave driver, but we're definitely busy. I know *The*

Advertiser is only a local newspaper, but I'm treated like a proper reporter, and I love it.'

'That's because you *are* a proper reporter,' Loveday said. 'And the sooner you start believing in yourself, young lady, the better it will be.'

She was still thinking about their conversation when Sam walked into their kitchen later.

'Maddie rang,' she said, stretching up to kiss him. 'She's coming down tomorrow.'

His face broke into a wide smile, but it didn't quite mask the weariness Loveday had spotted.

'That's great,' he said, heading to say goodnight to his daughter in the nursery.

'She says she'll babysit so we can go out for a drink or something.'

'I hope you bit her hand off.'

'All the way to the elbow,' Loveday called after him. She was itching to know how his day had gone, and more than curious about why he and Will had returned to the medical centre.

'Bad day?' she asked, following him into the nursery.

'Frustrating.' He released a deep sigh. 'Domestic murders are so much easier. Normally we have someone locked up within 24 hours, but this is different.'

'Because the murders aren't domestic, you mean?'

'Oh, I don't know, I think so. We have so many suspects, but they all have alibis.'

'Philip Dawson doesn't,' Loveday reminded. 'He got his wife to lie for him, saying he'd been on his travels when Teague was murdered, even though he'd been here all the time.'

'We've interviewed him since then. He was with Mellissa when Teague was killed.'

'He's using a dead woman for his alibi?' Loveday's voice rose in disbelief.

'The receptionist at the medical centre saw Mellissa getting into his car outside the building. They drove off together. The times checked. Dawson was telling the truth, Loveday.'

'What about his wife, Rachel? Where was she that morning?'

'She says she was at home, but she was alone.'

'She's probably relying on the fact that she's Teague's sister to rule her out of the case. But Teague's bitterness and blackmail threats to just about everyone could have destroyed Rachel's marriage. If he'd been prepared to do that, it might be a reason for his sister to kill him.'

'We're not ruling her out,' Sam said.

'And then there's Locryn Grantby,' Loveday went on. 'Teague went after him because he was at the wheel when his sister-in-law, Tamsin, died in that accident. It wasn't his fault, but we know how vindictive Teague could be. Maybe he was persecuting Locryn, and the man eventually snapped.'

'Locryn Grantby has an alibi. He was here in Marazion. Customers visiting his studio have confirmed it.'

'Are you still thinking Teague's killer also murdered his cleaner?'

'It's the only thing that makes any sense.'

Loveday paused before continuing. She had to choose her words carefully. Sam was bound to see her visit to the medical centre as going behind his back.

'What about Mellissa?' she started cautiously. 'Nessa Cawse still believes she was murdered.' She glanced up at him. 'Is that what you think, Sam?'

'It's what the pathologist tells us.'

'Really?' Loveday's eyes widened. 'So, it's official? Mellissa Grantby was murdered?'

Sam gave a weary nod. 'Dr Bartholomew took another look at those cuts on her wrists. He now says if they'd been self-inflicted they would have been angled differently.'

'Isn't that something that should have been immediately obvious?'

'If he'd been looking for it, then yes, but it looked so much like a suicide. We're now waiting for toxicology results.'

'Toxicology?' Loveday screwed up her face. 'Mellissa didn't take drugs, did she?'

'That's not why I requested a toxicology report.'

'Ah,' Loveday said, beginning to understand. 'You think Mellissa might have been drugged before her wrists were cut?'

'It's a possibility we're considering.'

'What about Gabriella's husband? Isn't he the one who found Mellissa's body? Will you be interviewing him again?'

'Already done. Will and I paid him a visit this afternoon.'

'And?' Loveday's eyes were wide again with questions.

'He was very engaging the first time we spoke to him, but definitely shocked. He seemed keen to help.'

'And this time?' She watched Sam go to the cupboard where his malt whisky was kept and pour himself a drink. It was unusual for him to have a dram before his evening meal, but Loveday could see how tired he was this evening.

Sam's eyes narrowed as he considered her question. 'We asked him to go over events when he found Mellissa. It was word perfect with his previous account. He looked genuinely surprised when I told him about her blood phobia. We put it to him that if Mellissa had wanted to kill herself, then she would surely have chosen a simpler way to go.

'But Bentley said Mellissa was all about the dramatic, and what could have been more dramatic than slitting her wrists right there in the medical centre?'

'I suppose he has a point,' Loveday said. 'Did you get around to asking about his marriage?'

'Only to establish that he's happily married, and happily childless – his words. He comes across as being a nice, genuine man.'

The oven timer pinged and Loveday went to slide out the chicken joints.

Sam sniffed. 'Smells great,' he said. 'I feel guilty that you're still doing all the cooking.'

'I like cooking.'

'It's still not fair. *I'll* do more when this case is over.' He grinned at her. 'I promise.'

CHAPTER 27

*P*riddy was settling Rosie in her corner when Loveday was called into Merrick's room.

'Has that rascal of a brother of mine apologized yet?'

'He did.' Loveday gave a smug smile. 'I haven't actually accepted it. I thought I'd keep him dangling for a bit.'

'Quite right. A bit of humility won't do him any harm.' He'd picked up a pen, twirling it in his fingers.

Loveday waited. She could see he wanted to say more.

'Was there anything else, Merrick? It's just that I have an article to write.'

Merrick dropped the pen and looked up at her. 'I know it's short notice, but would you and Sam be available to come over for supper this evening?'

She hesitated, the invitation took her by surprise. 'I'm not sure, Merrick. Sam's work is pretty full on at the moment. On the other hand, Maddie is coming today and she has offered to babysit. Can you give me time to ask Sam?'

'Of course,' Merrick said, his brow wrinkling.

'What?' Loveday said, narrowing her eyes at him. 'Why do I feel I'm missing something?'

'Connie has invited Gabriella Bentley and her husband. The women play golf together. They're good friends.'

'Ah,' Loveday said. 'And you're wondering if it will compromise Sam's case if he meets Dr Bentley socially?' She lifted her shoulders in a shrug. 'I can't see it being a problem, but I'd have to ask Sam.' The prospect of meeting the couple on the neutral ground of the Tremaynes' big, converted farmhouse was suddenly exciting. And then another thought struck. 'What about Cadan? Has he been invited to this supper?'

'Of course not.'

'Won't that be awkward? I mean, if Cadan knows the Bentleys are coming, and he really is having a fling with Gabriella–'

Merrick cut her sentence short. 'That's his problem. Clearly Gabriella doesn't think it'll be awkward or she wouldn't have accepted Connie's invitation.'

'But Gabriella knows I saw her and Cadan together in Aldo's.'

'It should be interesting then, shouldn't it?' Merrick said, his eyes twinkling with mischief.

Loveday rang Sam as soon as she left Merrick's office. To her surprise he picked up immediately. 'Everything OK? Is Rosie all right?' She could hear the flash of anxiety in his voice.

'Everything is fine, Sam,' she assured.

'Then why are you ringing me at…' He paused. Loveday guessed he was checking the time. 'At five past nine?'

'Sorry, but I had to catch you now before you got really busy.'

'I'm really busy now.' He sighed. 'What's this about?'

'I need to run something past you, and I don't want you to dismiss it out of hand.' She repeated Merrick's supper invitation, reminding him that Maddie was due to arrive later and had offered to babysit.

'It's a bit of a cheek walking out on her when she's only arrived.'

'Not a bit,' Loveday said. 'Anyway, I suspect she's more interested in seeing Rosie than chatting with us. If I double check with her that she's still coming, can I confirm with Merrick that we'll be there?'

'You're quite determined about this, aren't you?'

'Why not? It'll be fun to let our hair down for a change.'

'OK, tell Merrick we'll be there.'

Loveday blew out her cheeks as he ended the call. Plenty of time to mention the other supper guests later...when they were on their way to the Tremaynes' home.

Rosie was having her lunchtime feed when Loveday's phone rang, and Maddie's name flashed onto the little screen.

'Want me to take over with Rosie?' Priddy asked, her arms already outstretched.

'No, she's fine,' Loveday said, enjoying the feel of her daughter nestling so comfortably in her arms. 'Can you speak to Maddie? Put her on answerphone. She's probably ringing to confirm she's on her way here.'

Priddy took the call.

'Hi, Maddie. No, it's Priddy. Loveday is busy with Rosie at the moment. Yes, I'm fine. Hang on, I'll put you on speaker.'

Maddie's clear young voice rang out. 'Hi, Loveday. Is my lovely little sister behaving herself?'

'She's guzzled her way through the entire contents of her bottle in four minutes flat.' Loveday laughed. 'But yes, apart from needing to refine her table manners, young Rosie is doing really well. How about you? Are you still coming to see us?'

'Absolutely. I'm on the train,' Maddie said. 'Just wanted to say don't worry about arranging to pick me up at Penzance station, I'll get a taxi.'

'Are you sure?' Loveday said.

'Of course. Is the key still under that big blue plant pot at the back door?'

'It is. Rosie and I won't be there till around five, so make yourself at home.' She paused. 'We might take you up on that babysitting offer tonight. Would you mind?'

'Of course not. You and Sam deserve a night out. Hope you're going somewhere nice.'

'We are. Remember my boss, Merrick?'

'I do,' Maddie said.

'Well, he's asked Sam and I to join him and Connie for supper this evening.'

'Sounds lovely. I'll want all the details when you get back.'

'It's a deal,' Loveday said as Keri poked her head around the screen. 'There's a call for you. Shall I get them to ring back?'

'Who is it?'

'She wouldn't give her name.'

'I'd better take it,' she said, handing Rosie over to Priddy.

'Sorry, Maddie. I have to go.'

'No problem,' Maddie said. 'I'll see you later. Maybe we can catch up too, Priddy?' she called out.

The older woman's face broke into a delighted smile. 'I'd love that,' she said as the call ended.

LOVEDAY FOLLOWED Keri to her desk and waited until she'd transferred the call.

'Who am I speaking to?' she asked.

There was a pause at the other end of the line, and then a voice with a pleasant soft accent said, 'It's Gabriella Bentley. I apologize for ringing out of the blue like this but I was wondering if you could spare me a few minutes of your time. Perhaps we could meet for a coffee?'

Loveday needed to think. She had intended speaking to this woman, but in her own time. Was she ringing to dissuade her and Sam from attending the planned supper party?

Her brow furrowed. Was she to be accused of spreading

rumours about this woman and Cadan again? A speck of indignation was starting to flare.

'I wouldn't keep you more than a few minutes,' the woman insisted. 'If you're free now, I'm at Aldo's restaurant. I could wait for you.'

'Why can't you come to my office?'

The caller hesitated, the sound of a low, faltering breath coming over the phone. 'It's private,' she said.

Loveday relented. 'OK, I'll come, but it will literally be for a few minutes.'

'Thank you,' Gabriella said.

She was already regretting her decision to meet the woman before she'd even left the magazine office, convinced that her first assumption was right. Gabriella probably wanted to dissuade her and Sam from turning up at Merrick's place that night. If that was her game, she was out of luck.

Aldo's was busy as Loveday walked into the restaurant. It was hardly the place for a private conversation.

Gabriella had been watching for her and came forward, her hand outstretched.

Loveday took in the woman's elegant olive green suit, her professionally cut dark hair and careful make-up. Her whole appearance spoke of money and power.

'Thank you for coming. May I call you Loveday? I really appreciate this. We can use my father's office.'

She turned, leading the way between the tables and into a small room at the back of the restaurant. Loveday was surprised at how scrupulously tidy and organized it was.

Gabriella followed her gaze. 'My father is paranoid about running an orderly business,' she explained.

'Very commendable,' Loveday murmured, but she wasn't here to pass the time. 'I'm intrigued to know why you wanted to talk to me.'

The woman bit her lip. She looked nervous. 'Connie

'Tremayne tells me that you and your husband will be joining us for supper this evening. There's something you need to know.'

Loveday waited.

'I understand you saw me here with Cadan a few days ago, but despite how it may have appeared, we are not having an affair. Connie introduced us the last time Cadan was home in Cornwall some months ago. He was easy to speak to and I found myself confiding in him.' She leaned forward, meeting Loveday's direct gaze. 'I have a very jealous husband. If he gets the whiff of an affair, even though it's all in his mind, he…well, he'll make my life unbearable.'

'Are you saying your husband abuses you?'

'Not physically. He's much too clever for that. The abuse is more subtle. He takes his anger out on the man he's decided I'm involved with.'

'How does he do that?'

'He has them followed, making sure they are aware of this. Then the blackmail starts. He saves the anonymous threatening letters for the final blow.'

'I don't understand. Who are these men you say your husband targets?'

Gabriella gave a defeated shrug. 'He sees any man I've met more than once as fair prey. It's easier for him if they're married because he can then threaten to contact the wife with his wild accusations. Putting a seed like that in someone's mind is certain to be disruptive. No man wants that kind of trouble so they do what my husband tells them. They cut off any future contact with me.'

She gave a heartfelt sigh. 'I've lost my hairdresser, my personal trainer, and the professional at my golf club now gives me a wide berth. Even one of the young servers in the restaurant here left mysteriously when all he'd done was to collect some shopping for me.'

'And you shared all this with Cadan?'

Gabriella nodded.

'Weren't you worried about him being targeted?'

'The only times we met were at the Tremaynes' house, and my husband knew I was friendly with Connie.'

'But I saw you and Cadan together here.'

'That wasn't my idea. Cadan made it his business to discover when I'd be here at Aldo's.'

'Cadan said it was your suggestion to meet here.'

Gabriella's beautiful dark eyes blinked. 'Did he?' She looked confused. 'Oh, maybe he was right. I get so mixed up. Cadan wanted me to go to the police.'

'I'm inclined to agree with him,' Loveday said.

'No!' Gabriella shook her head. 'I can't do that. You don't know my husband. I'm only telling you this so you understand my position. I couldn't risk you casually mentioning that you'd seen me with Cadan.' She grabbed Loveday's hand. 'You have to promise me.'

Loveday sat back, trying to process what the woman had told her. 'All right, I promise, but only for this evening.' She didn't appreciate becoming involved in the woman's life, not if she wasn't prepared to help herself.

'But I will eventually have to share what you've told me with my partner.'

'I know,' Gabriella said quietly.

CHAPTER 28

'*L*ook who's here, Rosie.' Loveday threw out an arm to draw Maddie into a hug.

'Now that's what I call a welcome.' Maddie grinned. 'How are you both?'

'How do we look?'

'Fabulous,' Maddie said as Rosie's tiny fingers grasped her outstretched hand. 'How's Dad?'

'Sam's fine. Busy as ever, of course. He'll be delighted to see you.'

'What about you, Loveday?' Maddie's eyes were still on Rosie. 'How can you bear to concentrate on work when you have this little one with you?'

Loveday's mind went back to the guilt she'd felt earlier when it had been Priddy walking Rosie and not her. 'We have our moments,' Loveday said. 'But Priddy is wonderful, and she loves Rosie like her own granddaughter.'

'Can I hold her?' Maddie asked, making her arms wide to take her baby sister.

'Be my guest,' Loveday said, passing Rosie across.

'Are you sure you're OK to babysit tonight? I feel guilty leaving you on your first night here.'

'Rosie and I don't mind, do we, my darling?' Maddie said, bouncing the child in her arms.

The women were still having a good catch up when Sam burst into the kitchen later, a wide smile on his face. 'My three favourite ladies. How good is this?'

Maddie flew across the kitchen to embrace her father.

Sam hugged her back. 'How long can you stay?' he asked, disentangling himself to plant kisses on Loveday and Rosie's cheeks.

'I have to go home on Monday. Can you and Loveday put up with me that long?'

'Just watch us,' Loveday called from the other side of the kitchen.

'Well, let's start as we mean to go on. You two get ready for your big night out and Rosie and I will look after ourselves.'

'You're sure this is OK?' Loveday asked half an hour later, glancing at herself in the mirror as she passed. She was wearing a new, figure-hugging red dress and had paid more attention than she usually did to her hair and make-up.

'Of course it is,' Maddie said. 'And you look beautiful. Tell her, Dad.'

Sam raised an appreciative eyebrow. 'She's right, my darling. You do scrub up well. We should do this more often.'

Loveday was feeling good as they drove out of Marazion, but by the time they got to Morvah traces of unease had begun to filter through. She knew Cadan hadn't been invited to the supper party, but what if he turned up? He was more than capable of gate-crashing the evening. On the other hand, Gabriella was his friend. Surely he wouldn't risk making her uncomfortable in front of her husband? Her pulse was picking up as Sam parked in the drive and they walked to the house.

Merrick greeted them at the door and led them into the big, comfortable drawing room.

'Can I introduce Gabriella and Chris,' Merrick said as the couple came forward to be introduced.

'We meet again,' Sam said, shaking Dr Christopher Bentley's hand. 'This is my partner, Loveday.'

The man's charismatic brown eyes flitted appreciatively over her. She was waiting for him to say he'd seen her at the medical centre, but he didn't.

'Pleased to meet you,' he murmured. 'Have you met Gabriella, my wife,' he said, tuning to bring Gabriella forward. She offered her hand.

Loveday took it, aware that the GP was still smiling at her. He might be a ladies' man, but she was having difficulty picturing him as the cruel, abusive husband Gabriella had described.

'Your husband and I met when we interviewed staff at the Hilltop Medical Centre over that very sad death of Mellissa Grantby,' Sam explained.

Gabriella's huge brown eyes flashed surprise. 'You interviewed the staff? You mean you're a policeman? Merrick didn't say.'

'Is that a problem?'

'Of course not. I didn't realize.'

Dr Bentley was shaking his head sadly. 'Poor Mellissa. We still haven't got over her death. The entire medical centre is shocked.' His gaze went back to Loveday, and she knew he was remembering seeing her there with Nessa. She wished now that she'd told Sam about that. At any moment, this doctor would speak up, say he'd seen her there. She waited, but still he said nothing.

An uneasy atmosphere was settling over the room. Merrick's fidgety body language told Loveday he also felt it.

She looked around her. 'No Edward tonight?'

'My father has taken himself off on a cruise, would you believe.'

'A cruise?' Loveday's eyebrows rose in surprise. She remembered how frail the 88-year-old had looked last time she'd met him here at Morvah.

'It's a National Trust for Scotland cruise around the islands,' Merrick explained. 'When he heard about it at one of those talks on antiques he attends there was no holding him back.'

'Good for Edward,' Loveday said. She was fond of the old man, even if under his guardianship, the *Cornish Folk* magazine had almost been driven into the ground. It was only saved by the drastic staff-cutting measures Merrick had been forced to implement. It was still being run on a shoestring.

Merrick's voice brought her back into the room. 'I think Connie is treating us to her famous roast beef,' he said lightly as his wife entered, apologizing for not having been there to greet their guests.

'I don't know about famous,' she chided. 'I'll settle for it just being tasty.'

'You're a wonderful cook, Connie,' Sam interrupted, looking at the faces around him. 'Loveday and I can vouch for your roast dinners.'

She knew Sam was taking his cue from Merrick by keeping his comments light.

It didn't stop Gabriella looking uncomfortable. Her husband, on the other hand, appeared to be completely at home.

'How long have you been a GP, Dr Bentley?' Loveday asked.

Bentley turned his infectious smile on her again. 'Please call me Chris.'

Loveday nodded.

'I've been a doctor for ten years,' he said. 'The last four at Hilltop after meeting Gabriella.' His glance to his wife was affectionate. 'We met at the British Open in St Andrews and married weeks later in Bali.'

'Bali?' Connie exclaimed. 'How romantic.'

'It was,' Gabriella agreed, but there was a stiffness to her smile.

'So you met at the golf?' Merrick addressed Bentley. 'We should arrange a foursome.'

'Gabriella is the golfer. I'm afraid my interest is limited to being a spectator. I fear you would find me a clumsy partner.'

'Nonsense,' Connie said. 'Merrick and I are no experts, and I just hack about. Ask Gabriella.' Her nose twitched. 'Can anyone smell burning?'

A chorus of 'nos' went around the room.

'I'd better check,' Connie said, hurrying off to the kitchen.

'I'll come with you,' Loveday said.

'Maybe I can help, too.' Gabriella had already turned to follow the other women from the room.

'I shouldn't have come,' she whispered to Loveday when they were out of Connie's hearing. 'Chris knows something's wrong. I didn't realize your partner was a policeman, or that he had already met my husband.'

'Does it matter?' Loveday returned.

'Not as long as you believe what I told you. It's all true, although you'd never guess my husband was an abuser. Chris is very clever at hiding his real self under this cover of friendliness, he wants everyone to think of him as a caring doctor. Believe me, things are very different when we are alone.'

'You have to tell someone about this,' Loveday said.

'I told you.'

'But I'm not the professional help you need, Gabriella. You won't even let me tell Sam.'

'Going to the police won't do any good. They could interview him as often as they like and would still only see a perfectly charming man who is worried about his wife's mental health. He'd tell them I'm unstable and that I make up things.'

'The police won't take his word for that. They'll investigate.'

'And what do you imagine would happen to me in the meantime?'

'Are you saying your husband would harm you?'

'What do you think? Of course he would harm me.'

They hadn't noticed Connie standing behind them. She looked shocked. 'Good heavens, Gabriella.' Her hand was at her throat. 'Why didn't you tell me?'

'Connie is right,' Loveday said. 'You should have said something. You need to trust your friends.'

Gabriella looked away, touching her hair. 'Sorry, I'm all over the place.' She gave Connie a hesitant look. 'I don't suppose I could stay here tonight to clear my head?'

'Of course you can,' Connie said, putting a reassuring hand on her arm. 'When we've had dinner you take yourself off to the bathroom. Loveday will check up on you when you don't reappear. She will come back and tell us you were feeling faint and needed to lie down.'

Gabriella bit her lip, considering this. 'What if Chris insists on taking me home?'

'I'll insist you stay the night,' Loveday said. 'At least that will give you a breathing space until you decide what to do.'

'You're both being wonderful, but will it work?'

'We're not saying spending a night here with Connie and Merrick will solve anything, but it will give you some time to think, at least it won't do any harm. There's nothing to stop you going back to your husband tomorrow if that's what you decide.'

'Well?' Connie said. 'Are we agreed on this?'

Gabriella gave a silent nod.

Loveday returned to the men, bearing the roast beef on a warmed platter. 'I'm told you carve a mean joint, Merrick,' she said, placing the meat on the table in front of him. She was followed by Gabriella carrying a dish of roast potatoes and Connie with more dishes of vegetables.

Sam sniffed the air appreciatively. 'This smells like another treat, Connie.'

Bentley took the potatoes from his wife. Loveday saw him whisper in her ear. 'Are you OK?'

Gabriella smiled. 'A bit shaky, that's all.'

Merrick sliced the meat as Connie handed round plates, telling everyone to help themselves to vegetables.

The conversation mellowed to a lull as they ate. Loveday was waiting for the signal of Gabriella getting to her feet.

It happened towards the end of the meal, when she pushed aside her plate of hardly touched food and stood up, excusing herself.

Bentley looked up sharply. 'OK, darling?'

Gabriella nodded, flashing an apologetic look to Connie. 'It's a bit warm in here. I need to step out for a moment.'

Bentley jumped up. 'I'll come with you.'

'No, please. Don't make an issue of it, Chris. I just need a bit of breathing space.'

The other two men had also stood, but Gabriella waved them back to their seats as she left.

'I'm sure she'll be fine,' Loveday said, watching Bentley's eyes following his wife from the room.

'There's an arctic roll in the fridge,' Connie said brightly. 'I hope you've all left a space for it.'

Loveday was aware Sam was watching her. She tried to keep her eyes from straying to the clock. Hopefully, her body language would warn him to stay quiet. She waited until five minutes had passed before getting to her feet. 'I'll check on Gabriella,' she said, moving away from the table and slipping out.

The woman was waiting on the stairs. Loveday hurried her up to the agreed room where, still protesting, Gabriella sank down onto the bed. 'This won't work,' she said. 'Chris will never allow me to stay here. There's no way he'll go home without me.'

'Connie and I will insist that you stay. It *will* work so long as you keep your nerve.'

As Loveday spoke, the door behind her was slowly opening. A man was standing there.

Gabriella gasped, clutching her chest. 'Cadan!' Her eyes were wide with shock. 'You scared me.'

Loveday swung round, frowning. 'What are you doing here?'

Cadan stared back at her, his brow creasing. 'I live here, remember? What's your excuse?'

'I was feeling faint,' Gabriella said quickly, fingertips touching her forehead. 'Loveday was looking after me.'

'Faint?' He stepped forward. 'What's wrong? Are you all right?'

The concern in his voice sounded genuine, but Loveday was more interested in why Gabriella was maintaining the subterfuge. This was supposed to be the man whose friendship she relied on, the person she confided in. Maybe Cadan wasn't the trusted amigo he'd led her to believe.

'We should let her rest,' Loveday said, linking arms and leading him from the room.

His backward glance was unsure. 'I'll be fine, Cadan,' Gabriella called, her voice sounding weak. 'I just need to rest.'

Loveday closed the door after them, aware of Cadan's confusion. 'Something's going on here. Has Bentley been threatening her again?' He crooked his head. 'That's it, isn't it?' His nostrils flared with anger. 'I'll kill the bastard.'

'No you won't!' Loveday pulled him back as he attempted to head for the stairs. 'Don't interfere, Cadan. Connie and I are taking care of things.'

'Taking care of what?'

Loveday bit her lip. Could she trust Cadan? She needed to think.

'None of this must be repeated. Tell me you understand.'

Cadan gave an impatient nod.

Loveday glanced down the stairs, making sure they weren't being overheard as they moved away from the door. 'We know about the abuse,' she whispered. 'Gabriella told us.'

'She did?'

'Connie and I have advised her to get professional help. We

haven't completely convinced her, but I believe she's getting there. Gabriella is going to spend the night here to give her some thinking time.'

'I don't see Bentley going along with that.'

'He will if he wants to save face. Let's see what happens.'

'What can I do to help?'

'The best thing you can do is to stay out of the way. If Bentley even suspects there's another man in the house tonight he definitely won't agree to Gabriella staying.' She paused. 'Is it a deal?'

Cadan clapped his hand against the one Loveday held up. He clearly wasn't happy, but he repeated the word, 'Deal.'

Loveday took the steps slowly as she made her way back to the dining room.

'Gabriella's not feeling very well,' she announced. 'She's feeling a bit giddy and she's going to lie down for a while.'

'Giddy?' Bentley was on his feet again. 'Where is she?'

Loveday put up a hand. 'I should leave her for now. She's having a little nap.'

'I need to get her home,' Bentley said.

'I thought Gabriella was looking a bit peaky when she was in the kitchen,' Connie said.

'She said she was tired,' Loveday agreed.

'If she's comfy in bed I think you should let her sleep, Chris,' Connie said. 'In fact, she should stay the night.' She glanced to Merrick for support.

'Absolutely, Gabriella must stay,' Merrick said. 'We have plenty of room.'

Bentley was still not looking convinced. 'I need to see her.'

'I'll take you.' Loveday had sat down, but now she was on her feet again. 'We'll go quietly though, in case she's still asleep.'

She led the way upstairs, creeping into Gabriella's room.

The woman's eyes were closed and she was curled up in the bed. 'She looks really peaceful,' Loveday said. 'I'd say she's been overworking and needs a good rest.'

Bentley frowned at her. 'You're a doctor, are you?'

'No, of course not. But I can recognize when someone is exhausted.'

The man didn't look happy, but other than waking his wife and conducting a series of health checks, he had no reason to suspect she was seriously ill.

'OK, we'll leave her to sleep,' he said. 'But I'll be back first thing in the morning.'

Gabriella hadn't moved in the bed, and he took one last look back at her before following Loveday downstairs.

'Dr Bentley agrees his wife should stay here for tonight,' Loveday announced when they got back to the room.

'If you're sure that wouldn't put you out,' Bentley said.

Connie shook her head. 'She's more than welcome.'

'In that case, I'll be back to collect my wife in the morning.'

'Won't you stay for coffee?' Connie offered.

The man shook his head. 'Gabriella and I hadn't planned to stay late, and there are things I have to do at home.'

'We'll take good care of your wife,' Merrick assured, as the man excused himself and headed for the door, Merrick behind him.

'We'll help with the dishes,' Loveday offered as the men left the room.

'That's really unnecessary,' Connie said.

'No, please. We want to help,' Sam insisted.

'Has he gone?' Loveday asked, when Merrick came back.

'Yes, he's off. I'm more concerned about his wife.'

'Don't worry. I'll be keeping an eye on her,' Connie said, turning to Merrick. 'Why don't you help Sam with the washing up? Loveday and I will organize some coffee.'

'I'll make a quick check on your guest,' Loveday said, making for the stairs. She met the woman standing by the bedroom door.

'Has Chris really gone?'

'He has,' Loveday said. 'Use this time well to decide what you want to do.'

'And I really can stay here for tonight?' She was smiling now.

'Well, that's the idea. Sam and Merrick are downstairs. They know nothing of your situation, but I think you should trust them.'

Gabriella hesitated, apparently processing this. 'You're right,' she said. 'You can tell them. I've got to stop hiding this away.'

CHAPTER 29

Sam waited until they were through the gates of Morvah and heading for the A30, before sliding Loveday a look. 'Care to share what was going on back there?'

'I don't know what you mean.'

'I think you do. What was wrong with Gabriella? And why were you and Connie so keen for her to stay the night?'

'She wasn't well.'

'So why didn't her husband take her home?'

Loveday heaved a sigh. 'I've been biding my time before telling you about this.'

'About what, for heaven's sake?' His voice was rising. 'What's this great secret you women are keeping?'

Loveday fixed her sights on the road ahead, sucking in her bottom lip. 'Gabriella's husband is abusing her,' she said.

'What?'

'She's terrified of him, Sam, but she won't go to the police. Connie overheard us talking in the kitchen. Gabriella asked if she could stay the night, and of course Connie agreed. I went along with it because I thought it would be good for the woman to have some space from her husband. Even if only for a night, it will give her time to think. Hopefully by morning she will have decided to leave the man and get some proper help.'

'I didn't see any signs of abuse,' Sam said.

'Well, you wouldn't. He doesn't hit her. Gabriella says Bentley is much too clever for that. It's all psychological stuff.'

'I think you better tell me everything.'

The A30 sped past as Loveday talked. When she finished, she saw Sam blow out his cheeks. 'What will you do?' she asked.

'Why is Gabriella so reticent to come to us?'

'Why do you think? She doesn't want the police accusing Chris of abuse when she has no physical evidence she's being harmed. That would make everything so much worse.'

'We're not *that* insensitive,' Sam said. 'We need to interview Bentley again, anyway.'

'Please be careful, Sam. This could backfire on Gabriella if Bentley feels he's being accused of something.'

'I don't barge into sensitive situations, Loveday, your friend can trust me. But we are in the middle of a murder investigation, so I can't ignore what you've told me.'

Loveday stared at him. 'You think this might be connected to the murders?'

'That's not what I said, but Bentley did find Mellissa Grantby's body.'

All was quiet as they crept into the cottage later and peeked into the nursery at the sleeping baby. 'Ah, look at that,' Loveday whispered. 'She's smiling.'

'I'd be smiling too if everybody was dancing attention on me.'

'You don't do too badly,' Loveday said.

Sam put a finger under her chin and tilted her face up to him, his eyes serious. 'I know that,' he said quietly before he kissed her.

IT WAS six o'clock before Rosie woke next morning. Loveday was slowly sliding from under the duvet when Sam's mobile phone buzzed. She watched his expression turn from drowsy to interested. 'Tell Connie not to worry,' he said. 'I'm sure everything will be fine. I'll call by on my way to the nick.'

He looked up as he ended the call. 'That was Merrick.'

'I gathered that,' Loveday said. 'What's wrong?'

'It's your friend, Gabriella. She's gone.'

'Gone?'

'Apparently, Connie took her an early morning cup of tea, but when she went into the room, it was empty.' He pulled a face. 'Our bird had flown.'

'I don't like the sound of this,' Loveday said, as Rosie's cry became more demanding. 'Once I get Rosie sorted I'm coming with you.'

Half an hour later, as she settled Rosie back in her cot after feeding and changing her, Maddie emerged, tousled haired, from her room.

'I need a huge favour,' Loveday said. 'Could you keep an eye on Rosie until Priddy gets here?'

'Of course I can, but what's going on? I thought you were going into the magazine today? Although I'm not quite sure why you would on a Saturday.'

'There's a lot to catch up on at the office,' Loveday explained, biting her lip. 'But now there's been a bit of an emergency with one of my friends and I need to find out what's happened.'

'What kind of emergency?'

'She's disappeared,' Loveday said. 'Gabriella was spending last night at Merrick and Connie's place, but she wasn't in her room this morning. Sam and I are going over there now.'

'What about Priddy? Does she know about this?'

'Not yet, I'll call her from the car and explain everything. I'll ask her to come here when she's ready.'

'Great.' Maddie gave a wide smile. 'I love girlie days.'

'Thanks, Maddie. You're a lifesaver,' Loveday called back,

bumping into Sam as she headed for the shower. 'Ten minutes and I'll be right with you,' she said, rushing past him.

'We don't both have to go, you know. Why don't you stay here with Maddie. I'll explain to Merrick that you're not going into the office today.'

'Nice try, Sam, but I'm going with you. I may not know Gabriella all that well, but I feel responsible for her.'

After a quick shower, Loveday pulled on her jeans, teamed them with a white T-shirt and denim jacket, and went in search of Sam. She found him and Maddie in the nursery, watching a very active baby Rosie, kicking her legs and giggling up at them.

Loveday shook her head, laughing at the cooing noises Sam was making. 'I've no idea what you're saying, but it seems to be working.'

'I'm a good communicator,' Sam said, making a face that caused Rosie to giggle even more.

Maddie took her father's shoulders and turned him towards the door. 'Go,' she ordered. 'Rosie will be fine with Priddy and me.'

After assurances that she would contact them if any problem arose, they left the cottage.

THE RABBITS on the front lawn looked up as the old Lexus passed, but well used to the comings and goings on the drive, they dismissed the interruption and went back to their grazing.

'Shouldn't you send someone to the Bentleys' house?' Loveday asked, glancing at the rabbits as they passed. 'I can't give you an address, but Priddy mentioned they live in Crantock.'

'We have addresses for all witnesses. I'll send Will and Amanda out there.'

The gates to Morvah were open when they arrived. Merrick had been watching for them and was standing at the front door.

'Thank goodness you're here. We didn't know what to do.'

Cadan appeared in his dark checked dressing gown behind his brother. 'Bentley's abducted her. That's what's happened. We need to tell the police.'

'I am the police,' Sam said.

Connie looked distracted as she stood in the hall. 'There's a fire in the drawing room. I'll make some tea.'

'I'll help,' Loveday said, taking her friend's arm and steering her towards the kitchen.

'I don't understand. Where could she have gone?' Connie shook her head as she sank into a chair.

'I suppose you tried ringing her?' Loveday asked, filling the kettle and setting mugs on a tray.

'I did that as soon as I realized she'd gone and have been repeatedly ringing since then, but the calls all go to answerphone.'

'I wouldn't worry. The whole purpose of her staying here overnight was to give her time to think. Maybe she decided to leave Bentley, or she could simply have gone home.' Loveday hoped she sounded more confident than she felt. 'Sam has already sent two of his officers to the Bentleys' place in Crantock, so we should know soon if she's there.'

The three men were in the drawing room but still on their feet when Loveday and Connie appeared minutes later with the tea tray. Cadan was pacing the floor, his phone at his ear.

'Sit down please, gentlemen,' Loveday said, setting down the tray. She let Connie pour.

'Can we start at the beginning?' Sam tipped milk into his tea and looked at Connie. 'Merrick said you discovered Gabriella was missing when you took her an early morning cuppa. What time was that?'

'It was just before seven. When she wasn't in bed I assumed she was in the ensuite, but the door was ajar and she wasn't there.'

'Apart from that, was there any sign of disruption in the room?'

'If you mean did it look like there had been a struggle then the answer's no. You can have a look for yourself, Sam. We haven't touched anything.'

'Did Dr Bentley check up on his wife after he left last night?' Loveday asked.

'He didn't actually,' Connie said. 'That surprised us.'

'And you weren't disturbed during the night?' Sam asked.

'What d'you mean?' Merrick said. 'We didn't hear Gabriella wandering about, and we certainly didn't hear her leaving.'

Cadan rolled his eyes, releasing a sigh. 'I think what Sam is asking is did we hear Gabriella being abducted.'

'Abducted?' Connie's hand flew to her throat. 'You think she's been abducted, Sam?'

'Of course she has,' Cadan cut in. 'And we all know who is responsible. It was that husband of hers who did this.'

Sam glared at him. 'I take it there was no sign of anyone breaking into the house?'

'No, nothing,' Merrick said.

'Have you checked the key rack in the hall?' Loveday asked. She had a sudden vison of Bentley unhooking the front door key as he left last night and sneaking it out in his pocket.

'I'll check,' Connie said, hurrying out to the hall. Her look of dismay when she returned said everything. 'One of the keys has gone,' she said.

'I told you. Didn't I tell you? Bentley has abducted her.' Cadan's voice rose, as he threw his hands up in exasperation.

Connie bit her lip, her eyes wide with concern. 'He wouldn't hurt her, would he?'

'Let's not get ahead of ourselves,' Sam said. 'We don't know why Gabriella left.'

'Maybe she had an emergency call from one of her shops,'

Loveday suggested. 'She has three boutiques. I'll ring them.' She pulled out her phone and began scrolling for the Bonita website.

The others watched as she rang each boutique and asked for Gabriella. Staff confirmed she wasn't in any of her three shops.

'We still need to check them,' Sam said, as Loveday emailed the website details to his phone. She watched him resend the information to his sergeant, Will Tregellis's mobile, before he called him instructing that he organize officers to visit each of the three premises.

Sam glanced at Connie. 'Could I have a look at the room Gabriella used last night?'

'Yes, of course.' She turned for the stairs.

'I'll come with you,' Loveday said, hurrying after them.

When they reached the room, Sam put out an arm, stopping the women from entering it. Loveday shot him a surprised look. Was he thinking this could be a crime scene? She hoped Connie hadn't seen the involuntary shudder that went through her.

'Best not go in, not until our forensic team has checked it out.'

'Forensic?' Connie was staring at him. 'So you do think something terrible has happened to her.'

'I'm sure it's just a precaution,' Loveday said. 'Isn't it, Sam?'

He was scanning the room, taking in the chintz curtains and matching duvet, the little cream bedside cabinets and the louvred doors of the wardrobes. Everything looked exactly as Loveday remembered it from the previous night.

'What about that?' Sam asked, pointing to the filmy green scarf on the floor by the bed.

'It's Gabriella's,' Connie said, moving forward to lift it.

Sam's arm shot out again. 'Don't touch it!' His stern tone caused Connie to step back quickly. 'Is it important?' she said.

Loveday stared at the scarf. Connie hadn't noticed the staining at the edges, but *she* had – and it looked like blood.

. . .

Merrick was staring anxiously up at them from the bottom of the stairs. Sam had his mobile to his ear, organizing the forensic team as they went down. 'Can you make sure no one enters that room, Merrick?' he said, when he'd ended the call. 'Loveday and I are going to the Bentleys' house.'

Loveday's head came up sharply. 'Is she there?'

Sam shook his head. 'The house is empty.'

'I'll come with you,' Cadan said.

'No, that's not a good idea,' Sam said.

'But I know the cottage. I could take you,' he protested.

Merrick put a hand on his brother's arm. 'Leave it to them, Cadan,' he said, his voice gentle. 'They know what they're doing.'

CHAPTER 30

'Priddy said the Bentleys live in an old, converted farmhouse.' Loveday glanced at the roadside cottages they were passing.

'*Gwel an Mor*,' Sam said. 'It's Cornish for Sea View.'

'Given we're in Crantock, and the beach is over there.' She nodded to the blue horizon that kept appearing and disappearing at the end of the road. 'It doesn't really cut down the possibilities.'

'What else did Priddy say?' he asked, annoyed he hadn't got directions from the officers he'd earlier sent to the place.

'Only that the house was down a rutted track about a mile from the village.'

'Not very helpful,' Sam said, squinting along the length of each farm track they passed.

'Let's try that one.' Loveday pointed. 'At least it appears to be going in the right direction.' She peered ahead. 'Is that a signpost?'

'It's a postbox,' Sam said. 'And if I'm right it says, *Gwel an Mor*.'

They set off along the narrow lane, the car pitching them this way and that as they made slow progress along the track.

'No wonder they have a postbox,' Sam grumbled. 'I don't see the Royal Mail being happy to bump along here every day.'

'I can't see Gabriella and her doctor doing it either,' Loveday said. 'Are you sure this is right?'

'I am,' Sam said, staring ahead as the property came into view.

The house bore only a passing resemblance to the traditional stone cottage it must at one time have been. The original building would have been constructed so that the gable end took the brunt of the wild buffering from the sea.

More recently an extension had been added, allowing the owners to take advantage of the stunning ocean views. Extensions required planning permission, and the glass edifice she was staring at was hardly in keeping with the rest of the property. She wondered if Dr Christopher Bentley had a friend on the planning committee.

When no one answered Sam's knock Loveday squinted around the side of the house. 'I can't see a car, but there's a conservatory back here.'

Sam had appeared and was striding past her, trying the door to the conservatory. It wasn't locked, so he went in, making his way to the interior door into the building. It was locked.

Loveday watched, fascinated as Sam produced a pocket knife and manipulated it around the lock until the door swung open. She smiled. 'Are you supposed to do this, Inspector?'

'A woman is missing, so yes. We have every right to gain entry to this house.'

'You'll get no argument from me,' Loveday said, following him inside.

The corridor was at the back of the house and quite dark, but all that changed when Sam opened another door and light flooded in.

Loveday gasped as a huge open-plan white room was revealed.

'Take pictures,' he said.

Loveday took out her phone and began snapping. Her eyes went to the three large pale leather sofas grouped around two beechwood coffee tables. They had been placed to enjoy the best views through the bifold doors to the extensive lawn and the sea beyond.

'Wow,' Loveday said. 'I thought our place was fantastic, but this is something else.' She turned frowning at Sam. 'How much do GPs earn?'

'Not this much,' he said, his eyes going around the room. 'But it's a fair guess that his wife, with all those boutiques, is not short of a bob or two.'

The open-plan aspect led to a sparkling clean kitchen with white range and breakfast bar. Four stylish bar stools in green, blue, yellow and red added to the trendy image.

A large oval-shaped beechwood dining table was set for eight people and enjoyed the same views over the beach.

Loveday went to the fridge and was surprised to see it was well stocked with fresh food. She sniffed the milk carton. The 'use by' date was the following week. 'I was beginning to think nobody lived here,' she said. 'But this tells a different story. It's been recently filled.'

Sam was making his way up an elegant spiral staircase. Loveday followed. She counted four smart bedrooms. The biggest, and most luxurious had an ensuite. The door was open and she could see towels strewn on the floor. The duvet had been thrown over the bed, but not tidily. Loveday glanced out to the balcony where she could see a small round table and two chairs placed to look out to sea.

'Well the Bentleys aren't here,' she said. 'And I can't see any signs that they left in a hurry. So what do we do now?' Her brow creased. 'Could we have got the wrong house? This place looks like a show home.'

Sam's expression was thoughtful. 'Let's ask around the village.' They went out, securing the door behind them, and were driving back along the rutted road when Loveday called 'Stop!' She twisted round. 'Go back a bit, Sam.'

He reversed, stopping for Loveday to jump out. 'Look,' she said. 'It's a parking area.'

Sam left the Lexus and strode to join her.

'Well, what d'you make of that?' she said as they stared at the two vehicles hidden from the road.

One was a beaten up old Land Rover covered in mud splats. It was parked alongside a smart red sports car.

'I think this is Gabriella's car,' she said. 'But why would the Land Rover be here?'

Sam was still staring at the vehicles. 'What if the Bentleys parked their own cars here and used this one to ferry them to and from their property? It would make sense. I wouldn't want to drive up and down this road more than I had to.'

Loveday checked the vehicles. Both of them were locked. She took another picture.

Sam's phone rang, and he pulled it from his pocket. 'Yes, Will,' he said.

She watched him frown. 'We need to speak to him. I'll meet you at the nick.'

'What's happened?' Loveday asked, eyeing him as he ended the call.

'It's Dr Bentley,' he said. 'He's turned up at the medical centre.'

'Is Gabriella with him?'

Sam shook his head. 'He says he thought she was still at the Tremayne house.'

'I wonder what he was doing at the centre. It's Saturday. There are no GP surgeries today, at least that's what Nessa told me.'

'Well he was there. Will checked the place out when it was confirmed the Bentleys weren't at home. He's been taken in for questioning.'

'I don't suppose you'd let me sit in on the interview?'

'You know I can't do that. I'll drive you back to Merrick's place. He'll give you a lift home.'

THE SUNNY MAY morning had brought families out in droves and the drive to Truro took longer than the expected half an hour. Loveday called Merrick to tell him they hadn't found Gabriella. He still sounded worried.

'I'll explain everything when I get there,' she said.

Merrick and Connie were at the kitchen table, mugs of coffee in front of them when Sam and Loveday walked in. 'Your forensic people have just left,' Merrick said. 'It was weird knowing they were upstairs examining every inch of that room.'

'I'll get some more mugs,' Connie said, getting to her feet.

'Not for me, thanks.' Sam held up a hand. 'We have Dr Bentley back at the station. I don't want to waste any time getting back to interview him.'

'Does he know where Gabriella is?' Cadan had come running downstairs when he heard them arrive. 'Has anybody asked him?'

'He says he doesn't know. He thought she was still here.'

'He's lying.' Cadan's mouth curved into an expression of disgust. 'Of course he knows. You have to make him tell you.'

'We can't *make* him do anything,' Sam said stiffly. 'He'll be interviewed, but it will be done properly. We don't know he's done anything wrong.'

'All this talk is delaying things,' Loveday said. 'Sam knows his job, Cadan. Let him get on with it.'

Cadan shot her an exasperated look, but he backed off.

Sam nodded around the room. 'I'll ring as soon as we have any news.'

Merrick walked him to the door.

'This isn't looking good, is it, Sam?'

'Let's not jump the gun.'

'But that scarf…there was blood on it.'

. . .

Sam was thinking about that scarf as he drove to the station. The blood might not be relevant. Gabriella could have pricked her finger. The whole thing could be completely innocent. So where was she?

Dr Christopher Bentley had been given a mug of tea, but Sam noticed he'd barely touched it when he and Will entered the interview room. The man's head came up sharply as the detectives appeared. 'Well?' he demanded. 'Have you found my wife?'

'Not yet,' Sam said. 'We were hoping you might be able to help us.'

'I don't know where she is.'

'Let's take a step back,' Sam said quietly. 'Gabriella was feeling unwell and it was agreed she should spend the night with the Tremaynes. You weren't happy about that if I remember.'

'Of course I wasn't,' he retorted sharply. 'How would you feel if your wife wanted to spend the night away from you?'

'But you still agreed to it.'

'She was ill. I was worried.' He paused. 'My immediate reaction was wanting to take care of her, but she was sleeping when I saw her. Taking Gabriella home would have meant disturbing her. I agreed with your partner that it would be better to let her rest.'

'Did you ring later to check on her?'

'I did, but her phone was turned off.'

'And you didn't think that was strange?'

'I assumed she'd done it on purpose so she could sleep without interruption.'

'But you're her husband,' Will chipped in. 'She must have known you'd be concerned.'

'Gabriella is her own woman. I respect that.'

Sam's stare was probing. 'Is your wife in the habit of taking off like this?'

'Not really. But she's a businesswoman and often has to travel at a moment's notice.'

'Without telling you?'

'Sometimes. If she's caught up in phone calls she might not contact me until she reaches where she's going.'

'Do you think this is what's happening here?'

'I don't know.'

'But you must have been worried when you couldn't contact your wife. Why didn't you drive to the Tremaynes' house this morning?'

'I told you. Gabriella doesn't like me checking up on her.'

Sam was trying to imagine this man as the controlling, abusive husband Gabriella had described to Loveday. He was showing no sign of it, but Bentley might be a great actor. People with narcissistic personalities were often skilled at hiding domineering behaviour.

'There are no surgeries held at the medical centre on Saturdays. What were you doing there, Dr Bentley?'

'Just a bit of admin. I like to keep my files tidy.'

'Even when your wife is missing?' Will said.

'We don't know she is missing.'

'Well, she's not here,' Will retorted.

Sam kept his eyes fixed on Bentley. His sergeant's show of frustration was rare, but he completely understood it. The GP was hiding something, but they had no evidence to hold him.

Sam got to his feet. 'We will need to speak with you again, Dr Bentley. Please don't leave the area,' he said as he and DS Will Tregellis left the room.

CHAPTER 31

*L*oveday was scrolling through the images she'd taken of the Bentleys' cottage when her mobile rang. 'Hi, what's going on?' It was Cassie. 'Maddie told me Gabriella Ricci is missing.'

Loveday had been about to call Sam's daughter for a Rosie update. 'Why are you ringing? Is Rosie OK?'

She could almost hear the smile in her friend's voice. 'Of course she is. She's being spoiled rotten by her big sister. Priddy's there too, so mega spoiling going on.' Cassie lowered her voice. 'Can you speak? Are you still with Sam?'

'No, he's back at the nick. I'm at Merrick and Connie's place trying to organize a lift home. Merrick offered to drive me, but I think he should be here with Connie until this business has been sorted.'

'Maddie told me what's going on, at least as much as she knows. Is there any news?'

'If you mean has Gabriella turned up, then no.' Loveday hesitated. 'I don't suppose I could beg a lift back to Marazion?'

'You're in luck,' Cassie said. 'I'm here in Truro doing some shopping. What's Merrick's address?'

It was forty minutes before Cassie arrived at Morvah. 'Connie was all for inviting you in,' Loveday said, coming to meet her. 'But I told her we were pushed for time. I've already said my goodbyes.'

Cassie's face fell. 'Why did you do that? I was looking forward to a cup of tea and a natter.'

'Believe me, it's not a day for social chit-chat,' Loveday said, climbing in beside Cassie. 'And I need to get to a supermarket.'

Merrick had joined Connie at the window and returned their waves as the big four-by-four moved off.

'Nobody mentioned anything about a supermarket. I thought I was taking you home.'

'That's right. But I have to call at a supermarket first or we'll have no dinner tomorrow.' Loveday slid her friend a glance. 'You don't mind, do you?'

'Do I have a choice?'

'Not if you want to know about Gabriella.'

Cassie pulled a face. 'OK, supermarket it is,' she said as they drove through Morvah's impressive gates. 'So tell me. Has Gabriella been murdered?'

Loveday was used to her friend's no-nonsense approach to life, but her directness frequently surprised even her. 'Where did that come from? Gabriella has disappeared. No one is suggesting she's dead.'

'Nobody just disappears. And Sam wouldn't be involved if he wasn't concerned.'

Cassie had put into words something she hadn't dared consider. But the woman's husband could be a murder suspect. He worked as a GP in the medical centre where Mellissa Grantby was murdered, and he'd been the one who found her body.

'Sam had Gabriella's husband in for questioning this morning, but they had no reason to hold him,' she said. 'He rang me at Morvah to tell me Bentley had been released.'

'What happened last night?' Cassie asked.

Loveday sighed, then retold the story of the previous night's supper party.

'You can imagine how worried Connie was when she took the woman a cup of tea this morning and found the room empty.'

Cassie frowned. 'And there was no sign of a struggle?'

Loveday shook her head.

'And no one in the house heard anything during the night?'

Another shake of the head.

'How well have you got to know this woman?'

'I don't know her at all. You were with me the first time I set eyes on her that day in Aldo's.'

'So you didn't meet her again until last night?'

'Actually yes, she rang me after Cadan made that exhibition of himself in the office.'

'You didn't tell me.'

'She asked me not to repeat anything she said.'

'That was then,' Cassie said. 'Sounds like Gabriella needs all the help she can get now.' Loveday told her story and Cassie listened, her expression incredulous as she stared at the road ahead.

'Did you believe her husband was abusing her?'

'I had no reason not to.' She turned to her friend. 'Why? What are you thinking?'

'Abused women rarely run successful businesses. I thought I recognized Gabriella when we saw her in Aldo's. It's only now that I'm putting two and two together. I've seen her in Bonita's in Truro.'

'Go on.'

'Put it this way,' Cassie said. 'If I talked to my staff the way that woman was speaking to hers, they would no longer be working for me.'

'Really?' Loveday's brow creased.

'She was abusing them, Loveday.'

'You think she was spinning me a tale when she told me how controlling her husband was?'

'Well, you met her. What do you think?'

Loveday had bought the woman's story, but now she was rethinking that meeting. She'd felt sorry for Gabriella. Why would she lie? There had been no reason to disbelieve her. But that was before she knew about the Bonita business. Something was wrong.

'The Bentleys have a house in Crantock. Sam and I went there this morning. It's sumptuous, Cassie. Certainly not the kind of property a GP could afford.'

'You think the money comes from Gabriella?'

'Sam and I assumed so, but we thought it could also be family money with her father owning that restaurant.'

'And now?' Cassie raised an eyebrow.

'Now I'm wondering how profitable those boutiques are.'

'This is all very interesting but it still doesn't explain why Gabriella has disappeared,' Cassie said as they pulled into a space in the supermarket car park.

IT WAS ABOUT ninety minutes later when they took the roundabout that led down to Marazion.

Cassie's husband, Adam, appeared from the back of their house as they pulled up in the drive.

'D'you think Adam will mind if you come in for a coffee?'

'Of course he won't.' Cassie jumped down from the four-by-four and went to plant a kiss on her husband's cheek.

'You look busy,' Loveday called, nodding to the spade he was holding.

'Just a bit of weeding, but I'm done now. There's a cold beer waiting for me inside.'

'What about the carrots?' Cassie asked.

'The seeds are in the ground. I've also sowed some lettuce.'

'You're my hero.' She grinned up at him. 'I'm going to nip into Loveday's to grab a coffee. You don't mind, do you?'

Adam gave an exaggerated sigh. 'Would it matter if I did?'

Cassie's eyes twinkled with mischief. 'But you don't, do you?'

Adam shook his head, laughing. 'Be off with you, woman,' he said as Cassie followed Loveday into her kitchen.

'Hi.' Maddie came to meet them. 'Have you found your missing woman yet?'

'Not yet,' Loveday said. 'Has Rosie been all right?'

'A perfect little treasure.' Priddy beamed, joining them. 'Come through and see for yourself. She's sleeping now.'

Maddie organized the drinks as the three other women crept into the nursery.

Rosie had thrown her covers off and was fast asleep, spread-eagled in her cot.

'Aw, bless her,' Cassie said. 'She looks so relaxed.'

'Doesn't she just.' Loveday grinned, satisfied that her daughter was safe and well. 'Let's have that drink.'

'And talk about our missing Gabriella,' Cassie said.

'Should I take notes?' Maddie wanted to know.

'Good idea.' Loveday said, directing her to the fresh supply of stationery she kept in the study. 'Let's start by listing everything we know about Gabriella.'

Maddie's pen flew over the page as everyone contributed information.

'I don't like this talk of abuse,' Priddy said. 'That husband of hers needs locking away.'

'If it's true,' Cassie said. 'We only have Gabriella's word for it.'

'Why would she lie?' Maddie said.

'Well, she would if she had something to gain,' Cassie said. 'We need to think about this.' She turned to Loveday. 'You've seen her with her husband, did it look like she was afraid of him?'

Loveday's mind went back to when she and Sam had turned up for supper at Merrick and Connie's house. Gabriella had appeared uneasy from the start, but Loveday had put that down to the woman's surprise that Sam was a police officer. She wondered now why that had been an issue. She screwed up her face. 'It's difficult to say. She had certainly appeared upset when she was in the kitchen with Connie and me. But Dr Bentley had been in the other room then. All I can say is that he seemed genuinely concerned when he was told she was unwell.'

'Did Sam say anything about his interview with this doctor?' Cassie asked.

'He didn't go into any detail. There's only a certain amount of information he passes on when he's in the middle of a case.'

'But Dr Bentley was the one who found Mellissa Grantby's body?'

'That's right. He said how shocked everyone at the medical centre still was...' She looked up at Priddy. 'Hannah knew Gabriella. What did she think of her?'

Priddy put down the coffee mug she had been nursing. 'She was grateful for the job offer, and she liked working in the Truro boutique, but there was a different atmosphere when Gabriella was around.'

'Different?' Maddie had stopped writing and was chewing the end of her pen. 'What was different?'

'Apparently, the woman was quite strict. Some of the staff thought she was...' She bit her lip. 'Well, Hannah said some of the staff felt she bullied them.'

'That doesn't sound like a woman who is being abused,' Cassie said.

'Gabriella is a businesswoman. Maybe she had to crack the whip now and again if her staff were taking advantage,' Loveday said. 'It can't be easy to keep three boutiques running successfully.'

'I think there was more than three,' Priddy said. 'Hannah got the impression Gabriella had other business interests abroad... Italy, I believe.'

They were all staring at her.

Loveday's mouth had dropped open. 'She has more businesses in Italy?'

'That's what Hannah said.'

Ideas were beginning to fall into place in Loveday's mind. She was remembering the opulence of the Bentleys' home in Crantock.

'I don't suppose she said where in Italy these business interests were?'

Priddy pulled a face, trying to remember. 'What's that place where all the film stars go to buy their fancy outfits?'

'Do you mean Milan?' Loveday ventured, all sorts of scenarios chasing around her head.

'Yes, Milan, that's the place.'

Maddie had been writing again, but now she stopped. 'Maybe Gabriella has gone there,' she said.

Loveday could tell by Cassie's expression that she had reached the same conclusion.

Maybe Gabriella wasn't missing at all. She could be in Italy!

'Milan's a big place. We need to narrow down the possibilities,' Cassie said.

Maddie glanced around the faces. 'How do we do that?'

'We ask her father,' Loveday said, scrolling the restaurant website for Aldo's phone number.

CHAPTER 32

*P*hilip Dawson raised frustrated eyes to the ceiling. 'It's Saturday, Rachel. Even detectives get some weekends off.'

'Mr Kitto said I could contact him any time.' She waved the business card Sam left with her. 'I need this thing to be over.'

'That won't happen if you keep chipping away at it.' He scowled. 'Please leave it.'

'Don't tell me what to do, Phil.' Her eyes glinted with anger. 'It wasn't your brother who was murdered.'

'And how will talking to the police again help? It's not as if you have anything new to tell them.'

But his wife was already on her phone, tapping in DI Sam Kitto's mobile number.

SAM WAS thoughtful as the call from Rachel Dawson ended.

Will Tregellis raised an eyebrow 'Anything interesting?'

'I'm not sure. That was Brian Teague's sister. She wants to speak to us.'

'About what?' Will's brow wrinkled.

'She wouldn't say, at least not on the phone.' Sam was reaching for his jacket.

'Are we going somewhere, sir?'

Sam nodded. 'It's time we paid Mrs Dawson another visit.'

SAM STOOD ON THE DAWSONS' path and gazed out over the rooftops at the impressive view of Falmouth Harbour. He thought again that such a fantastic outlook was significant compensation for living in a hilly town. The downside was probably the high sloping garden, and the 12 steps he and Will had to climb to the front door of the couple's bungalow.

Rachel Dawson, dressed in jeans and blue checked shirt, pushed a strand of fair hair from her face as she stood by the open door. She gave them an uncertain smile. 'Thanks for coming. I hope I'm not wasting your time.'

Sam gave her an encouraging nod. 'You said there was something you wanted to tell us about your brother's murder?'

'Come through,' she said, brushing past her husband in the dark hall. 'I'll speak to these officers in the front room. Could you keep an eye on the children, Phil?'

Sam shot Will a look, his eyes registering interest that the husband was not to be included in whatever this was about.

The room they were shown into was tidy and smelled faintly of furniture polish. A wall of shelves on either side of the fireplace displayed rows of paperback romances. Rachel indicated the two large, upholstered chairs. 'Please sit down. Can I get you some coffee...tea?'

'Good idea, but let my sergeant make it.'

'What? No.' She looked uncertain. 'I can do it.'

'DS Tregellis doesn't mind, do you, Sergeant?' He flashed Will a smile. Sharing a drink was an accepted way of relaxing an interviewee, but he didn't want this woman disappearing into the kitchen. He turned back to her. 'Please sit down, Mrs Dawson.'

She sank onto the sofa, her expression cautious.

'Now what is it you want to tell me,' he said kindly.

'It's about Brian. I should have told you before.' She hesitated. 'I was worried about him. He wasn't a well man.' She looked up.

Sam waited for her to continue.

'Brian never really got over losing Meredith and the twins. And he never forgave Lawrence Kemp for killing them.' She shook her head. 'And poor Tamsin dying in another car crash just about finished him. She was Meredith's sister, and I think Brian saw her as his last remaining link with his dead wife. He was really fond of Tamsin. We all were. She was a lovely girl.'

Sam's mind was scrolling through the findings of the inquest into Tamsin Lamphier's death.

'I believe the inquest found it was an accident.'

'It *was* an accident, but Phil and I were in the vehicle that struck Tamsin. We were all there, Nessa Cawse and her partner, Kenan Retallick. Mellissa Grantby and her husband, Locryn. It was Locryn who was driving. You know he's an artist?'

She shot Sam a questioning look, and he responded with a silent nod.

'It was the opening day of his exhibition in Plymouth and we'd all gone to support him. The wine was flowing and we were all a bit tipsy. Except for Locryn, of course. He'd stayed off the wine because he was driving.' She swallowed, apparently reliving the tragedy.

'Anyway, we'd left the gallery on the way home. It was early evening, but the city roads were still busy. We'd turned a corner at some traffic lights when suddenly Tamsin was there, in the middle of the road, right in front of us. She had run out, trying to beat the lights. There was no way Locryn could have avoided hitting her. He didn't stand a chance.'

'All this was said at the inquest,' Sam said.

'It was,' Rachel agreed. 'But what wasn't there was the effect it had on Brian. He flipped. It was like Tamsin's death had cracked his mind. He blamed us for the accident, well the other five, not me.'

Will came back into the room carrying a tray of coffee. His expression confirmed he'd heard what had been said.

'Tell us more about Brian,' Sam encouraged, moving a mug in front of her.

Rachel sighed. 'He was my older brother, but it never felt like that. Brian was a sensitive soul, family meant everything to him. Meredith's death still affected him, even though it was years ago. He totally blamed Lawrence Kemp and was so full of hate for the man that it knocked his balance of reality.'

'In what way?' Will asked.

Rachel wrapped her hands around her coffee mug, staring across the room. 'Brian used to follow him. He made it his business to find out when Kemp was released from prison so he could be there.'

'You mean your brother was stalking Lawrence Kemp?' Sam said.

The face Rachel pulled confirmed it. The detectives shared a look. Sam hadn't known about this.

'It was all still eating away at him when Tamsin was killed.' She looked from one to the other. 'Can you imagine what that did to my brother? Her death broke him completely. All he could think about was revenge.'

'But it was an accident,' Will said.

'Not in Brian's mind. He held everyone in that vehicle, apart from me, responsible. I was only there because of Phil. Those people were his friends, not mine. I'd met them of course at that party Phil had insisted throwing for them at our house. Brian was there too, so he knew all of them.

'He was good at digging out people's secrets. He watched them and followed them. It was easy because they were all up to something.' She shook her head. 'Even my Phil. Yes, Brian told me all about my darling husband's fling with Mellissa Grantby. Such a bitch. I'm not sorry she's dead.'

She looked from one to the other. 'And before you ask, the answer is no, I didn't kill her and neither did Phil. He was here with me the night she died. I heard it was Dr Bentley who found her. Poor man, he didn't deserve that.'

Sam's head snapped up. 'You know Dr Bentley?'

'Yes, of course. He was at our party with that snooty wife of his. Phil knew him from the medical centre.'

'You didn't like his wife?'

'She only came so she could look down her nose at everybody.' She paused. 'Well, except for Locryn. She liked him.'

Sam frowned. 'Are you suggesting Gabriella Bentley was flirting with Locryn Grantby?'

'That's a nice way of putting it. She was quite blatant. It was embarrassing.'

'How did Grantby react to that?' Will asked.

Rachel rolled her eyes to the ceiling. 'He's a man. How'd you think he reacted? It was her husband I felt sorry for. He pretended he hadn't noticed how his wife was behaving, but he must have known. I saw Nessa Cawse giving them the eye. There was a lot of hanky-panky going on that night.' Rachel paused for breath.

'All of this was like a godsend to Brian of course. I could see he was squirrelling away all this stuff to use against them. I thought he was intending to blackmail them, but his reaction later made me worry.'

She bit her lip. 'I can still see that chilling look in his eyes when he said he would make each of them pay.'

Sam sat up, meeting her eyes. 'What did you think he meant by that?'

Rachel stared back at him. 'I thought he was going to kill them.'

'I heard that.' Philip Dawson burst into the room. 'So your

brother was going to kill us, was he? What a crackpot. No wonder somebody topped him.'

Sam was on his feet. 'That sounds like you think Brian Teague got what he deserved.'

'The man was an idiot.'

'He was also my brother.' Rachel spat out the words. She was on her feet, moving towards him, fists clenched. 'And he got the measure of you, didn't he, Phil? Did he spoil your little affair with Mellissa Grantby?'

'Shut up, Rachel. You're talking nonsense.'

'Am I?' She advanced on him, her eyes glinting with hostility. 'Did she threaten you too? Is that why she's dead?'

Dawson raised his hand to strike her, but Sam intervened. It was like they had forgotten the detectives were in the room.

'I think you should come with us, Mr Dawson,' Sam said.

'What? You're arresting me?' The man's eyes bulged with rage. 'You can't believe what this silly bitch says.'

Will was already on the phone requesting back-up.

'You'll be helping us with our enquiries.'

A police car arrived outside the house within minutes and Dawson was put into the back.

Rachel stood by the window watching him being driven away, swiping at sudden tears. 'I shouldn't have said that. I was hitting out. Phil hasn't killed anybody.' She sighed. 'But our marriage is over, and that's completely down to him.' She looked up at Sam. 'What will happen now?'

'Your husband isn't under arrest, Mrs Dawson, but we will interview him.' He paused, watching her. 'You suggested Mellissa Grantby might have threatened him. Why did you say that?'

Rachel moved back to the window, staring out into the street. 'Phil has his secrets. Mellissa wasn't the first woman he's had since we've been married.'

'You know of others?'

She turned, lifting sad, defeated eyes to his. 'Ask Gabriella,' she said.

'I CAN'T HELP FEELING sorry for that woman,' Will said, as they drove away from the Dawsons' house. 'If what she says about the doctor's wife is true, she's not the wilting violet she would have us believe.'

Sam had been thinking the same thing. If it was true, it put Gabriella Bentley's disappearance in a whole new light.

Philip Dawson had been driven to the police station in Truro and was waiting for them in an interview room when they arrived back. He inclined his head to the detectives as they entered.

Sam was in no mood for pussyfooting around. They had wasted enough time.

'Did you murder Mellissa Grantby?' he asked.

Dawson's eyes were wide with apparent shock. 'You surely didn't believe what Rachel said. She's a very bitter woman.'

'Why would that be?' Sam narrowed his own eyes at the man.

Dawson glanced away, avoiding Sam's stare. He held up his hands in a gesture of surrender. 'I like the ladies. I don't boast about it, and it doesn't hurt anybody.'

'Apart from your wife,' Will threw in.

The man sighed. 'OK, so I'm not the best husband.'

Sam gave Dawson a hard stare. 'Mellissa was one of your *ladies,*' he emphasized the word, 'and now she's dead.'

Dawson was out of his chair. 'I told you!' he shouted. 'It wasn't me who killed her!'

'Gabriella Bentley was another of your conquests. And now she's disappeared.' He paused, watching the man. 'Your ladies don't have much luck, Mr Dawson.'

'Gabriella's missing?'

'Where is she, Mr Dawson?'

The man looked genuinely shocked. 'I've no idea. I know nothing about that.'

'But you don't deny you had a relationship with her?'

Dawson shrugged. 'Hardly that. A couple of nights, maybe. And it was her who came on to me.'

'How did you meet her?'

'At the Hilltop Medical Centre. Gabriella had called in to see her husband. He's a GP. But you know this. Anyway.' He waved his hand. 'Gabriella was in the car park when I came out. She had a flat tyre, and I changed it for her. She insisted on buying me a drink.' He shrugged. 'We met a couple of times after that, but she did all the running.'

'Was this before you had an affair with Mellissa Grantby?' Will asked.

'No.'

'So, you were having sex with Mellissa *and* Gabriella?'

Dawson's face coloured. 'I told you, I like the ladies.'

Sam struggled not to show his dislike of the man. He stood up. 'You can go now, Mr Dawson.'

CHAPTER 33

The A30 was busy with Saturday afternoon traffic as Sam drove to Marazion. He relaxed into the journey, allowing the new information about Gabriella Bentley to filter through his mind. If what they'd been told was true – and he was inclined to believe it – they had to view the woman in a different light. He went back over what Loveday told him about her. According to Gabriella, she was married to a very jealous, controlling man who invented relationships of which she was innocent. She said Bentley threatened men to stay away from her, inferring that he was making her life a misery.

Sam went over the various times he had met Bentley. When he'd been interviewed after finding Mellissa Grantby's body at the medical centre, he had appeared genuinely upset. And then last night at Merrick and Connie's house, wouldn't he have insisted on taking Gabriella home if he had been the controlling man she had suggested? His subsequent interview at the police station had rung no warning bells either. On the other hand, people with controlling, abusive traits were very good at hiding them.

Sam was hoping Locryn Grantby could shed more light on

what Gabriella was really like. Rachel Dawson had accused the woman of setting her cap at Locryn. If it was true, how far did things go? Did Locryn know where Gabriella had gone?

Loveday had called earlier before Sam left the station, suggesting she might have gone back to Italy where she could have more business outlets. He'd asked Amanda Fox to check that with her father, Aldo Ricci. They were reportedly close.

And then a thought struck him. Why had Bentley not mentioned his wife had business interests in Italy? If they existed, then surely she must make regular trips there?

The tide was on the turn as he drove down the hill into Marazion, but a crocodile of people was still making its way across the causeway to St Michael's Mount. He wondered if they realized the causeway would soon be under water and that returning to the mainland would have to be by boat. He smiled, remembering the last time he and Loveday had crossed to the Mount. They had misjudged the tide on the way back, and laughing, had to make a dash for it hand in hand, splashing through the water as it crept up the causeway.

Locryn Grantby's studio was in one of the white-painted shops coming up on his left. He had to drive past it to find a parking space. It was late afternoon, but the town was still busy with visitors. They clogged the narrow footpath, causing Sam to step onto the road to pass them. Some visitors had paused by Grantby's studio, studying the collection of blue and aquamarine beach scenes on display. They looked specifically created for the holiday market.

The artist, in a paint-splashed T-shirt, was working at an easel as Sam walked in. He jumped up, concern crossing his face as he recognized the detective. 'Is this about Mellissa?' he asked sharply. 'Have you caught her killer?'

'We're making progress,' Sam said, aware that a couple who'd been browsing the canvases for sale had looked up at them. 'Is there somewhere we can speak in private?'

'Come through,' Locryn said, leading the way into a back room.

The window had a view across the bay, but it was the bed in the corner that drew Sam's attention.

'I moved in here when Mellissa and I split up. Our marriage was over long before she died. I've already given your people a statement.'

'This isn't about Mellissa,' Sam said, choosing his words carefully. 'I understand you knew Gabriella Bentley.'

The artist's head came up. 'Gabriella? What does she have to do with this?'

'She's missing,' Sam said, watching the man's face for any sign of recognition, but he saw only surprise. 'We were wondering if you knew where she is?'

'Me? How would I know?'

'You were friends, weren't you?'

'What?' Then Locryn began to smile. 'Ah, I see where this is going. Someone's told you Gabriella and I had something going. Well, it wasn't even that. We had sex a couple of times. Neither of us was in the market for a relationship.'

'What about her husband? Didn't you feel guilty having a fling with another man's wife?'

Locryn shrugged. 'Gabriella wasn't bothered. I'm sure I wasn't the only man. We're talking about a very promiscuous lady.'

'Dr Bentley didn't approach you then, didn't warn you off?'

'No.'

'And you have no idea where Gabriella could have gone?'

The artist shook his head.

'You must have shared some conversation when you were together. Think, man, did she tell you anything about her life?'

Locryn sucked on his cheeks, thinking. 'I think she had a child.'

Sam narrowed his eyes at the man. 'She told you that?'

'Of course she didn't. It was the great secret nobody was supposed to know about, but I heard her on the phone.'

'Go on.'

'She was here,' his eyes slid to the bed, 'when her mobile rang. She shot up when she saw who was calling her and scrambled out of bed naked, saying she had to take the call. She said it was private and went into the front studio. I listened of course but I only caught her end of the conversation.

'She was telling the caller to stay calm. She would deal with it. But the caller must have persisted because Gabriella was getting angrier by the second. I heard her say *"The child is yours now, do what you've been paid to do, and if you try to squirm out of that you'll both be sorry."* Her voice sounded so chilling. I'd never heard Gabriella speak like that.'

'You think the caller was a woman?'

'That's the impression I got. It sounded like this person had been paid to take the child off Gabriella's hands, but somebody had discovered their secret and was threatening to expose them.

'Anyway, I'd skipped back into bed by the time she ended the call, looking like I hadn't heard a thing. Then Gabriella said she had to leave and began to get dressed. It was the last time I saw her.'

'Why have you not mentioned any of this before?'

'Because it has nothing to do with the murders.'

'That's for us to decide. You should have told us,' Sam said grimly.

The more he discovered about this woman the more confused he felt.

He could think of a number of reasons why a mother would want to keep her child a secret. Perhaps the baby wasn't Dr Bentley's child. But if Locryn Grantby's view of Gabriella's behaviour was true she hadn't been concerned about her husband's feelings.

Could it be that a baby would affect the success of the

woman's fashion business? Sam couldn't see why that would matter.

SAM ARRIVED home to find Cassie and Priddy were leaving. 'I hope you're not going because of me?' He grinned at them.

'Don't worry, we'll be back,' Cassie said airily. 'Your very hospitable wife has invited us for Sunday lunch tomorrow.'

'Oh no, she hasn't, has she?' Sam slapped his hand over his forehead.

Cassie gave his arm a thump as she passed him. 'Just for that you can do your own washing up.'

'That'll teach you to tease my friends,' Loveday said, reaching up to give him a peck on the cheek as he came into the kitchen.

'Where's Maddie?' he said, looking around.

'She's in the nursery with Rosie. She's been amazing, Sam. She won't let me do anything for the baby. I think we'll have to check her bags before she leaves or she'll be taking her little sister home with her.'

Sam laughed, going through to see how his two girls were getting on.

Loveday was opening a pack of ham slices to include in their teatime salad when he came back into the kitchen. 'How did it go today? Have you found Gabriella yet?'

'Not yet, but we have made a few discoveries. It would seem our Gabriella is not the lady she would have us believe.'

'Really?' Loveday looked up. 'Do tell.'

'Later. I'm still processing everything I've heard today.'

IN BED LATER, Loveday listened in silence as Sam reported, first what Rachel Dawson had said about Gabriella and her husband being at their party, and then how she had flirted with Locryn Grantby.

Her eyebrows rose in surprise when he told her Philip Dawson also had a fling with Gabriella.

But she stared at him in shock when she heard Grantby's story.

'A baby? You think Gabriella has a child?' She blinked, clearly trying to take this in. 'I take it Dr Bentley is not the father?'

'Whoa.' Sam put out his hand. 'We don't know if any of this is true yet. It's only what Locryn Grantby said. The conversation he lugged in on could mean something completely different.'

'He could have been lying.' Loveday screwed up her face. 'We don't know we can trust him. If, as he said, it was the last time he saw Gabriella he might not appreciate getting dumped.'

'You mean he was trying to cause trouble for her?'

'It's possible.'

Sam nodded. The idea had also occurred to him, but he was willing to keep an open mind. 'Let's assume he was telling the truth, and this *was* a woman Gabriella was speaking to. Could she be someone we know?'

The faces of the women he'd interviewed flitted through his mind. Rachel Dawson had two older children. He supposed it was possible she was also looking after a third child, although there had been no sign of a baby in her house.

'What about Nessa Cawse?' he said. 'I know she's Adam's receptionist and works next door, but it doesn't rule out the possibility of a baby. She could have childcare.'

Loveday shook her head. 'I can't see it.' Then a light came into her eyes. 'What about the female staff at the medical centre? We know from what Philip Dawson said that Gabriella used to drop by to see her husband. Could she have befriended one of the staff in particular? When did this conversation Grantby says he over-heard take place?'

Sam cast his mind back to the murder wall in the incident room. 'The Dawsons' party was on April 18 and Grantby said his affair with Gabriella ended with that phone call on May 8.'

Loveday was still screwing up her face. 'That's very specific.'

'It was his birthday.'

'So, well before Mellissa was killed,' Loveday said, chewing her bottom lip. 'What if Gabriella was paying Mellissa to look after her child?'

Sam blew out his cheeks. 'From what I've heard about Mellissa Grantby, she was a full-on professional. She wouldn't have had time to care for a child.'

'Like we said, she could have had a childminder looking after the baby while she was at work.'

'Why would she have wanted to help Gabriella?'

'Well, that's what we have to find out,' Loveday said, wriggling into a more comfortable position. 'Suppose it was true, and Mellissa saw Gabriella throwing herself at Locryn at that party? I know she was in a relationship with Philip Dawson, but Locryn was still her husband, so maybe she was jealous. And then she heard Dawson was also having a ding-dong with Gabriella.' She met Sam's eyes. 'D'you see where I'm going with this?'

'Not really,' Sam said, rubbing his hands over his tired eyes. 'I think it's time we got some sleep.'

'No, listen,' Loveday said. 'All that would have been enough to make Mellissa good and mad at Gabriella. What if she was the woman who rang Gabriella when she was with Locryn?'

Sam considered this. 'Locryn got the impression the caller was panicking because someone had discovered whatever arrangement they had.'

'What if this person was threatening to tell the authorities about Mellissa having a baby that wasn't hers? Maybe they even suggested she had abducted the child. She'd be on her own then, wouldn't she? If everything we've heard is true I can't see Gabriella rushing in to help.'

'If there really is a baby, and Mellissa was looking after it, where is the child now?'

'Maybe it's back with Gabriella, and that's why she's disappeared. She could have taken the baby to be looked after by relatives in Italy.'

'So why involve Mellissa? Why didn't she do that in the first place?'

'I don't know,' Loveday said, flopping back on her pillows. 'I'll need to think about that.'

CHAPTER 34

*I*t was almost six when Loveday woke next morning to the sounds of Rosie's lusty cries. There was a pattern to Loveday's mornings, which revolved around feeding and changing a hungry baby.

She got up and popped her head into the nursery, but her assurance that the desired bottle was on its way only made Rosie's cries even more demanding.

Loveday headed for the kitchen, half expecting to find Maddie already there making Rosie's bottle, but she wasn't, and her bedroom door was firmly closed. Loveday smiled as she scooped milk powder into the measuring jug, wondering why she was the only one tuned into the hungry cries of a baby.

She cooled the milk under the running tap before taking it to the nursery and lifting her daughter. Crying had made the little face red with impatience and Rosie's mouth was already working, anticipating that bottle.

'What a fuss.' Loveday held the warm little bundle in her arms. 'It's here, look, your breakfast is here.' The child's face immediately changed to a picture of contentment when presented with the all-important bottle. Loveday gazed down at her daughter and wondered again how any mother could give away her child, but according to Locryn Grantby, it was exactly what Gabriella had done.

Loveday frowned as she went over last night's discussion with Sam but now, in the cold light of day, everything they'd considered seemed improbable. From what she'd learned of Mellissa, she hadn't been a woman who loved children. Locryn clearly hadn't believed she was the woman who'd called Gabriella that night, or he would surely have mentioned it.

If it hadn't been Mellissa, then who? She and Sam had already decided it was unlikely to have been Nessa or Rachel.

Memories of the day she'd visited the medical centre with Nessa returned as she remembered the three admin women she'd met. Gabriella must have known them.

Loveday estimated the oldest woman Helen Wright, to be in her mid-fifties. She had mentioned grandchildren. Surely she was an unlikely candidate for taking on a baby?

Her colleague Sally Richards was a young mum of two children. Would she take on someone else's child for money? Loveday didn't think so.

That left Merryn Lawry, a pretty young woman with a crush on Dr Christopher Bentley. Loveday screwed up her face. Could this be important? If the GP had fathered this child maybe a besotted Merryn would agree to be its surrogate mother. She was jolted from her reverie when Sam poked his head into the room. 'How are my two favourite girls?'

Maddie appeared behind him and gave her father a poke in the ribs. 'You mean your *three* favourite girls.'

'That's exactly what I meant,' he said, an arm around her shoulders. 'I'm on breakfast duty this morning. How does bacon, sausage, tomato and scrambled eggs sound?'

'You do know it's only seven o'clock on a Sunday morning?' Loveday said, her eyes narrowing suspiciously.

Sam flashed her a guilty look. 'I might have to go into the station for an hour or two, but I'll definitely be back in time for lunch.'

'Promise?'

He laid a hand on his heart. 'I promise.'

'In that case, I accept your generous offer to cook, although I'll settle for just the scrambled eggs,' Loveday said.

'Me too,' Maddie said, heading for the bathroom. 'And if it's all right with you, Loveday, I'll change and dress Rosie after I've showered.'

Loveday nodded enthusiastically. 'We're going to miss you when you go back later.'

'Ditto,' Maddie called over her shoulder as she went out.

AFTER BREAKFAST, and feeling pleasantly full, Loveday took a cup of coffee into her study. She had been hoping to share ideas with Sam, but she hadn't been surprised when he'd said he was going into the station. Sunday mornings at home during a murder inquiry simply didn't happen. And this time there were three murders, and he was no closer to solving them than on day one. She could imagine Sam's frustration.

Loveday opened her computer, she needed to give more thought to who might take on Gabriella's child. She began to type a list of the candidates she had previously considered.

She'd put Mellissa's name at the top, but the more she thought about it the more unlikely it seemed. She'd heard nothing about this woman to suggest she was the motherly kind.

Rachel Dawson came next. She could have been a possibility, except for Sam describing her hatred of Gabriella for bedding her husband.

Nessa Cawse. *No.* Loveday was making notes beside each name. Her thoughts went back to the party. Were she and Locryn

Grantby an item back then? She was picturing Nessa's reaction if she saw Gabriella making a play for her lover.

She listed the other women – Helen Wright? Sally Richards? But screwed up her face at the likelihood of it being either of them.

The most interesting was still Merryn Lawry. Loveday was remembering how the young woman's face had lit up when Dr Bentley appeared in the waiting room. Nessa had tutted when the GP smiled back at Merryn, accusing him of being a ladies' man. But men who flirted with women didn't necessarily have affairs with them. Could Nessa have misjudged the man? What if he had a genuine affection for Merryn? She could definitely see Merryn with a child.

She and Sam had agreed that childminders were not out of the question for a working mother. It was exactly the arrangement she had with Priddy, except she kept her daughter with her at work.

Merryn struck Loveday as the homely kind of girl who might still live with her parents. If that was the case, it was entirely possible for her to have a child that Merryn's mother looked after when she was at work.

Loveday threw up her hands in exasperation. She was making all these assumptions when she didn't even know if there was a child. Only one person could confirm that – and she was missing!

Priddy looked a little flustered as she hurried up the drive to Loveday and Sam's cottage. She wasn't used to having lunch with her GP, although Dr Adam Trevillick was also Cassie's husband. Did that justify her treating him like a friend? She was still considering this when Maddie answered her knock and the wonderful smell of roasting chicken reached her.

'Come in, Priddy,' Loveday called, her cheeks flushed from the heat of the oven. 'Cassie and Adam are in the sitting room. Maddie will get you a drink.'

'Can I help?' Priddy asked, glancing at the serving dishes warming on top of the stove.

'No thanks, I think I'm organized.' Loveday used the back of her hand to push back an escaping strand of long, dark hair as she looked around the kitchen. 'You go through to the others. I'll join you in a minute.'

Priddy followed Maddie into the big sitting room and stopped, surprised as she caught sight of the colourful back garden. Her recent visits to the cottage had been restricted to the kitchen and Rosie's nursery, so she hadn't often been in this new extension.

'Impressive, isn't it?' Cassie said, following her friend's gaze. 'Who'd have thought Loveday would be such a great gardener.'

'It's only bedding plants,' Loveday said, coming into the room and sweeping away the compliment. 'Anyone can grow them. All I do is a bit of weeding now and again.'

'Don't listen to her,' Adam said. 'I've seen her out there with her spade.'

'So have I,' Sam said, stepping into the room and smiling around the faces.

'You made it!' Loveday cried, going to him and stretching up to give him a peck on the cheek. She knew he would make a special effort, not just because their friends were here, but it was also Maddie's last day with them.

'Does this mean you've solved all those murders?' Cassie quipped.

'Sadly no, but I am taking a couple of hours off.'

'How is the investigation going?' Adam asked.

Loveday watched Sam rake his fingers through his hair as he shook his head. 'It's tricky. We seem to take one step forward and then three back. When we think we've tied up one loose end, another presents itself.'

'Is Gabriella Bentley still missing?' Priddy asked, her brow lowering in concern at Sam's weary nod.

Loveday had caught Adam's frown and wondered if he wanted to say something but wasn't sure he should. 'What is it, Adam? You look worried.'

'It's probably nothing,' he started with an unsure shrug. 'But that artist chap, the one whose wife died with her wrists cut, he was in the surgery yesterday.'

'Locryn Grantby? He's a patient?' Loveday's brow arched.

'No, not a patient. I don't think he knew I'd spotted him. It was Nessa he'd come to see. I saw them talking.'

'What d'you mean talking?' Loveday cut in quickly, aware that Sam was eyeing her. 'Were they arguing?'

'Not that, no. They were being quite covert, actually. Their heads were together and they were whispering.' He looked at Sam. 'Could it be helpful?'

'It might be. I'll look into it,' Sam said.

Through in the kitchen a pinger sounded. 'That's the roasties done,' Loveday announced. 'Come on, Sam. You can help me dish up.'

It WAS after three o'clock before their guests started to leave. Cassie hugged Loveday. 'That was a fabulous meal.'

"I'll echo that,' Adam said. 'Thank you for inviting us.'

'That goes for me, too,' Priddy said. 'I couldn't have done better myself.'

'That sounds like high praise.' Sam smiled, an arm around Loveday's shoulder.

'He's sussed us.' Cassie laughed. 'He knows we're only angling another invite.'

Priddy looked shocked.

'Cassie's joking,' Loveday said. 'Pay no attention to her. I never do.'

Cassie shook her head. 'You'd never think she was my best friend.' She winked at Priddy.

Maddie joined Loveday and Sam at the door to wave everyone off.

'I'm not sure Priddy knows what to make of Cassie,' she said.

Sam's frown was teasing. 'That makes two of us,' he said.

CHAPTER 35

Sam had still not left the house when Priddy arrived at 8.30 the next morning. Loveday knew he'd stayed behind because he wanted to question Locryn at his studio in Marazion, and Nessa at Adam's surgery. It was clear he wanted to know more about that covert meeting between the two of them Adam had mentioned. She was also curious about that. Her head was full of questions as she drove to work in Truro.

'THAT WOMAN'S on the phone for you again Loveday,' Keri said as they arrived at the office.

'What woman?'

'I don't know. She wouldn't leave a name, but she's rung twice and she's on again now.'

Loveday blew Rosie a kiss and crossed the office to pick up her landline. 'Loveday Ross,' she said crisply. 'How can I help you?'

'Loveday?'

Loveday's pulse quickened at the sound of the soft Italian accent.

'Gabriella?'

'Can we meet, Loveday? I need your help?'

Loveday steadied herself. 'Gabriella! Where are you? We've all been worried about you.'

'I'm here in Truro,' she said. 'There's a landing at Malpas, down from the Heron Inn. Can you meet me there?'

'Malpas? Well, yes, but…'

'You mustn't tell anyone about this, Loveday,' Gabriella said sharply. 'I need your word.'

'You have it,' Loveday said, not sure what she was agreeing to. She had no time to dwell on her response because Gabriella had ended the call.

Loveday stared at the phone. She knew Sam would not appreciate being kept in the dark. He was probably still in Marazion, speaking to Locryn and Nessa. Her loyalty to him was more important than this woman who apparently had no qualms about lying. She reached a decision, pulled out her mobile and began texting.

'Gabriella just rang me. She's in Truro. I've promised not to say where, but I'm on my way to meet her now. Turning off my phone, so please don't call, Sam. I'll contact you as soon as I can.'

There were only two vehicles in the car park when Loveday arrived at the Heron Inn. She reversed alongside one of them, remembering previous difficulties getting out of this awkwardly shaped place when it was busy.

The distinctive squawking of young birds in the heronry opposite drifted across the water and for a second she stopped, surveying the picturesque scene where the Truro and Tresillian rivers met.

She glanced around to get her bearings. The road still glistened from earlier rain as Loveday walked, searching for a gap in the fence that could lead to the landing Gabriella mentioned. What she found was more than a landing, there was a timber-built house nestling down by the water, and completely unseen from the road. She approached gingerly, careful not to miss her footing on the slippery wooden steps.

The house door opened before she reached it, and Gabriella stood there, but this wasn't the smartly dressed, professionally made up woman Loveday remembered. This woman was in jeans and a scruffy navy T-shirt, her previously sleek black hair now looked lank and unwashed.

'You weren't followed, were you?' she asked, squinting anxiously to the stairs.

'No one followed me, everything's fine, Gabriella.' Loveday stepped past her into a small front room with a picture window that looked out across the water. 'Is this your place?' Loveday asked, glancing to the balcony she could see through the glass doors.

'It's a holiday rent. I have it for the week.'

'What's going on, Gabriella? What's this all about?' Loveday turned, at the same time discreetly slipping a hand into her pocket to activate the recording device on her mobile phone.

'The last time I saw you was in Connie and Merrick Tremayne's home when they kindly allowed you to stay the night. Why did you disappear like that?'

Gabriella fixed her with a stare. 'Chris is trying to kill me.'

'He's What!' Loveday stepped back, frowning.

'Look, I'm sorry if Connie feels I let her down, but surely you understand why I couldn't stay. It wasn't safe.'

Loveday was desperately trying not to let her mouth drop open.

The woman's attention had darted to the river, scanning the water as though she expected some evil, disturbing image to appear from the waves.

'OK, let's stay calm,' Loveday said, hoping her voice sounded more reassuring than she felt. 'What makes you think your husband is trying to kill you?'

'Because he's killed before. I told you what kind of man he is, I'm not safe with him.'

'Wait a minute.' Worrying pictures were racing through Loveday's mind. 'What are you talking about? Who did Dr Bentley kill?'

Gabriella moistened her lips, her eyes moving everywhere. 'Brian Teague. He killed him, and then he had to murder the woman who cleaned for Teague. She died because she could identify him.'

Loveday's mouth was dry, her heart felt like it might hammer right out of her chest. Could this be true? She had to keep her composure. She was remembering that first meeting with Gabriella when the woman described how controlling her husband was and how he'd virtually stalked her, threatening any man she spoke to. Back then she'd appeared chaste and innocent, but that was before she'd been revealed as a man-eating, cheating wife. Was this accusation another lie?

This wasn't something Loveday could deal with on her own, she wished Sam was here. She swallowed. 'How do you know this?'

Gabriella's brow furrowed as though she didn't understand the question. 'How do you think I know? He told me, of course.' She shook her head. 'Poor Mellissa. She didn't deserve to die. Chris didn't have to kill her.'

An icy chill ran through Loveday. She took a steadying breath. 'You're saying Dr Bentley also murdered Mellissa Grantby?'

'He did, and now he's after me.' She began to pace the room.

'You have to tell the police,' Loveday said.

'They won't believe me. You've met my husband. You've seen how plausible he can be. Ask your partner, Sam, he's interviewed him.'

'There's no proof your husband has done these terrible things,' Loveday said. 'He's probably only trying to frighten you.'

'But I do have proof,' Gabriella said. 'That's why he's after me.

He took something from Teague's house. Something that will prove he was there.'

Loveday felt her pulse quicken again. 'What did he take?'

'It's a photograph of Teague's late wife. He took it as a kind of trophy.'

'Do you know where this photo is now?'

Gabriella nodded. 'I have it.'

Loveday's mind was in turmoil, but she concentrated on keeping her breathing easy. 'Did he take any other trophies?'

'He kept the hammer he used to kill Teague's housekeeper. I know where it is.'

'You definitely have to tell the police about this. They will get DNA from the hammer.' Loveday leaned forward, her body language insistent. 'Don't you see, Gabriella, this could be the proof the police need. If your husband's DNA is on that hammer, he'll have some explaining to do.'

Gabriella turned wide eyes on Loveday. 'Do you think so?'

There was something in that look that made Loveday start. Everything the woman said was plausible, so why did she feel there was more to it than what she'd been told?

'Ring the police. Tell them what you've told me.'

'I can't. Chris may be a killer, but he's still my husband, it's difficult for me to betray him.' She looked up, meeting Loveday's eyes again. 'Will you do it for me? Will you tell the police?'

But as Loveday took her phone from her pocket, Gabriella leapt forward. 'Not on the phone. I don't want that. You must go there in person. Tell your Sam, he'll know what to do.'

Her eyes were imploring. 'Please, Loveday. You have to help me.'

'Calm down, Gabriella. Of course I'll help you. I'll go right now.' She reached out to touch the woman's arm. 'Promise me you'll stay here until the police come.'

Gabriella nodded. 'I'll be here.'

Loveday hurried back to her car, stopping the recording and

switching over her phone as she went. There were numerous missed calls from Sam. She clicked on his number. He responded immediately. 'Loveday! What the hell is going on?'

'Gabriella is here!' Loveday gasped out the words. 'I've spoken to her. She's staying in a house down by the river in Malpas, near the Heron Inn.

'Oh, Sam, she says her husband murdered those three people.'

She could see the road from where she sat in her car. Gabriella was emerging from the house and crossing to a vehicle parked by the wall opposite. Loveday's brows knitted. What on earth was she up to?

'Are you still there, Sam?'

'Yes, what's happening?'

'Gabriella is on the move. I'm going to follow her. I'll get back to you.'

'No!' he shouted. 'Don't hang up. Put the phone on hands-free.'

She did, keeping a safe distance behind the woman's car as she followed her along the narrow winding road.

'Where are you now?' Sam's voice was urgent.

Loveday slowed down. 'I'm passing the Radio Cornwall studios, the roundabout is just ahead.' She was on familiar ground now. The first turning would take them onto the Falmouth road, while the final exit led out of Truro, heading south. But Gabriella surprised her by negotiating the turning into the centre of town.

'I don't know what this woman is playing at, Sam. We're in the town centre.'

'Don't lose her,' Sam said.

'I wasn't planning to,' Loveday muttered under her breath.

And then she realized where the woman was heading.

'You won't believe this, Sam, but Gabriella Bentley has just driven into your car park.'

'She has?' He sounded as surprised as she felt. 'Right, park in the road, we don't want her to see you. I'll be right down.'

Loveday's brow creased as she watched the woman drive into a parking space and get out of her car. She bent her head, hiding her face as Gabriella walked to the front of the police station and went in.

What was she up to? Why was she here when she had explicitly asked her to contact the police? Loveday hadn't noticed Sam's approach and started when he tapped the car window, beckoning for her to follow him.

'Take this,' he instructed, thrusting a visitor badge into her hand as they entered the building by the back door. 'We'll go to my office.'

Loveday knew Sam was controlling his impatience as she produced her phone and scrolled for the recording where Gabriella had accused her husband of murder.

She watched him stare at the phone as she replayed it, his lips pursed as he listened. He looked up when it ended. 'Well, what do you think? Did you believe her?'

Loveday shrugged. 'There's no reason not to believe her. She's very plausible. Will you speak to Dr Bentley?'

'Definitely,' he said.

CHAPTER 36

Sam had sent DC Amanda Fox to meet Gabriella in reception and take her to an interview room with the instruction she was not to be let out of her sight.

And then he instructed Will to send DCs Rowe and Carter to the Hilltop Medical Centre to bring Dr Christopher Bentley in for questioning.

Loveday watched Will stride away, his phone at his ear, and made sure no one was watching before she stretched up to plant a kiss on Sam's cheek. 'Let me know how those interviews go,' she said over her shoulder as she made for the stairs. 'I'll be at the magazine if you need me.'

Sam's composure as he watched Loveday leave gave no hint to the turmoil going on in his head. Gabriella Bentley had accused her husband of being their killer. Could it be true? Why would she lie? Three victims, and no one yet in the frame for their murders. It was more than two weeks since Brian Teague was killed. Were they at last in a position to bring this case to a successful conclusion?

A frisson of excitement began to stir inside him as he got to his feet. 'Come on, Will,' he called across the room. 'Let's see what this lady has to say for herself.'

GABRIELLA'S APPEARANCE took Sam by surprise. She looked nothing like the glamorous woman he'd met at Merrick's house. The previously chic dark hair had been scraped back in a harsh, unflattering bun and her pale face was free of make-up. Her shoulders in the denim jacket she wore looked broader than he remembered.

She looked up at him, her huge eyes anxious as her voice shook. 'Please help me, Sam. I'm so afraid my husband means to kill me.'

A frown was etched on Sam's brow as he leaned forward. They might have been on first name terms at the supper party, but this was a different matter and he had no intention of allowing the interview to stray from the professional.

'Many people were worried about you, Mrs Bentley. Where have you been?'

Gabriella bit her lip and looked away. 'I needed time to think. I couldn't go back to my husband, he–'

'Tell us about your husband,' Sam interrupted. 'Why do you think he means to harm you?'

'Chris hates me, you don't know how he tries to control me. He won't let me out of his sight. He treats me like I'm having affairs with every man I meet.'

'Are you?'

She flashed him a horrified stare. 'Of course not. How could you even ask that?'

She was biting her lip again. 'You won't believe how many men Chris has threatened. I'm not allowed to have any male friends. He even warned off my hairdresser.'

'Why do you think he behaved like that?' Will asked.

'Isn't it obvious? My husband is an insanely jealous man.'

Sam met her eyes. He was remembering how Rachel Dawson had talked about Gabriella, and then there was that fling with Locryn Grantby. 'Are you saying he has no cause to be jealous?'

'Of course he doesn't. I have always been faithful to my husband, but his twisted mind conjures up these fantasies and I don't know what to do any more.'

Sam tilted his head at her, trying to figure out why she was lying. She was clearly an intelligent woman. She ran fashion businesses in Cornwall and possibly even Italy. What was she up to?

He decided to change tack. 'You said you left the Tremaynes' place because you felt you were in danger from your husband.'

Gabriella nodded.

'You haven't told us how you managed that. Morvah is pretty remote and you didn't have transport.' His stare was questioning.

The woman sighed. 'OK, I'll tell you.' She paused, her look sliding from one detective to the other. 'I planned it. Connie and Loveday agreeing I should stay the night was a bonus because I had already organized what I was going to do that night. Everything had been previously arranged. I had ordered a taxi to pick me up at a house half a mile from Morvah, so even if you did check, there would be no record of anyone being collected by taxi from the Tremaynes' place in the early hours.'

'Where did you go?' Sam said, curious to see if she would stick to the same story she told Loveday.

'A holiday cottage in Malpas,' she said. 'I stocked it with food in advance so I didn't have to go out.'

'But you did have transport. Your vehicle is in our car park,' Will said.

'A hire car. I paid a bit extra to have it delivered to Malpas.' She reached across for the bottle of water on the table and drank down a few inches.

'So all the time we were searching for you, you were right here in Malpas?'

She nodded, squinting a guilty look at him. 'Sorry.'

Sam glanced down, frowning. He flipped open the folder he'd brought with him and removed three photographs.

Gabriella gasped as she was presented with the dead post mortem images of Brian Teague, Janet Harris and Mellissa Grantby.

'Do you recognize these people?'

She nodded, her hand at her throat. 'I haven't seen these pictures before.'

'Who are they, Gabriella?'

'I'm sorry,' she said, a tear springing to her eyes. 'It's a shock seeing these poor people like this.'

'Who are they?' he repeated, ignoring the quickening of his pulse as he watched her.

Gabriella looked back at the photos. 'These are the people my husband murdered,' she said.

Sam sat back, his eyes not leaving her face. 'Tell us about that.'

She glanced away, swallowing. 'You have to understand how difficult this is for me. I'm betraying my husband.'

'What's difficult for us to understand is why you're protecting a man you believe is a killer. If you're right, there's nothing to stop him killing again.'

'The only person Chris wants to kill now is me.'

'Why would he want to do that?'

She buried her face in her hands and began to sob.

The detectives waited.

Gabriella lifted her head, tears cascading down her cheeks. 'He was right.' Her voice shook. 'I had an affair with a man I met at a party. I knew it was wrong but he was kind, understanding, and I needed that.' She reached for her bag, pulled out a tissue and blew her nose. 'When I realized Chris was having me followed, I was terrified of what he might do.' She looked up. 'That's the real reason I left the Tremaynes' house in the middle of the night. I had to get away from him.'

'It's time you told us everything,' Sam said, his tone gentler.

Sam and Will listened as Gabriella talked. It was practically a replay of what Loveday had recorded.

'You say your husband kept the hammer he used to kill Janet Harris?'

'It's in the shed in our garden.'

Sam knew she'd seen his nod to Will and watched her eyes follow the sergeant's movements as he got up and left the room. Seconds later he returned, having passed on instructions for a warrant to search the Bentleys' cottage in Crantock.

'What about the photo of Brian Teague's wife?' Sam asked.

'I've got it here.' Gabriella reached into her bag again and took out a photograph. She put it on the table.

Sam glanced down at the image of a pregnant Meredith Teague. The woman was smiling up at the photographer, a glint of pride in her eyes as her hands wrapped around her swollen belly.

It was a happy picture, and Sam felt a sudden surge of emotion as he looked at it. Only weeks later, this young woman and her unborn babies would be dead, and an innocent Lawrence Kemp would be imprisoned for years convicted of causing the deaths.

'What about Mellissa Grantby?' he asked, aware that Will had produced an evidence bag from his pocket and, without touching the photo, was sliding it inside.

Gabriella blinked. 'Well, he must have killed her. Who else would have done it?'

'But you have no evidence of this?'

'Well no, but why else would Chris have been at the medical centre so early in the day? Don't you see? He made sure it was him who found the body. That way he could ensure his DNA was legitimately all over it, so swabbing him as a suspect would be pointless.'

Sam's eyebrow arched. She had it all worked out, but she hadn't finished.

'In Chris's damaged mind he may also have thought that if it was him who found the body then the police would rule him out of the killing.'

'I'm not sure I understand that.'

'Chris would know that the obvious person is seldom the killer, he'd be banking on that.'

Gabriella had jumped to her feet. 'You have to arrest my husband.' Her voice was rising. 'I know he murdered these people. Do you really imagine he will let me live?' She stared at them, wide-eyed. 'You must see that I'm not safe as long as he is out there.'

The detectives exchanged a look. 'Please sit down, Mrs Bentley,' Sam said, waiting until she had complied before going on. 'We will deal with this. You need to trust us. Now go back to that cottage in Malpas and stay there until you hear from us.'

'You'll arrest him? You'll arrest my husband?'

'Dr Bentley will be brought in for questioning. The information you've provided is really helpful. In the meantime it would be useful if you agreed to having your fingerprints taken before you leave.'

Gabriella narrowed her eyes. 'I don't understand. Why is that necessary?'

Sam smiled. 'It's our routine I'm afraid, but we need to be able to rule you out of our investigations. You did handle that photograph after all.'

'Well, I suppose...'

But Sam gave her no time to further question it. He was already calling in a constable to escort the woman away.

Will held up the Meredith Teague photo. 'I'll have this tested for prints.'

Sam nodded. 'And get Amanda to keep an eye on her.'

'You really think she could be in danger?'

'Just belt and braces, Will, but I'm taking no chances.'

'What about Dr Bentley? We've got him in another interview room.'

'He'll have to wait,' Sam said thoughtfully. 'Let's recover that hammer from their cottage first.'

CHAPTER 37

'You have a visitor,' Keri Godden told Loveday. 'She's at the front desk. She wouldn't give her name.'

Loveday finished the paragraph she was typing and saved her work before looking up and frowning. Was this Gabriella? She was curious why she'd gone to the police when she'd been adamant Loveday should do it on her behalf. Perhaps she'd come to explain? Sam hadn't contacted her so she had no idea what the woman told him. A growing unease was beginning to envelope her as she went downstairs.

Gabriella was on her feet, staring through the glass doors of reception to the busy Lemon Street. She swung round at the sound of Loveday's approach.

'Forgive this intrusion. I know you're busy. I need to apologize for asking you to go to the police on my behalf, and then going there myself. Look, can we talk?'

'Of course,' Loveday said, making to sit.

'No, not here.' Gabriella stepped forward. 'I have the car outside.'

'Well, I...' Loveday started.

'It won't take long, I promise.'

Loveday shrugged, following the woman outside and into her car, assuming she wanted to talk in the privacy of the parked vehicle. But Gabriella started the engine. 'Let's get out of the city,' she said. 'I know a place.'

'I don't have a lot of time,' Loveday protested. 'What's this all about, Gabriella?'

'I've told the police everything. They know my husband murdered all those people. I can't tell you what a relief it is.'

'That's great, but I don't see how I can be of any more help.' They were passing the city hospital, heading for the A30. 'Where are we going? I have to get back.'

'Have patience, my friend. We'll soon be there.' They were across the main road, following the sign to Newquay.

Loveday frowned. Why were they going to the coast? And then she knew...she was being taken to the Bentleys' cottage in Crantock.

'HAVE YOU FOUND HER?' Dr Chris Bentley had jumped to his feet as the detectives entered the interview room. 'Have you found my wife?'

'Sit down please, Dr Bentley. Your wife is safe. We've spoken to her.'

Sam watched relief flood over the man's face as he sank back down onto the seat. 'What's she told you?'

'What do you think she's told us?' Sam batted back.

'Gabriella's not well. She needs careful handling.'

Sam opened his folder and took out the same victim photographs he'd shown Gabriella. 'Do you recognize these people?'

Bentley's gaze flicked over Brian Teague and Janet Harris, lingering on the slumped and bloody image of Mellissa Grantby. He looked sad. 'That's my colleague, Mellissa.'

'What about the others?'

'We met Mr Teague once at a party in his sister's house. She's married to Philip Dawson who is a rep for a pharmaceutical company that sells products to the medical centre.'

'I don't know this lady.' He pointed to Janet Harris's photo. 'But I've seen her picture in the newspapers.'

Sam blinked, focusing on the man's concerned face. 'Did you kill these three people?'

Bentley leaned back, covering his face with his hands. 'Is this what Gabriella told you?' He was shaking his head. 'You didn't believe her?'

'Why would she lie?'

'To protect herself.'

'Care to explain that?'

The detectives' eyes followed Bentley as he got to his feet and began to walk about the room. 'I don't know where to begin, I've already told you my wife is not a well woman.' He paused, turning to Sam. 'Gabriella poisoned Brian Teague because he was blackmailing me.'

Sam showed no emotion. 'Go on.'

'Mellissa and I were friends and colleagues. She didn't have many friends, so she confided in me. She told me Teague was threatening to expose her love life. It's what he did, he pried into people's lives.'

'What was he blackmailing her about?'

'She was having an affair with Philip Dawson.' He paused, the tip off his tongue coming out to moisten his lips. 'But that wasn't it. Teague had got it into his head that Mellissa and I were lovers. It wasn't true, of course, but Gabriella got an anonymous letter full of disgusting accusations. She showed it to me, and completely ignored my protests that it was all lies. Even when I told her what Teague was like, she refused to believe me.'

'Are you telling us that your wife murdered Brian Teague because he wrote that letter to her?'

'That's exactly what I'm saying, but you have to understand that Gabriella has not been in her right mind.'

'Your wife has an alibi for the day Teague died. She was in her boutique here in Truro. We checked.'

Bentley came back and slumped into his chair. 'You don't know how the poison that killed Teague was administered. Gabriella is clever. She had it all worked out. She broke into Teague's cottage the night before he died.' He shook his head again. 'The poison was in the ice tray. She emptied the tray, refilling the cubes with fresh water, and dripped the poison into them. She only half-filled half the tray because she couldn't chance any of the cubes being left for police to examine.'

'Where did she get the poison?' Will asked.

'In our garden shed. It's rat poison. It was there when we bought the place and we never got rid of it. It's probably still there. You can check.'

The sergeant's brow creased. 'How do you know this?'

'Gabriella told me. She was gloating. She said Teague had to be taught a lesson.' He took a breath and met Sam's eyes. 'His poor cleaner had nothing to do with this, but her dog had been ill and she'd taken it out for a walk the night Gabriella broke in. Mrs Harris saw her in the lane and recognized her, so she had to die.' Bentley sighed. 'She told me she had set everything up to frame me for both murders, so I shouldn't go to the police.'

'What about Mellissa Grantby?'

'Gabriella killed her because she believed we were having an affair. You have no idea how insanely jealous my wife is.'

'But it was you who found Mellissa's body,' Will said.

'That was also part of the plan. Gabriella told me what she'd done, knowing I would immediately go to help Mellissa.' He drew in a shuddering breath. 'But she was already dead.'

Sam gave the man a hard stare. He was fighting to control his frustration. 'Why didn't you come forward with this information before?'

'I know, I should have come to you. I suppose I was trying to shield my sick wife from the inevitable.'

'Would it surprise you to know that your wife has accused you of murdering these people?'

'No, it's exactly what I would have expected. But Gabriella is lying to you.' He paused. 'What happens now?'

'Now we investigate all these claims. And as far as what will happen to you, Dr Bentley, you may be charged with murder, or at the very least aiding and abetting murders.'

Bentley's shoulders slumped. He looked like a defeated man.

'I should have come to you,' he sighed. 'I should have told you about Gabriella. I'm sorry.'

LOVEDAY LOOKED around her as they bumped along the rough track to the Bentley's cottage. Gabriella stared ahead, her grip tight on the car steering wheel.

'What are we doing here?' Loveday demanded. 'I have no time for this. Take me back to Truro immediately.'

'Not so friendly now, are we? I saw how you and Chris were eyeing each other up at the Tremaynes' place. I know what's been going on. Do you think I'm stupid?'

Loveday blinked, not believing what she was hearing. 'There is nothing going on between your husband and me. You're talking nonsense, Gabriella.'

'I don't think so, but it stops right now. Nobody fools around with my husband. I don't allow it.'

The car came to an abrupt halt outside the cottage. Loveday grabbed the door handle and leapt out.

'Take another step and I'll shoot,' Gabriella shouted after her. 'I mean it, I'll shoot you!'

Loveday stopped in her tracks, glancing over her shoulder. The woman was standing, feet apart, and both hands around a gun that was pointed at Loveday's chest.

Heart thumping, Loveday raised her arms. 'OK, take it easy, Gabriella. I'm doing what you say.'

'I should just shoot you anyway, but I'll give you a chance. You can have a ten second start and then I'll be after you.' She waved the gun towards the sand dunes. 'Well, what are you waiting for? Move! The clock's ticking. Did you hear me?' she yelled. 'Run, you bitch, run!'

Loveday took flight, aware how unstable the dunes were. Gabriella was only feet behind her, but she stumbled, and the gun went off with a loud rapport. Loveday heard the scream, turning in time to see the woman fling out her arms as the clifftop parted and Gabriella disappeared into the void.

Loveday stared after her in horror. Twenty feet of clifftop had just disappeared before her eyes. The beach below was where children played, families picnicked and dog owners exercised their pets. Oh my God! Were more people lying beneath that mountain of sand? She had to do something, but what? The rest of the cliff might collapse if she moved.

She was trapped, but she had to do something. She began to back away gingerly, testing the ground with the toe of her trainers as she moved.

'Loveday?' The voice calling her name sounded distant. She cocked her head to one side, listening. It came again, closer now. 'Loveday! Oh my God, Loveday. I thought you'd gone over.'

Detective Constable Amanda Fox was running towards her.

Loveday threw out her arms. 'Stay back,' she shouted. 'Don't move! This whole cliff could give way.'

'What happened?' Amanda called. 'Where is Gabriella Bentley?'

'Down there somewhere.' She nodded to where the bank had collapsed. 'We need to get help. Call Sam, and get an ambulance.'

Amanda was already on her phone. Loveday could tell the detective was trying to keep the panic from her voice. 'Help's on the way,' she called back to her. 'I've got a rope in the boot of my. Will you be OK till I fetch it?'

Loveday gave a distracted nod, praying the little island of clifftop she was trapped on would hold firm. Out at sea, the waves continued to roll in, giving no hint of the drama unfolding on the dunes. Had Gabriella survived this devastation, or was she lying dead, entombed somewhere under a moving mountain of sand?

Beside her, more debris slipped away, widening the gap that surrounded her. Where was Amanda with that rope? All around, she could hear the rippling sound of sand trickling away. Her island of safety was getting smaller by the second.

'Are you OK over there?' Amanda was back, ginger curls bobbing and a rope swung over her shoulder. 'I'm going to tie the rope to that fence post over there and throw the other end to you. Will you be able catch it?'

'I'll try,' Loveday said, aware that any sudden movement on her part could send the whole clifftop crashing.

'Are you ready?'

'Yes,' she called. 'Throw the rope.'

It landed at her feet, but it slid away before she could grab it. She steadied herself.

'It's coming again,' Amanda shouted, throwing the rope. It clattered into the gap, releasing a chunk of marram grass before falling away. Loveday held her breath, feeling the movement under her feet again. Her time was running out.

She swallowed. 'One more try,' she yelled. 'Throw the rope again, Amanda!'

The rope came flying across and she made a grab for it, clinging to it as the sand beneath her finally gave way, leaving Loveday dangling over the edge of a cliff face.

'Try to get a foothold,' Amanda shouted, struggling to hold the rope. 'You'll have to help me. Can you pull yourself up?'

Loveday scrambled, fighting for purchase on the moving wall

of sand. Then she found a ridge, jamming in her foot, praying it would hold.

Using the rope, and with Amanda's help, she slowly yanked herself to the top, crawling on her stomach to reach the safety of the fence before she collapsed, gasping for breath.

Amanda raced towards her, throwing her arms wide to grab Loveday in a bear hug.

'We did it!' she yelled. 'We bloody did it.'

Loveday winced as pain shot along her arm.

'Oh, sorry. Are you hurt?'

'I think I've sprained my arm.' She began to grin. 'You saved my life, Amanda.'

The detective blushed as the flashing blue lights of coastguard vehicles approached.

'There's a woman down there,' Loveday called to the officers. 'She was caught in the fall.'

'We've already got people searching the beach,' the coastguard officer said, as the stamp of more feet sounded behind him.

Suddenly Sam was there, racing forward, his shocked face full of concern. He gathered Loveday into his arms. 'Oh, my darling. What are you doing here? Amanda told me what happened.' He was stroking her hair. 'Are you all right?'

'I am now,' Loveday said, throwing an embarrassed-looking Amanda a grateful look.

'I didn't follow Gabriella, you know. She insisted on bringing me here. I really wasn't interfering, not this time.'

Sam held her at a distance, looking down at her. 'We'll deal with the excuses later,' he said, but a wide grin was spreading across his face.

CHAPTER 38

*L*oveday took a sip of the hot chocolate Sam made, and sat back with a sigh. 'I really thought Gabriella had died back there today.'

'Well, she didn't,' he said, coming to put his arms around her. 'But you had a lucky escape. I don't think you should go into the office tomorrow.'

'We'll see,' Loveday said, knowing full well she would definitely be at work the next day.

'I want to know about Gabriella. Was she badly hurt?'

Sam went back to his chair, puffed out his cheeks and exhaled.

'Enough to scare the wits out of her,' he said.

'She had a gun, Sam. She was going to kill me. She thought I was having an affair with her husband.'

'The woman's a fantasist,' he said. 'But we did find that gun. We also recovered the hammer used to kill Janet Harris. Gabriella's prints were all over it. Same with that photograph of Meredith Teague.'

'Her prints were bound to be on that photo because she handled it at the police station,' Loveday said.

Sam smiled. 'It's the prints that weren't on it that are important. There was no sign that Chris Bentley had ever touched that photo, or the hammer.'

'So she really did kill Teague and Mrs Harris,' Loveday said quietly, taking another sip of her drink. She didn't notice Sam looking away.

'What about Mellissa? Did you find any evidence linking her to that killing?'

'The only prints on the knife used were Mellissa's. We believe it had been wiped clean and then put into her hands.'

'It's hard to believe anyone could be that calculating,' Loveday said. 'What about the baby Locryn Grantby overheard Gabriella talking about on that phone call?'

'Just another bizarre twist to the story,' Sam said. 'There is no baby, but Gabriella told Merryn Lawry that she was pregnant and suggested she should look after the child once it was born.'

Loveday stared at him. 'So Gabriella *was* pregnant?'

Sam shook his head. 'No, that was another of her fantasies.'

'But that's ridiculous. Why would she say such a thing?'

'She told Merryn that Bentley wasn't the baby's father and she feared that if he discovered this it might put the child in danger. It was all about strengthening her story that Bentley was a killer.'

'And Merryn fell for that?'

'No, that's the point. Gabriella chose the wrong person to involve in her weird make-believe. She hadn't realized that Merryn was besotted with the doctor, and the girl told Bentley everything.'

'Did Merryn tell you this?'

'No, Bentley did during that last interview. He said it proved how deranged his wife was.'

Loveday shook her head, sighing. 'What happens now? Will Gabriella be charged with the murders?'

'We're waiting for the forensic medical assessment.'

'So that's it? Dr Bentley was innocent all along. I knew

Gabriella was spinning us a yarn. Blaming her husband for those murders came too easily.'

Sam had got up and took a bottle of wine from the fridge. He offered to pour Loveday a drink, but she refused, so he filled a glass for himself, fingering the stem as he sat back in his chair. 'I thought exactly the same thing when we interviewed Chris Bentley. Neither Will nor I trusted his insistence that Gabriella was wholly responsible for the killings. His story sounded as unlikely as the tale his wife was spinning. It was all too easy.'

She watched as he lifted his wine and took a sip. 'Take those fingerprints on Meredith Teague's photo, for instance.'

'You said only Gabriella's were on that,' Loveday interrupted.

'Exactly, and that's what raised our suspicion. At the very least, we would have expected to find Brian Teague's prints there, but they weren't. The photograph had been wiped. It was the same with the hammer, but this time the only prints we found there were Gabriella's.'

Loveday's brow wrinkled. 'I don't understand. Isn't that proof that she's the one who handled the weapon used to murder Janet Harris?'

'Think about it. Do you imagine a killer as organized as this wouldn't have worn gloves?'

'Well yes, but…'

Sam didn't give her time to finish the sentence. 'We didn't find any other prints in the kitchen either, or even at the front door. This killer knew what they were doing. Believe me, gloves were worn.'

Loveday frowned. 'Hang on,' she said, pushing her fingers through her hair. She blinked. 'I'm really confused now. Are you saying even though Gabriella's prints are on that hammer it doesn't prove she was the killer?'

'That's exactly what I mean,' Sam said, pausing to look up at her. 'We're being set up.'

'Wait a minute.' Loveday held out a hand. 'So, which one was it? Did Bentley kill those people, or was it Gabriella?'

Sam was still meeting her eyes. 'It was both of them,' he said.

Loveday's gaze widened. 'They admitted it?'

'Finally, yes. It was Gabriella getting caught in that landslide that changed everything. Will had gone to the hospital to check on her condition when she called him to her bedside, saying she couldn't face any more lies. She said the killings had been her idea, but Bentley had been more than keen to go along with it. They had planned it all together, even down to each one accusing the other. Apparently leading us a dance was all part of the fun.'

'What about Bentley? Surely he didn't admit that?'

'Not at first, but once we'd told him about Gabriella's confession he just kind of caved in. The plan always was that they should accuse each other. Pitting their wits against the police had been like a game to them, but their pack of cards collapsed when Gabriella almost died in those sand dunes.

'Bentley admitted everything after that, but said it was Gabriella who killed Mellissa Grantby, although he'd been involved. He'd teased her that he'd had sex with Mellissa, which apparently threw his wife into a jealous frenzy. She said she'd make sure Mellissa didn't try to break up any other marriages.'

'Nessa Cawse warned me about Bentley,' Loveday said. 'She said he was a womanizer and not to be trusted. It looks like she was right.'

'She certainly was,' Sam agreed. 'It was Bentley who tricked Mellissa into meeting him at the centre and he drove Gabriella there, but said he didn't go inside. He said his wife later shared how she'd killed the woman. According to him she told him how she'd held Mellissa at knifepoint while backing her into the rest room before striking her on the back of the head with a stone she'd brought with her.

'Once the woman was unconscious on the floor Gabriella

slashed her wrists. She also smeared her blood on the wash basin to make it appear she had struck her head as she fell.'

Loveday was still frowning. 'Surely if she battered Mellissa with a stone the post mortem would have revealed fragments of it in the wound?'

'Not if the stone was wrapped in plastic and everything pointed to it being a suicide.'

'Gabriella wrapped the stone in plastic?' She couldn't hide her gasp of disbelief.

Sam nodded. 'It was only after Nessa Cawse alerted you to Mellissa's problem with blood that we took a second look at things and requested a new post mortem. Dr Bartholomew wasn't happy but he did it anyway.' Sam pulled a face. 'He was rather chaste when it revealed tiny flecks of plastic in the wound.'

Loveday shook her head. 'Why did they do it, Sam? How could the Bentleys kill three people and apparently enjoy it?'

Sam lifted his glass and took another sip. 'I didn't tell you Aldo Ricca came to see me.'

'Aldo, Gabriella's father?'

'He isn't her real father.'

'What?' Loveday screwed up her face. 'You mean she was adopted?'

Sam nodded. In his mind's eye he was back in the interview room listening to Aldo's story. He could still hear his words.

'Gabriella is not our natural daughter. Maria and I adopted her when she was six years old. She was a difficult child with a chip on her shoulder, and who could blame her.' He'd sighed, his dark eyes meeting Sam's. 'What I am going to tell you will sound stark, but it's true. You can check it. 'Gabriella was born into one of Italy's most feared Mafia families. She was taken into care when her father, Vito De Marco

was killed in a shoot-out with the Carabinieri.' He looked up at Sam. 'You're familiar with that name?'

Sam had nodded. He knew the Carabinieri was an Italian

military corps with police duties. They also carried arms and investigated terrorists. If they killed her father it's not surprising she would have animosity against them, but it didn't explain her hatred of all police.'

He remembered how Aldo had put a hand on his chest, as though trying to calm a fast-beating heart. 'There's more,' he'd said, his expression of sadness turning to pain as he slowly shook his head.

'Gabriella's mother, Lia De Marco was arrested and put into a police cell, and while she was there...' He'd swallowed. 'She hanged herself.'

Sam looked at Loveday as he repeated the man's words and heard her intake of breath. 'I know,' he said. 'I hadn't expected this either, but shocking though the man's story was, and no matter how much sympathy we might have for a child who loses her parents in such a way, three innocent people had died at the hands of Gabriella Bentley. And she had been aided and abetted by her husband, a practicing GP that people had trusted.

'I told Aldo I hoped he wasn't suggesting what happened to his adopted daughter's blood parents in any way absolved her of blame for the terrible things she's done. He said of course he didn't, but he thought it might help me to understand Gabriella's state of mind.'

'And does it...help you to understand her state of mind I mean?'

'Whether it does or not is completely immaterial. That's a decision for the court. I fully expect Gabriella to have a psychiatric assessment.'

Sam took another sip of wine, draining the glass and put it back onto the table. 'It was almost four murders. I haven't told you everything Bentley said in that last interview.' He looked up and met her eyes. 'Gabriella was going to kill you, Loveday.'

'I was never in any doubt about that,' Loveday said, remembering the look in the woman's eyes when she pointed that gun.

'You don't understand,' Sam said, holding her gaze. 'It was all part of their plan. Killing you would have been the icing on the cake.'

'Really? But Gabriella threatened me because she believed I was having an affair with her husband.'

Sam shook his head. 'The plan to kill you was about scoring points against the police.'

'I still don't understand. Why me, I'm not a police officer.'

'But I am. Think about it, Loveday. If you want to hurt someone you don't kill them, you target the people they love.' He paused, and she saw his expression turn to a grimace. 'You were set up, my darling. Until then it had a been like a game to them and the more they could run circles around us the more successful it was.

As soon as Gabriella realised your partner was a copper the wheels began to turn in her brain. She hated every kind of authority, but especially the police. Killing you would have been the embellishment on the crimes of two seriously damaged people.'

'What monsters,' Loveday said. 'I might be dead if Amanda hadn't turned up. I'm guessing that wasn't a coincidence.'

Sam shook his head. 'Gabriella thought she was so clever, but I never trusted her, so I had Amanda follow her when she left the station.' He smiled. 'I'm very glad I did.'

'Me too,' Loveday said.

She screwed up her face. 'I've been wondering how Merrick's brother will feel when he hears about this. He was besotted with the woman.'

'I shouldn't feel too sorry for him. He's treated plenty of women badly and not given them a second thought. Gabriella turned the tables in him. It suited her to have Cadan at her beck and call. She knew he could be trusted to supply her with an alibi if it was needed.'

'Cadan is a proud man, and he won't take kindly to being used,' Loveday said.

'I'm afraid this pair didn't give a hoot about who they used.'

Loveday frowned. 'Gabriella always said Chris was the controlling one, but they're the same, aren't they? They are both narcissists.'

'What do you know about narcissists?' Sam raised an eyebrow.

'Quite a bit actually. I researched the subject for an article I wrote last year. People like the Bentleys are charmers, it's the honeypot they use to attract their prey. They feel superior to the rest of us, that everyone else is inferior to them.' She stopped, staring at Sam. 'They probably believed the people they murdered deserved to die.'

'It's a bad business,' Sam agreed. 'I didn't know Mellissa Grantby, but Will and I had met Janet Harris. She was a nice woman.'

Loveday held out her hand to him. 'Come on, let's say good-night to our daughter.'

Rosie had kicked away her cover, and a tiny smile was twitching at the corners of her mouth as she slept. Sam wrapped his arms around Loveday as they stood by the cot, looking down at their daughter.

'Do you like being a police officer?' she asked quietly.

'Not always.' He sighed. 'But on days like this, when we remove two evil killers from society, the world feels like a better place.'

Loveday snuggled closer into his arms and laid her head on his chest. 'It is a better place, Sam, because you make it better.' She smiled down at the sleeping child. 'I'll have that glass of wine now,' she said.

YOUR FREE BOOKS

If you enjoyed this book and would like to read more of Loveday and Sam's adventures, sign up for *Rena Writes* and collect your two free books in *The Loveday Mysteries Series.*
Your free copies of *A Cornish Kidnapping* and *A Cornish Vengeance* are waiting at
www.renageorge.net

Happy reading,
Rena

ALSO BY RENA GEORGE

THE LOVEDAY MYSTERIES

A Cornish Revenge

A Cornish Kidnapping

A Cornish Vengeance

A Cornish Obsession

A Cornish Malice

A Cornish Betrayal

A Cornish Deception

A Cornish Ransom

A Cornish Evil

A Cornish Guilt

A Cornish Anguish

A Cornish Intrigue

THE JACK DRUMMOND THRILLERS

Stranglehold

Deadfall

Entrapment

Witchling

Inverness

Monster

THE MELLIN COVE TRILOGY

Danger at Mellin Cove

Mistress of Mellin Cove

Secrets of Mellin Cove

The Mellin Cove Trilogy (Boxset)

THE ROMANCE COLLECTION

Highland Heart

Inherit the Dream

Fire in the Blood

Where Moonbeams Dance

A Moment Like This

LEAVING A REVIEW

Can you spare a few minutes to leave a review?
Reviews are important to everyone as they help readers to find
the books they love. They are the lifeblood for authors and the
best way for readers to express their thoughts about a book.
Reviews can be long or short, it really doesn't matter so long as
they are fair. This author would be very grateful if you could take
a few moments to leave a review.
Thank you.

Printed in Great Britain
by Amazon

33665983R00154